CINDY VILLANUEVA

A THISTLE *in the* CEVENNES

Book Three
BLOOMING
The Series

ISBN: 979-8-9929057-1-7 (paperback)
ISBN: 979-8-9929057-2-4 (ebook)

This novel is entirely a work of fiction. The names, characters and incidents portrayed in it are the work of the author's imagination. Any resemblance to actual persons, living or dead, events or localities is entirely coincidental.

Cover design by Samantha Sanderson-Marshall, www.smashdesigns.co.uk

To Cathie and John

Forty years plus and counting. You inspire me and I love you.

1

Susana slid the business card out of the box and ran her finger over the raised type. She gazed at the paper's linen finish and elegant font, and her chest swelled with delight.

"Susana Cortéz-Guerrero," she whispered. "Senior Vice President, Miles Porter Gelbarr."

I did it.

She set the box on the kitchen counter and kicked off her Jimmy Choo pumps, her feet cooling instantly on the Saltillo tile. Sighing contentedly, she poured herself a glass of lemonade, then stole another glance at her new business cards. She had signed off on the compensation package a week earlier, but somehow having the physical cards made the promotion more real. *It'll be even better when the website is updated,* she mused. The executive team sat for new headshots just that morning, and she was eager to see the results.

Still smiling, she padded down the hall to her bedroom where she quickly stripped and put on a bathing suit, knotted her hair in a messy bun, and grabbed a towel. The housekeeper had been in today, she remembered, noting the gleaming bathroom mirror and the perfectly fluffed pillows on the bed. It was a luxury Enrique insisted upon, telling her he wanted to spend time on the weekends with her, not scrubbing toilets.

She had an unexpected memory of her grandmother. When Susana was a small girl, her *abuela* would braid ribbons into her long hair, telling her in broken English, "You so pretty, *mija*. You gonna get a rich husband." The tiny woman had worked as a housekeeper when she came to Florida, her hands rough and calloused as she worked long hours to provide for Susana's mother and uncles. Susana had never met her grandfather—he died in an accident in Mexico when her mother was small—but her grandmother fiercely led the family, sending three of her four children to college and one into the military. Why she had thought Susana's path to success would only come from marrying well, her granddaughter didn't know. Instead, she'd mirrored her grandmother's impressive work ethic and concentrated on building a career and her own wealth. And Susana had called her *abuela* first, even before her parents, after every win, every promotion. She relished the pride in the woman's aging voice.

She wondered what her grandmother would have thought of today's accomplishment—SVP *and* a successful husband. Susana looked down at her manicured hands, then back at the tidy bedroom and whispered her thanks. "*Gracias por todo, abuelita.* I wish you were here."

She took her lemonade and the box of cards outside. The Florida afternoon humidity struck her as soon as she opened the sliding glass door, and she wasted no time diving into the swimming pool. After baking in the sun for months, the water felt like a bath, yet it was still refreshing. Susana lay back and floated, her eyes closed as she relaxed in the sunshine. She idly thought she probably should have put on sunscreen but couldn't muster the energy to go back inside. For the millionth time in twenty-five years, she appreciated their decision to buy this house. The pool had made the home nearly too expensive for the young couple, but Enrique had crunched the numbers over and over and convinced her it was a good investment—*And he'd been so right,* she thought.

She swam languidly to the side of the pool and climbed out to sit on the shaded patio. She wiped her hands on the towel and took out a single business card. She snapped a quick photo, then texted her parents.

Hola Mami y Papi, she wrote. *Mírame! Tu hija es la jefa =)*

She waited a moment for their reply, knowing it would come immediately. Her father wasn't much for texting, but she was certain her mother would show him the message. Learning of their daughter's promotion to "the boss" would thrill them both.

Ay, princesa! Estamos muy orgullosos!

Susana grinned. Even at fifty-four years old, she loved to be the princess making her parents proud. She took a quick selfie blowing them a kiss and sent it off. Then she texted the photo of the card to her friends.

So this happened, she wrote. *I think it calls for a celebration, amigas!*

She wasn't surprised to see Azalea's response pop up first.

Suze! Congratulations! I am thrilled for you—I know how hard you've worked for this. We definitely need to celebrate. Can we all get together before the wedding?

Azalea and her husband Esteban were due to leave for Spain in just a few days, delaying their return to Barcelona so they wouldn't miss Sara and Terrence's nuptials. Before Susana could respond, Sara chimed in.

That is so great! And yes—this deserves a celebration for sure. How's Thursday? Where shall we meet? I'm so happy for you xo

Susana marveled at Sara's generosity. While another woman might have resented having her wedding bumped to second place—even for a moment—Sara's congratulations were sincere and heartfelt. Again, Susana was poised to respond but then burst out laughing as she read Lauren's text.

OK, here's my first answer as your employee: Congratulations, Susana. Very well deserved and I'm proud to work in your organization.

And now for my second answer as your friend: About fucking time! What took them so long? And where/when is the party?

Lauren had recently returned to the marketing agency as an account director after spending a year with a startup. It hadn't taken long to regret the move, but it took several months before she asked Susana and MPG to rehire her. She knew Lauren had dreaded the conversation—knowing Susana wouldn't allow their friendship to soften the encounter. *She took her ass-chewing well,* chuckled Susana.

The truth was, she was thrilled to have the talented marketer back with the agency and was happy to help shepherd the younger woman's career. She wished she'd had a comparable mentor over the past twenty years. It had been brutal proving herself and earning her way to the SVP tier and she was glad to have the chance to help her friend.

She looked back at her phone and the laughing emojis her friends were adding. *Let's meet at my house Thursday night,* she texted. *Cava and take out. Bring your swimsuit. Can't wait to see you all!*

She heard the sliding glass door open and looked up to see Enrique. Her smiling husband wore board shorts and carried a towel and two cold bottles of Dos Equis. Even after almost thirty years, that smile caused her heart to flutter and she smiled in return.

"Hey, *guapo,*" she said. "You're home early."

He set the beers down and leaned over to kiss her. "Had a client meeting nearby and decided to come home instead of going back to the office." He glanced down at the business card on the table and grinned. "So they came, huh?" He picked it up and read it, then looked back at his wife. "I am so incredibly proud of you, *mi corazón.* You deserve this."

Susana reached for him, sliding her arms around his neck and pulling him in for a kiss. She gasped as he lifted her out of her chair, scooping her into his arms and striding to the edge of the pool…

Where he jumped.

She had only a second to hold her breath before they went under the water. Sputtering and laughing, she slapped at his shoulder. "Next time warn me!"

"Where's the fun in that?" Enrique kissed her soundly. "Congratulations, Madam Senior Vice President." Then he laughed. "I guess this means you're buying dinner?"

Susana slid her arms across his shoulders, then kissed him as she moved to wrap her long legs around his hips. "I thought we could stay in tonight," she murmured. "Just a quiet celebration?"

Enrique chuckled as he nuzzled her neck. "Since when are you quiet when we're…celebrating?"

She grinned. He had a point.

2

Two days later, Susana sat with Enrique, Azalea, and Esteban at Sara and Terrence's beach wedding. A bamboo arch was set up a few yards from the surf, the wooden beams festooned with pink and white flowers. A soft breeze ruffled the tulle streamers and the groom's shoulder-length hair. She was glad the wedding was early in the evening, the ocean breeze cool enough to keep the usually oppressive Florida heat at bay. Behind them, the sun began its descent and the clouds glowed with soft pinks and blues, making everything just slightly hazy and romantic. Her design team called this "the golden hour," their favorite time of the day to shoot outdoor client videos.

The Fort Lauderdale beach was still full of people, many within a hundred yards of the ceremony. Some, she noticed, had cameras out. *Who takes pictures of someone else's wedding?* she wondered. "Tourists," she muttered, and Enrique chuckled.

The music started and the ceremony began. Susana looked down the aisle as the first pair of attendants approached. Savannah, Terrence's youngest sister, clearly enjoyed the spotlight. She wore a strapless pink chiffon gown with a sweetheart neckline and snug bodice over a huge skirt. Her groomsman partner smiled down at his wife as he escorted her toward the arch, the waves gently lapping in the background. Susana nudged her best friend and whispered, "Can you say, 'Disney princess'?"

Azalea covered her laugh with a hand and the two looked back toward the next bridesmaid. Talia, the middle sibling of the Billings clan, was likewise dressed in pink. Her gown was a one-shoulder satin column with a tasteful slit—elegant and simple. The bridesmaid seemed to glide across the sand and she glanced at the groomsman next to her with a loving smile. "That's her husband, right?" whispered Azalea and Susana nodded.

"Yup. That's Darren."

The two pair of bridesmaids and groomsmen veered apart as they reached the arch, moving into their respective places.

She looked back to see Lauren. The maid of honor was wearing a leaf green halter column, its fabric skimming her tall, lithe frame. Her dark hair was swept to the side in glamorous Hollywood waves, her makeup perfectly applied. As she approached Susana and Azalea's row, she glanced over and winked at the women.

"How does she do it?" Susana whispered to Azalea. "She's always so chic. And you know she probably had a triple cheeseburger right before sliding into that dress."

Enrique nudged her. "Shhh," her husband said softly, trying not to laugh.

As Lauren took her position, Susana noticed Talia's smile brighten, and looked back to see two children, the ring bearer and flower girl. Oliver and Mackenzie Dumont walked down the sandy aisle, their little faces beaming. At six years old, Oliver took his duties very seriously, keeping his eyes glued to his groomsman father. But Mackenzie had a dazzling smile for everyone, lagging behind as she tossed rose petals from the basket she swung perilously close to her brother's head. When the pair walked past Susana's row, the little girl's smile grew even larger and she whispered loudly, "Hi, new aunties!"

Talia looked mortified, but Susana and Azalea laughed. "Hello, Mackenzie," they whispered in unison. The child waved brightly and hurried to catch up with her older brother, then stood next to Talia while Oliver took his place next to Darren.

The music changed and everyone stood for the bride and her daughter. Susana took a moment to glance at Terrence before Sara and Natalie got close. He stood next to the pastor and to his best man, his mouth agape. Susana giggled as she noticed his friend nudge Terrence with an elbow and the groom's mouth abruptly shut. Yet he never took his eyes off his bride.

Sara and Natalie walked slowly down the aisle, Natalie's eyes glowing with pride as she gazed at her mother. They were hand in hand, their love for each other palpable. Natalie also wore pink: a simple, off the shoulder tea-length dress, her dark hair caught up in a casual chignon at the base of her neck. She carried a smaller version of her mother's bouquet—pink tiger lilies for her, white for Sara, with cascading greenery and fragrant jasmine.

"They look so much alike," Susana whispered to Azalea. "They could be sisters."

Sara was incandescent, her wavy, sun-kissed hair grazing her shoulder blades and threaded artfully with babies' breath. Her gown, a simple white silk dotted with embroidered pink roses and green leaves, set off her curves and her tan. Susana looked again at Terrence. He was mesmerized. She was certain he was completely oblivious to anyone or anything around him. He only had eyes for his bride.

She felt Enrique's hand in hers and glanced down at the tissue he'd placed in her palm. She looked questioningly at him, then shook her head. "You've met me before, right?" she whispered, then grinned. "If anybody's gonna cry at a wedding, it'll be you."

Her husband shrugged and pulled her close to his side, his lips pressing her cheek before murmuring, "I know…I'm the hopeless romantic and you're the tough one. But you love me, *mi cardito*."

My little thistle.

After the ceremony, the sun began to set. Susana stood with Enrique, Azalea, and Esteban, watching as restaurant employees lit tiki torches along the patio, adding to the tropical ambience. The wedding had been simple and beautiful, and the reception was a modest affair, with drinks and appetizers at a pub walking distance from the surf. She was thinking about another glass of champagne when the bride and groom approached them.

Sara had become like a younger sister to the older women and Susana's heart warmed to see her so happy. When she and Azalea learned about Sara's teen pregnancy and the heartbreaking way her parents had torn the baby from her, they were appalled. But when Sara told them the good news that her daughter had found her all these years later, they were thrilled. They met Natalie only weeks before the wedding but fell in love with her, occasionally including her in their ladies' night events—typically sangria and guacamole on Azalea's patio. She was a welcome addition to the group and seemed eager to embrace the older women as they shared their lives.

As much as we can, now that Azalea and Esteban live half the year in Spain, thought Susana. She wondered if she'd ever get used to her best friend's new life.

She shook off the unwelcome thought and hugged Sara. "You look absolutely radiant, my friend," she said. She glanced at Terrence. "You do know how lucky you are, right?"

Terrence beamed. "I am the luckiest man in the world," he said, hugging his new wife tight to his side.

"And we're very lucky to have you guys," Sara added. "We can't thank you enough for the gifts. You're so generous."

Azalea and Esteban were leaving directly from Fort Lauderdale the next day to return to Spain for the autumn and winter. They knew the young couple—on their paltry teachers' salaries—likely could not afford an expensive honeymoon, so their gift to them was two weeks at Azalea's beach house. Terrence and Sara had been overjoyed—and even more so when Susana and Enrique added a gift certificate to the Ritz-Carlton honeymoon suite for their wedding night.

"We planned to just drive back home after the reception," Sara had confessed. "We figured we could have more of a staycation before school starts in a couple of weeks." Susana and Enrique had insisted they stay in Fort Lauderdale for their wedding night. They could drive back north the next day and the couple was delighted.

As the friends chatted, Lauren approached with her date. "You remember Susana, my boss?"

The handsome man reached out a well-manicured hand, gold cufflinks glinting in the light of the torches. "Of course," he said with a pleasant smile, shaking her hand firmly. "It's nice to see you again."

Jayson Rivera was the vice president of marketing for Thompson Toys, a top client of Miles Porter Gelbarr. Susana had pulled Lauren off the account several weeks earlier when it became clear she and Jayson were interested in each other. It appeared the relationship was now serious enough that Lauren brought him to her best friend's wedding.

Lauren was introducing Jayson to Enrique, Azalea, and Esteban when Terrence's best man approached the group.

"I don't think you've met my brother Corey," Terrence said, his arm around the broad shoulders of his friend. He clapped Corey's back and added, "We're not blood brothers, but we've known each other since we were kids. Went to high school and college together."

Corey shook hands all around. He was taller and wider than Terrence, with a surfer's shaggy blonde hair and a mischievous grin. "I couldn't miss this, although I'm not sure how this Neanderthal ended up with such a fabulous wife." Sara grinned up at him as Terrence glared. "Anyway, very nice to meet all of you." He looked back at Terrence and asked, "Where can a guy get a beer around here?"

Sara patted her new husband's arm. "Go on—get the man a beer." He grinned and the two friends headed off for the bar. Sara smiled, then looked back at the others. "They haven't seen each other in two years," she said. "Corey moved to California after college—he's a high school English teacher in the Bay Area." She looked fondly at the men laughing at the bar. "I think he'd probably like to move back here, but he got divorced and they have an eight-year old daughter. He would never leave her."

Sara still grieved over the miscarriage she suffered earlier that year, and Susana heard the note of sadness in her friend's voice. She reached for Sara just as Lauren did, with Azalea a beat behind. Esteban and Enrique looked knowingly at each other, then beckoned Jayson. The men stepped away as the four friends pulled each other close, their foreheads touching, their arms around each others' waists.

It's so much better when we're together, thought Susana.

3

"Babe? Susana? We were supposed to be down there ten minutes ago."

Startled, Susana looked up from her phone. "Huh? Oh—one sec." She finished typing out a response to an email and then stood. "Sorry. I had to answer that. Peter's being his typical jackass self."

"Even on Sunday?" Enrique asked.

"Jackasses don't know the meaning of weekends," she answered. "Remember Bernard when you were coming up? I swear the guy worked twenty-four hours a day and expected you to keep up."

Her husband frowned. "I guess there are workaholics in every company. Thank God I don't work for him anymore."

Susana tucked her phone into her pocket. "The people who work for you are lucky."

The couple left their room and she covered a huge yawn as they approached the elevator. "I'm starving. Sorry for making us late for breakfast."

Her husband hugged her, brushing his lips on her cheek. "If you were on time, I'd wonder who was sleeping next to me last night," he said with a smile. She elbowed him with a scowl, but knew he was right. Promptness wasn't her strong suit.

The couple entered the café and saw their friends already seated in a booth, sipping coffee.

"*Buenos días, amigos*," said Esteban, rising as Enrique held Susana's chair. She appreciated their Latin manners—*Somebody's Mami raised 'em right*, she thought as she sat down.

A waitress approached and the two newcomers requested coffee. They all perused the menu and ordered when she returned with the steaming cups.

"Sleep well?" asked Azalea.

"Not great," admitted Susana.

"I hoped being away for the weekend might help," said Azalea. "When is the last time you got a decent night's sleep?"

Susana unsuccessfully tried to stifle another yawn. She'd had trouble sleeping for months and it was taking a toll. "It'll pass," she said. She grinned at her husband. "I'll sleep in the car while Kique drives us back to Orlando."

Azalea frowned. "Is it the new job?"

"Nah. Been busting my ass a long time before the promotion. You know the drill. If a woman's gonna be taken seriously, she has to work twice as hard as the men." She shrugged. "Some things never change, but at least it paid off this time."

The waitress returned with their orders and when she set down a huge plate of pancakes, Susana laughed, "See? I'll be in a sugar coma within the hour."

Azalea rolled her eyes. "You're incorrigible."

Susana opened her mouth to retort, but Enrique spoke first, deftly changing the subject. "So you go back to Spain today?"

"We do," said Esteban. "Our flight leaves at four o'clock, so we have a bit of time this morning to do some shopping before we leave for the airport." He smiled at his wife. "Seems there is a type of… body scrub?" His brows scrunched together. "I think that's it—anyway, it's only here in Florida and we are going to buy a suitcase full to stock our bathroom in Cadaqués."

Azalea looked at her friend. "It's the key lime one. You know what I'm talking about, right?

Susana nodded, her mouth full of pancakes. When she swallowed, she said, "Buy two suitcases' worth. That stuff is magic."

The four friends continued chatting as they finished their meal. When the waitress removed their plates and refilled their coffee cups, Azalea asked, "So next month is a really big deal for you guys. What are you planning for your thirtieth anniversary? You should do something amazing."

Enrique grinned at his wife. "Yes, *amor*. What are we doing?"

Susana shook her head. "I have no idea. I can barely plan what I'm doing tomorrow." She laughed, but it was weak and she knew it. She didn't know what Enrique had in mind, but she hadn't planned a thing.

Esteban reached for Azalea's hand and leaned forward. "We have a proposition for you," he said, his Spanish accent deep and melodious. "We'd love you to come to Spain and stay with us for a month."

Azalea smiled and nodded. "Please say you'll come," she said, her enthusiasm palpable. "We really want you to visit."

Enrique's brows rose in surprise. "That's quite the proposition." He looked at Susana, eyes questioning. "What do you think—"

"A month? Are you kidding me?" She was already shaking her head. "You know I just got this promotion, *'mana*. There's no way MPG is gonna let their new senior vice president go to Europe for a month." She looked at her husband. "And how could you leave for that long? Don't you have projects here?"

Enrique took her hand. "Susana," he began, his serious tone startling her. "I'm an architect. I can work from anywhere. I have a laptop and a pencil…I'll be fine." He looked at their friends. "How soon do we need to let you know?"

Esteban smiled. "Any time, my friend. We know you need to talk about it—"

Azalea reached across the table to grab her friend's other hand. "C'mon, Suze. Early autumn in Spain! It will be amazing. I have so many things I want to show you. You can work during the day and we'll have fun nights and weekends. Please say you'll come."

Susana looked around the table at the people she loved. She wasn't sure how Steven Miles would feel about his best employee leaving the office for a month, especially so soon after her promotion. She was quite certain how Peter and Jonathan would react.

Then again, she and Kique hadn't been on a vacation for…well, for a long time. She supposed she could work remotely and take the weekends to enjoy Spain. She gently pulled away from Azalea while she studied Enrique.

Thirty years is worth celebrating, she told herself.

She knew Enrique was thinking the same thing. "You're sure you can get the time away?" His eyes were solemn as he nodded. Praying she wouldn't rue the decision, she nodded in return and held his gaze. "Okay…. Assuming my boss agrees, let's go to Spain."

Azalea and Esteban burst into laughter and smiles and Enrique hugged her tight.

"*Gracias, mi amor*," he whispered into her ear as he held her close. "*Gracias*."

Enrique loaded their bags and held the door open for Susana. He kissed her cheek as she slid into the car and she looked up at him, surprised. "What was that for?" she asked.

"Do I need a reason? I love kissing my wife."

Susana yawned and then smiled. "Lucky for you, your wife loves getting kissed."

"Hmm," he responded. "Are you sure I'm not boring you? Yawning doesn't usually mean anything good." He laughed as he walked around the car. "But seriously, why don't you just put the seat back and sleep? We have a few hours and you need the rest. I'll listen to the football game on the radio."

She rarely slept in the car, but she had to admit the idea appealed to her. The next week promised to be busier than the last, and she wasn't about to let a little lack of sleep derail her. The promotion to SVP was significant—one she'd worked hard for, but the workload was brutal. She'd take advantage of the drive to bank some rest.

"Thanks, babe," she said, reclining the seat. "Maybe just half an hour or so, okay?"

Enrique nodded and squeezed her hand.

Three hours later, Susana awoke to her husband stroking her cheek. "We're home, *mi corazón*."

She stretched and looked around her, surprised to find them in their garage. "Are you serious?" she asked. "I slept the whole trip?" She knew it was unreasonable, but she felt annoyed. "Why did you let me sleep so long?"

Enrique looked long at her before answering. "You're completely wrung out, Susana. You need the rest and I was glad you could sleep." He got out and came around to open her door, but she got out first.

"Stop treating me like I'm gonna break," she groused. "I'll be fine."

He didn't answer, instead opening the trunk for their suitcases. He looked as if he wanted to say more, but walked into the house without another word.

Susana followed, trying to dispel her foul mood. She was embarrassed at the way she snapped at Enrique. He didn't deserve her ire.

They walked upstairs and he set the suitcases down. "I'm gonna go for a quick run," he said, kicking off his sandals. "I need to loosen up after that drive."

She stood and looked at the man she'd loved for over thirty years. *The man I still adore*, she reminded herself. He was older, grayer, and only slightly less fit than he'd been when they met in college. His smile still thrilled her and his touch still sent fire through her veins.

He finished lacing up his running shoes and turned to leave their bedroom. "Kique?" she murmured, reaching for him. She slid her arms around him, nestling her cheek between his shoulder blades. "I'm sorry."

He turned in her arms and pulled her close. "I know, *mi tesoro*." He stroked her hair and kissed the top of her head. "I'll be back soon."

She released him with a wan smile. She still felt drained and tears threatened as she watched him leave the room. She angrily shook off the unexpected and unwanted emotion and began to unpack, hurling dirty clothes across the room and slamming drawers.

Then she lay down on the bed. *I'll just close my eyes for a minute.*

4

Despite her exhaustion, the next month went by in a blur as Susana dove into her new responsibilities. She'd been a vice president for three years, leading the account teams for the business-to-business side of the house. She had a global team of designers, writers, and account executives and she loved the intense nature of the work.

Now, though, she took on a much greater role. Sitting in nearly daily meetings with the partners, she oversaw the business-to-business *plus* the business-to-consumer teams. Each had a vice president who was keen to impress her—and who, she was certain, also looked for the opportunity to take her job. She'd worked in agencies her entire career and knew the life was cutthroat. At MPG, it was less so, but the competition never waned. She couldn't let up, not for a moment.

If her grandmother could clean toilets, she sure as hell could do this job.

"BD says we can get more out of Thompson Toys and Liscia," growled Peter Gelbarr. He'd been harping on business development for the better part of thirty minutes and Susana was ready to scream.

"I'm scheduled to meet with Janice Thompson on Thursday," she said, keeping her voice calm. *How many times have I said that?* she wondered crossly. "I'm sure we can get more than this rebranding project with them. They love the video work we've done and they've already added social media. She knows they need new packaging and they might as well go with us on this new line of baby toys." She'd reviewed all the previous design work for Thompson Toys and knew the founder was delighted with the results. "I'll do my best to nail it down this week." She worked hard to control her features, wanting nothing more than to snap a sarcastic reply at the annoying partner.

"You mean before you go gallivanting off to Europe for a month?" groused Jonathan Porter. The second of the three MPG partners hadn't been in favor of Susana's request to work abroad for a month, following Peter's lead, as usual. Steven Mills, the third partner and Susana's direct supervisor, cajoled the other partners into letting her go. She knew Steven had to lobby heavily to get Peter on board with the decision—it had been no easy feat.

Her eyes tightened. "Galli—"

"Oh, c'mon, Jon," soothed Steven. "We've been over this. She's going and she'll work US hours from Spain. It's not a big deal." He winked at Susana. "Right?"

She plastered a smile on her face and said brightly, "Right!"

"It's not just Thompson Toys. What about Liscia?" snapped Peter, ignoring Steven. "Their new CEO will want to put her stamp on the company. It's like a dog pissing on a bush to mark territory. That should mean new work for us."

Susana bit the inside of her mouth to keep from reacting to the crude remark. "My team is all over their changes," she said. The Liscia board had appointed the new CEO the same week Susana had been promoted, and she'd spent an entire week studying the tier one client's history to prepare for her new role. Learning about the fashion industry in general was a gargantuan project by itself, but Susana also had to understand the company's emphasis on sustainability, its unique position in the market, and its culture. It had been like drinking from the proverbial firehose. The upscale women's clothing manufacturer, renowned for its elegant fabrics and delicate pleating, had undergone a significant leadership change. To make matters worse, rumor had it there was bad blood between the chief marketing officer and the chief operating officer, who'd been tapped to fill the top job. Susana frowned. She had no interested in getting enmeshed in Liscia's office politics, no matter what the benefit to MPG's project pipeline.

"Geneva seems to be taking a measured approach to her promotion," she continued. "I'll get more involved, but I think it's a long game with them. There's plenty of upside if we're patient."

Peter snorted and Jonathan shook his head. "Now isn't the time for patience, Susana," groused Peter. "Siestas are for Hispanics, not for MPG."

Was that a slam on my heritage or my trip? she wondered, clenching her jaw against a fiery retort. *I'm going to need a transfusion from biting my tongue.*

"Well, that should do it for today," broke in Steven, pushing back his chair. "Thank you for the update, Susana. Safe travels."

This is a mistake. I shouldn't go. I really shouldn't go.

Susana slammed the front door and threw her bag on the sofa. Enrique walked into the room with a concerned look. "Rough day?" he asked.

She sighed and nodded. "Peter and Jon are pitching a fit about me leaving for a month. The busdev people are convinced I'm not squeezing every single dollar out of our current clients, and the partners are pushing for big revenue increases this quarter." She frowned. "Maybe we should postpone—"

Enrique enveloped her in a hug. "We aren't postponing. We've already paid for the tickets and we're leaving on Saturday." He brushed her long hair behind one ear and bent to kiss her lobe, nuzzling her neck. "It's gonna be okay, *mi amor*—"

Susana pushed away, shaking her head. "Not now, Kique. You don't get it—these guys are putting a ton of pressure on me and I have to deliver. I don't know how I'm gonna do that from Spain. Am I supposed to close deals on fucking Zoom?"

Her husband stood quietly, then reached for her. "Susana. Listen to me. I know you're stressed and I know they're pressuring you to deliver. I do get it, babe. And I also know you are the smartest, hardest working person at that firm. You'll be amazing no matter what continent you're on." He leaned over to kiss her cheek. "I believe in you."

Susana looked at him, her eyes narrowing. "You're my husband. You have to say that." She walked toward the kitchen and glanced back at him. "Is there any more of that *arroz con pollo* you made? I'm starving."

"Ah, *mi cardito*," she heard him murmur. "I made plenty."

They cobbled together a dinner of leftovers and Enrique made a salad. As he set her plate on the table, he asked, "Did you eat anything today?"

"I was so busy I kinda forgot," she answered, scooping up the hot chicken and rice with a tortilla. "I had some toast this morning before I left and I drank about a gallon of coffee at the office." She forestalled his next comment. "I know, I know—I have to take better care of myself. I will." She laughed, but Enrique didn't smile.

"When?" he asked. "It's not like we're college kids anymore."

Susana swallowed and frowned. "What's got you so serious?"

He gazed at her before answering. "Thirty years, Susana. That's a long time. Have you thought about that?"

She *had* thought about it. She knew how unusual it was for a couple to stay married for any length of time these days, much less three decades. She took another bite before answering.

"I have," she said at last. "Pretty impressive, aren't we?" She tried for a lighthearted note, but it sounded more sarcastic. She put down her fork. "I do think about it, Kique. I'm proud of what we've built and I love you as much today as I did when met in college."

He reached for her hand. "Let's just leave the dishes," he said, pulling her to her feet and wrapping his arms around her.

She was shaking her head even as he held her. "I can't tonight," she said. "I have to get this presentation together for tomorrow. I'll be up for at least a couple of hours." She saw his disappointment and nearly gave in. "I'm sorry," she whispered.

Enrique released her and turned back to the table. "Go ahead, finish your dinner and I'll clean up."

They ate in silence until Susana was done. "Thank you for dinner," she said, her voice flat.

"You're welcome. And I do understand, *mi amor*. I remember those days and—" He hesitated as if unsure whether to continue. "It makes me wish I'd drawn better boundaries back then. Would have been easier on both of us."

"'Drawn better boundaries'? Is that an architect joke?" Susana's attempt to lighten the conversation fell flat and she found herself growing angry. "I guess you have the benefit of hindsight, but I'm stuck in the middle of it. And it's different for me. You've never been a woman and you've never had to wonder if you were good enough. You've always been good enough." She was shaking with the revelation, wishing she could take the words back.

Her husband looked at her, confusion all over his face. "What are you talking about? You're amazing. You're good at everything, Susana. How can you say that?"

She stared at him, then turned to leave. "Don't wait up."

The next morning Susana awoke to the smell of coffee and a kiss on the cheek. Enrique didn't say anything but set her mug on the nightstand. "Thank you," she mumbled, her voice rough after another late night. She noted her husband's soft smile as he turned and left the bedroom. *He knows me so well*, she mused. Never one for morning chatter, she appreciated the quiet.

She sat up and sipped her coffee while she scrolled through her phone. It was only seven thirty in the morning, but her inbox was already full. While she was a night owl, often working until past midnight, Peter was the stereotypical early riser, sending out terse emails before dawn. Today was no different, as he demanded yet another update on the Liscia account.

She'd worked until two that morning on the presentation— *What is it with Liscia? He knows it's coming today*, she thought crossly. *What the hell is he so anxious about?* She was excited about the company and the work and was certain she crafted a solid plan. There was ample opportunity to expand MPG's efforts on the account and she was eager to deliver her presentation to the partners that afternoon, in spite of Peter's annoying behavior. *It's like he's not happy if he's not ruining someone's day.* Sighing, she got up and began to make the bed.

Enrique came back in. "Just leave that, babe. I don't have to be in the office for another hour. I'll make the bed." He smiled at his wife. "And I made you some lunch. Just pop it in the microwave so you don't go all day without food again."

Susana knew she needed to take better care of herself. The long hours and hit-or-miss meals during the day were taking a toll on her. Her jokes didn't sway her husband—*He really is worried,* she realized.

She came around the bed to put her arms around him. "Thank you, *amor*," she said. "*Gracias por todo.*"

Enrique laughed and nuzzled her neck. "Ah, *mi cardito.* Are you trying to get me back into bed by speaking Spanish in that husky morning voice of yours?"

She hugged him, then released him with a frown. "I wish," she replied. "It would be a lot more fun than a slow death by PowerPoint with the partners." She kissed his cheek and walked to the bathroom to shower, his affection already forgotten by the time the water was running, her mind racing through a to-do list that seemed to grow by the minute.

How on earth am I going to leave for Spain in four days?

5

"You'll be able to reach me the entire month," repeated Susana, looking around the conference table at her team. "I know the emphasis is on Liscia and Thompson Toys, but don't forget we have a full roster of clients who deserve our attention. Today's tier two client is—"

"Tomorrow's tier one," intoned the group.

She grinned. "All right—I know you guys are gonna be fine." She waved a hand at the door. "Get out of here." She gathered her notebook as the team left, then looked up to see Lauren lingering at the doorway.

"Got a minute?" the younger woman asked.

"Of course. Walk with me." The two walked to Susana's office, and Lauren closed the door behind her.

Susana tilted her head, her eyes narrowing. "What's up?"

"I know you're slammed so I won't take a bunch of time. Here's the deal: I want to take on more responsibility, but I don't know if it's possible in this environment." Lauren paused, then continued. "It seems like if you're not in tight with the partners, it's hard to get noticed, but if you are—well, there are ample opportunities. I guess I need your guidance and your help."

Susana took a moment before answering. Lauren was technically her employee, yet the two had been friends for longer than they'd worked together. They'd successfully balanced the personal and professional aspects of their relationship and neither woman was eager to blur the lines. "You aren't wrong," she began, thinking quickly. "What do you want to do?"

"I want to work on the Liscia team." Lauren moved to the chair opposite Susana's desk. "But that…*dude* Peter put on the account—" She threw her hands up in exasperation. "Seriously? Just out of school and he ends up with them? He knows nothing about fashion unless it has a helmet and pads. He's an arrogant prick and he—"

Susana laughed. "Okay, okay! I get it." Part of her longed to go to lunch with her friend and just spill her guts—her annoyance with the partners and their endless condescension, her worries over leaving for a month. But no. This was the MPG office, she was a senior vice president, and Lauren was still her employee…as was the "dude."

"Let me think this through," she hedged. "I'm still getting my feet under me with this new job and Liscia is at the top of my very long list of priorities." She forced a laugh. "Unfortunately, my number one priority right now is packing to leave in four days."

Lauren smirked. "You poor thing. A month in paradise looming over your head. And here I am, nagging you about work."

"Get out of here, smartass." Susana smiled fondly at her friend. "I promise—I'll think about it and we'll get you somewhere you can make a difference. If it's not Liscia, there are plenty of other great accounts where I know you can add a lot of value. Just give me some time."

Four days came and went, and Susana was nowhere near ready to leave.

On their departure morning, she overslept, exhaustion finally claiming her after weeks of long hours. When she awoke, she was out of sorts—and irritated when she saw her suitcase packed and sitting by the door.

"Did you pack for me?" she snapped. "Why didn't you just wake me so I could pack my own suitcase?"

Enrique looked at his wife and sighed. "Susana, you were exhausted. Azalea sent me a list of things you should bring and I just did it for you." He shrugged. "And if I've forgotten anything, that's what credit cards are for."

She gaped at him, astonished. The truth was, she'd never gone anywhere without having to purchase items while she was away. She knew detailed planning wasn't her strong suit and she didn't mind the seat-of-her-pants approach—her spontaneity and willingness to take risks had been a hallmark of her work at MPG, and she'd always hired people who complemented her skills. But not having the opportunity to throw her things together—admittedly, at the last minute—sparked a flare of anger. "May I at least pack my own computer bag?"

Her husband didn't answer, just looked long at her. At last, he said, "The cab will be here in an hour," and left the bedroom.

"Fine," she muttered to his back. She yanked the bedding into a semblance of order and tossed the shams on top without a care for where they landed. Her heart hammered and she wanted to throw a pillow across the room. Or a lamp. Anything to relieve the pent up energy she felt. She knew she should be excited about this trip. She'd be in a beautiful country with the man she loved and her dearest friend. But right now she couldn't muster anything other than dread.

Her phone buzzed and she looked down to see a message from Peter. *I assume you're working on the plane, so make sure you send that updated sales plan to me today. I'm working this weekend and I'd like to have it for reference.*

She forgot about throwing pillows. She really wanted to smash her phone.

Within minutes after the plane reached altitude, Enrique was asleep. He'd surprised her with first class seats—"Just the first anniversary gift," he told her as they boarded the plane. She swallowed a pang of guilt. If he hadn't made the reservations, they wouldn't even be on the plane. The first gift? She hadn't bought him anything yet.

It felt odd having the panel between them. She was used to them traveling side by side, each having an aisle seat in coach. They'd reach across the space to touch hands or share a snack, always glancing at each other with a smile. Today's seats prevented them from touching, but Susana supposed she could reach over the barrier if she really needed to. *Like I can't go eight hours without touching him?* she scoffed to herself. She sighed and pulled out her laptop.

Thirty minutes later, she was finished, the sales plan sent winging its way across the ether to Peter's inbox. She was certain he was up and working and she wondered idly what his family did while he was engrossed in MPG business. She knew he was married with adult kids, but didn't know their ages. She'd met his wife—*Patrice? Patricia?*—at an agency holiday party but couldn't remember much about her. *Trophy wife*, she'd thought at the time, but perhaps that was unfair. Who really knew what people were like in real life? The statuesque blonde dressed head to toe in Chanel could have been a champion college volleyball player and a volunteer math tutor at a disadvantaged elementary school.

Probably not, she giggled. Then she wondered, *Why wasn't she wearing Liscia?* Surely the partner's wife ought to wear clothing from the agency's top client. The Gelbarrs could certainly afford the pricey pieces.

Good grief, she was tired, laughing to herself over the stupidest things. She rarely slept on planes, preferring to work or read, but the seat was so comfortable. Susana knew she was sleep deprived and pushing herself too hard, but she really had no other option. The partners were watching every move she made, and two of them were eager to see her fail. Maybe after the dinner service she'd nap. She glanced at Enrique, his easy breathing as familiar to her as her own. She was filled with a sudden urge to clamber over the half wall between them and curl up in his arms. Her husband had made partner in his architecture firm three years earlier and everything in his career now seemed stable and calm. He worked from home three days a week, only picked projects that interested and challenged him, and spent time mentoring the younger architects. She was just the tiniest bit jealous—*Okay, maybe a lot jealous*, she admitted. His career was golden while hers was nonstop pressure and grueling work.

She joined MPG nearly twenty years ago, rising from an account coordinator writing ad copy for her clients to her current role. She long ago transformed from the carefree university student who leaned heavily on Azalea's perfectionism and dean's list grades to get by. Now she was known throughout the agency as a relentless driver, a tireless researcher, and a brilliant strategist, someone who was determined to give clients the very best. Not always what they wanted, but always what they needed. She was a legend among the younger account teams for her insight and ability to zero in on the marketing trends to ride and those to abandon. She was at the pinnacle of her career and was proud of what she'd accomplished.

And, if she were honest with herself, she was absolutely burned out and wondered if she had what it took to succeed at this level.

Or if I even want to.

She awoke slowly, stretching and leaning into Enrique's palm on her cheek. When she realized where she was, she sat up with a start.

"*Cuidado, querida*," soothed her husband. "Good morning." He was leaning over the divide, brushing a lock of hair off her face. "Did you sleep well? Breakfast is coming and I thought you might be hungry."

Apparently, she'd fallen asleep before the dinner service and slept straight through the flight. She yawned as her stomach rumbled. "I guess I am," she said. "How did you sleep?"

"Like a baby," he grinned. "I woke up when they brought dinner but you were sleeping so soundly, I told them to let you be. It was nice to see you curled up and peaceful for a change."

After they finished eating, she rose to use the restroom. She gazed at her reflection and was surprised at how alert she looked—ordinarily she'd feel like a wrung out rag after a transatlantic flight. She mentally thanked her husband for the ridiculously overpriced seats. It was nice to feel semi-human now before they landed.

Susana brushed her teeth and smoothed her hair, then slicked some lip balm on her dry lips. She knew Azalea would be picture perfect when she got to the airport. Her best friend was effortlessly chic no matter where she was, and Susana had stopped trying to keep up with her decades before. The truth was, she just didn't care enough to be as fastidious as Azalea. She smiled at her reflection and made her way back to her seat where Enrique was returning after his morning ablutions. Before they sat, he leaned across the divider to kiss her.

"*Buenos días, Señora Cortéz-Guerrero,*" he murmured against her cheek. His morning beard scratched at her but she smiled at the sensation.

"*Buenos días, Señor Guerrero,*" she answered, reaching up to scratch his jaw.

They sat quietly and she sighed, feeling content for the first time in months. *Maybe this will turn out all right,* she thought, hoping she could hold onto the feeling. She watched as her husband folded his blanket and picked up his book. He was reading Ken Follett's *Pillars of the Earth* and earlier in the week she'd teased him about the size.

"Why don't you read it on your laptop?" she'd asked. "That thing must weigh ten pounds!"

He'd smiled and tried to explain to her how he loved the feel of a book in his hands and how he was learning so much about medieval cathedral architecture through the novel. "It's perfect for our trip," he'd told her. "We'll get to see churches in Spain and I'll know more about them when we get there. There's a lot more to see than just La Sagrada Familia."

Now he set a bookmark into the pages and looked up. "So how do you feel?" he asked.

"Fabulous," she answered. "I feel human this morning. It's wonderful." She stretched her neck and grinned. "You've ruined me, my love. I may never be able to fly coach again."

After getting through customs and retrieving their luggage, the couple entered the international terminal reception area. Their friends were in the front row of the crowd and Susana's smile matched Azalea's as they made eye contact. "I know it's only been a month, but I've missed you so much," she said, squeezing her best friend in a tight hug.

The four made their way to the parking garage and were on the road in no time, chatting about the flight and all the things the Obregons planned to show them. "Do you normally suffer much from jet lag?" asked Esteban.

"I do, especially the first day." Susana glanced at her husband and squeezed his hand. "But Kique splurged on first class tickets and I slept almost the entire flight. I feel great."

Azalea's eyes widened and she looked behind her at Enrique. "Well done, you," she said. "That's quite a kickoff to anniversary month."

Enrique smiled and squeezed Susana's hand back. "Thirty years is a miracle in this day and age," he said. "I think we should celebrate in a big way the entire month."

Susana noticed her friends glance at each other, a suspicious smile on both of their faces. "What are you two grinning about?" she demanded. "I saw that look."

Esteban responded first, his deeply accented voice rich and warm. "We are very happy you are here, Susana. And we're thrilled to see you so in love after all these years." He leaned over to kiss Azalea's cheek, then returned his gaze to the road. "I look forward to our own thirty year anniversary."

Enrique leaned over and whispered to Susana, "That will be sixty for us, *mi amor.*"

Susana leaned into his shoulder when her phone vibrated. Without thinking, she reached into her purse and pulled it out. Grimacing, she read the WhatsApp message.

Surely you've landed by now, Peter's message read. *Didn't you see my email? These numbers are not making sense, Susana. You're leaving out the possibility that Liscia gets acquired within the next year. I need more rigor from your analysis.*

She straightened and began typing. She glanced at Enrique. "Sorry," she muttered. "I have to answer this."

Her husband nodded. "It's your job, babe—I get it."

Susana noticed a slight edge to his voice, but pushed aside her concern. *He's just jet lagged.* She took a breath and continued typing.

6

The friends arrived at Esteban and Azalea's house and Susana and Enrique were given a quick tour. Susana noted Azalea's touch over the entire flat—her taste was impeccable, and the home managed to be both stylish and inviting. Azalea showed them to the spare bedroom, a small space decorated in soothing grays and blues. "This is lovely," Susana said, determined to put Peter's demands out of her mind.

"I hope you'll be comfortable. Let us know if you need anything at all." Azalea pointed to the towels folded at the foot of the bed. "Let me know if you need another blanket or more towels—the guest bath is just across the hall. Take your time," she told them before closing the door. "We'll head out for lunch in an hour."

Enrique opened his suitcase on the bed and began unpacking. Now that they were alone, the silence grew more awkward between them. At last Susana spoke up. "I'm sorry about the text messaging. I know I need to set some better boundaries with Peter." She worried that her husband didn't look back at her. "It's just this new job. I'm trying to meet their expectations and—"

"No, I understand," he interrupted quietly. "Babe, I know you've wanted—hell, you've *deserved*—this promotion. And I know what working at this level means. It's not like we're on a month-long vacation, as wonderful as that sounds. You have responsibilities and I need to be more patient."

Susana sat heavily on the bed. "Remember before you made partner? You worked crazy hours and took on projects you hated." She shook her head and muttered, "You weren't all that fun to be around then, to be honest."

His eyebrows raised at her comment and she turned away. She knew she wasn't being fair—Enrique was the most even-keeled person she'd ever met and he'd rarely been cross even during his most challenging career transitions. She ruefully acknowledged she'd been the grouchy one, loudly complaining at what she perceived were slights to her husband and the firm's unreasonable expectations. "*Ay, gruñosa*," he had soothed her many evenings. "All will be well, you'll see. It's just a season."

And he'd been right. She *was* grouchy and it *did* turn out well.

She lay back on the bed and patted the pillow next to her. "Come here," she said. She wasn't eager to start their trip debating over her job, and hoped she could snuggle her way clear of any tension. She smiled as her husband rolled his eyes, set the suitcase on the floor, and dropped onto the bed, his head snug against her breast.

"Oh, very well," he said theatrically before rolling over and clasping her in a firm embrace. "You know you can always win me over with that smile." He nuzzled her chest, then pulled her down for a kiss. His fingers laced through her hair and his warm tongue slid into her mouth.

Susana moaned and leaned into him. "Oh, Kique," she whispered. Her body molded to his and she felt the familiar yet still exciting heat for her husband of three decades.

The knock on the door startled them. "You guys decent?" called Azalea. "What about a walk around the plaza before we have lunch? It will help with the jet lag."

Susana stifled a laugh as she reached down to stroke Enrique's inner thigh. His eyes widened and he slapped her hand away. "Sure, Azalea. We'll be out in a second."

"You are terrible," murmured Enrique as he kissed her again.

"The worst," she agreed, smiling against his lips.

The weather was perfect—fluffy white clouds lazily drifted across a bright blue sky, and Susana took off her cardigan ten minutes after they sat down. The boulevard hummed with activity as hundreds of people meandered down the street. The couples had been lucky to find a table, wedging themselves amongst the other hundreds—thousands?—of people strolling along Las Ramblas.

Susana savored the sights and smells and felt her entire body relax. She loved the feel of the plaza, the unique Spanish juxtaposition of bustling energy and relaxation. She glanced over and saw Enrique smiling at her. He winked and squeezed her hand under the table, then lightly stroked her thigh. She knew he was still thinking of their brief interlude and she wondered how they would manage intimacy while staying in her friends' home for a month. *Shoulda thought about that before we left Florida*, she scolded herself, stifling a grin.

They looked over the menu and she laughed at the size of the drinks. Las Ramblas cafés were famous for the gigantic glasses of sangria, margaritas, daiquiris, and other exotic libations. They resembled fish bowls more than glasses. She knew drinking on the first day would make staying awake more difficult, but—

"I know drinking on the first day makes it a bit harder to stay awake," said Azalea, "but the sangria here is divine." Susana grinned. She and her closest friend had been sharing thoughts for over thirty years and it didn't surprise her to find Azalea speaking aloud what was in her head.

She set the menu down and nodded. "I'll go for the *sangria blanca*," she answered, then looked at Enrique.

"*Lo mismo. Estamos en Barcelona, querida.*" He looked around the table. "*Debemos hablar in español, no?*"

"We *should* speak Spanish, but it's gonna take me a few days for it to just flow," answered Susana.

Esteban leaned over to kiss his wife's cheek, then replied. "*Ambos lenguas, si? Mi esposa* still struggles a bit, but if we use both languages, it helps."

Azalea made a face. "I don't know what it is about speaking it. I read it just fine, but I get all tongue-tied when I try to speak Spanish."

Susana looked at her friend and smiled. "We'll help you, *hermana*. Don't worry about it—it will come." She looked up as the waiter approached with their huge drinks. "But for now, let's dive into these fish bowls.

Lunch finished, they sat back and relaxed. Susana grimaced as the couple at the next table lit cigarettes and blew the smoke her way. Living in Florida, she'd grown used to few people smoking outdoors but in Spain it was everywhere. She turned her chair slightly to avoid the smoke, but knew it would end up in her hair. *Chill out, chica,* she told herself. *You're in Spain with family and a little smoke isn't going to kill you.*

"…and so we added some temporary staff to the Cadaqués café and we're fine to stay here in Barcelona for a month," finished Esteban. He smiled at Azalea, then brought her hand to his lips. Susana's heart melted. Azalea had experienced profound heartache with her unfaithful first husband and she deserved a good man. *He loves her so much,* she thought.

Susana glanced at Enrique. She had a good man, too. Their thirty years hadn't been perfect, but they had been happy. She knew she was a handful—everyone, from her parents to her closest friends, told her that. But Kique had been there for every dream, every adventure, every disappointment, everything. He never turned away. Never.

Her husband seemed to intuit exactly what she needed, no matter how wild her mood or crazy her ideas. Enrique Guerrero was the rock she clung to in hard times and stood upon in good. From the moment they'd met, she had been certain of him. *There is just something so solid about Kique,* she mused. Words like *reliable, predictable,* and *stalwart* came to mind.

She stifled a chuckle. *I make him sound like a washing machine.*

Enrique and Esteban were chatting but she wasn't paying much attention. The jet lag was beginning to kick in, despite the luxury class seating, and the afternoon sun and gargantuan sangria wasn't helping. A pleasant languor overtook her when her phone abruptly buzzed, interrupting her thoughts.

She noticed a flicker of annoyance on Enrique's face but it vanished before it could take root. She glanced down and saw an incoming call from Steven Miles.

"Sorry," she said to the table. "I need to take this." She tipped her head at Enrique. "It's Steven."

He nodded and Susana rose to step away from the table.

"It's her boss," she heard Enrique say as she moved a few feet from the diners.

"Hi, Steven," she said. "What's up?"

"Hi Susana, sorry to interrupt your first day away. I hoped to leave you alone for at least a week." His chuckle sounded forced. "Anyway, Peter called and said he's very concerned about the Liscia account. He's decided he wants you to take personal charge of it. I don't think Doug is his favorite person right now."

Susana stifled a sigh. It was an open secret that Douglas Albrecht III was a good friend of Peter's eldest son, and Peter had pushed through his hiring as a favor to his boy. Now it looked like being his kid's college roommate—or "Peter's dude," as Lauren dubbed him— wasn't enough of a résumé boost to be successful at MPG.

"So what exactly does that mean? Does Douglas report to me now?" she asked, trying to keep her voice level.

"He does. Start with a full debrief from him. Get all his notes and review what's been done over the past month. I'm afraid you'll need to be pretty hands on, Susana. I get the impression he's made a bit of a mess over there."

"'Bit of a mess?' What is that supposed to mean?"

Steven sighed and grew silent.

"How bad is it?" she asked.

"Well, in addition to offering very junior-level advice to a premier client, evidently he got involved with one of their employees. It was brief, didn't end well, and she's complained to their CMO. They want him off the account immediately and they're seriously considering not continuing with MPG. I'm not trying to be dramatic, but we're relying on you to get this under control—maybe even consider flying out there for a couple of days."

"Steven, Liscia is headquartered in Palo Alto. That wouldn't have been a problem when I was in Florida, but it's a bit inconvenient now."

The silence lingered and then Steven answered. "Would a few days be that big of problem? I'm sure you're aware that I went to bat for you when it came to you working from Spain, Susana. Jonathan wasn't thrilled with the idea and Peter was downright hostile." *How many times will you remind me?* she wondered. She knew the other two partners hadn't supported her request and was thankful that Steven had. But his constant reminders were wearing thin.

"I do know that, Steven. And I'm grateful. I have no intention of letting the agency down or of losing an important client." She took a deep breath, trying to rein in her emotions. *Cuidate, loca,* she cautioned herself. It wouldn't do to alienate the one partner in her corner. "Why doesn't Peter talk directly to them and make nice?"

"Peter is convinced they're going to merge or sell. He believes the new CEO is just a placeholder and the board is quietly seeking a buyer. He was pretty dismissive of her when Geneva took the reins and I doubt he'd have much luck fixing this rift.

"Look, Susana, if they do sell, it won't be a quick deal—luxury brands aren't hot right now, but Peter's not budging from his opinion. I think we need to get ahead of this and be prepared if they get acquired or if they merge with another design house." Steven's voice was grim. "Whatever happens, MPG needs to retain that business."

Susana closed her eyes to steady herself. "I understand."

Twenty minutes later, she returned to the table and forced a smile. "I'm sorry. I didn't think that would take so long." She sat down and looked at Azalea. "This new job is more demanding than I expected." She shrugged, trying to adopt a lighthearted tone. "Evidently only I can salvage a problem client, who of course has to be in California. He even suggested I go out there, which of course is crazy."

"Are you serious?" Azalea asked. "Who's the client?"

"Liscia. It's a—"

"Oh, I know Liscia," her friend laughed. "A bit pricey for me, but I love the brand. Gorgeous stuff"

"Why would the client need you out there?" asked Enrique.

"It's the not the client," answered Susana. "This is all the part-ners. Peter screwed things up with Liscia and they expect me to clean up the mess." She took a deep breath. "I'll probably have to take some evening calls for the next week while I calm them down. I'll get it sorted as quickly as I can so it doesn't mess up our evenings."

Enrique frowned, but didn't respond.

Esteban nodded and stood up. "Shall we stroll a bit along Las Ramblas? It's such a lovely afternoon." He glanced at Enrique and then at Susana. "Do you need to take another call or are you free?"

She answered quickly. "No, I'm free. Let's look around—maybe grab a coffee? Isn't your café nearby?" She reached for Enrique's shoulder. "You up for a coffee, Kique?"

At last her husband looked at her, his look indecipherable. "Sure. I'd love to see the café." He stood and stretched, then reached for her hand. "Let's go see how the other half lives."

And what the hell does that mean?

7

The bedroom door closed behind her and Susana took a deep breath. Enrique stood next to the bed and began to undress, his back to her. She walked to him and slid her arms around him, laying her cheek on his smooth back.

"Susana—" he began.

She slid her hands along his stomach, kissing his back softly.

"Susana," he said, his voice tight. He turned in her arms, pulling away. "Can we please talk about today? We can't just pretend everything is all right." He ran his hand through his dark hair, and the sorrowful look on his face gripped her heart.

"What do you mean?" she asked. She sat heavily on the bed. "What's got you so wound up?"

He was silent for a long moment, then sat next to her. "I'm not trying to be a jerk about this, but what's going on with MPG?" He took her hand. "Now Steven wants you in California? Are you seriously considering going?"

A spark of anger flared and she snapped, "I didn't agree to go out there, but if that's what's required to salvage this client, that's what executives do. *You know this, Kique.* You've already achieved everything you wanted in your career. Why is it now a problem when it's me?" She knew she needed to dial back her anger but she was tired and frustrated. *Why did we even come here?* she thought. *I should have stayed home.*

Enrique looked at her for a moment before responding. "Is that what you think? That I don't value your career like I do mine?"

The hurt on his face was palpable but Susana pressed forward. "I didn't say that. But I do think maybe you forgot what it's like to grind. To want something so bad and to sacrifice whatever it takes to make it happen." She shook her head angrily as the words spilled out. "You've been a partner for what? Three years? It must be nice to sit in that ivory tower and judge me for trying to get to it myself."

Way to take it from zero to sixty in two seconds flat.

Enrique stood gaping at her, then took a deep breath. When he finally spoke, his words were measured, his voice soft. "Susana, you are the love of my life. You know that. I'm just worried when I see you working so hard for what I believe are unreasonable demands. I know you want this job, *mi amor*, but at what cost? You know I will always support your dreams."

"That's not what it sounds like, Kique. I know you love me and I know you support me. But I think now that you're enjoying the fruit of all your hard work, you don't appreciate what I'm going through. I'm not where you are and you don't like it. I'm still making the sacrifices you made years ago and somehow that's not okay?" She shook her head and frowned. "Never expected the stereotypical double standard from you."

Enrique looked away and didn't answer.

They undressed and got into bed, the inches between them a chasm she wondered how they would ever traverse.

"I'm sorry." His voice was soft in the dark. "I just want more for you and for us."

When she awoke, Susana sent a meeting invite to Douglas, scheduling it for four o'clock. *Might as well get this done today,* she thought. *That's ten in the morning for him. Easy.*

By three thirty, she was ready for a break and went to the kitchen for a glass of water. She stretched her neck, rolled her shoulders, and smiled at Azalea. "How's your day going?"

"Very well," answered her friend, closing her laptop. "Just finished a messaging document for a new client and I am very ready for a siesta."

Susana laughed. "Ah, the beauty of living in Spain. So where are the guys? I sort of remember saying good bye but I was knee deep in researching Liscia's distribution plans."

"Out for a run. They'll be back soon." Azalea smiled. "Seriously, I'm gonna go nap for half an hour. You done yet?"

"Nah…one more call. Go get your beauty sleep and I'll see you in a bit."

Azalea nodded and walked to her bedroom as an MPG instant message notification flashed on Susana's screen. She read, then reread Doug's note. *Is he for real?*

Sorry for the last minute change but I need to reschedule our meeting. I'm free at 4 pm today. See you then.

She looked at the clock again. It was five minutes until four—in Spain. He had accepted the invite immediately that morning and, while she thought it was odd that he was answering emails at one in the morning Florida time, she brushed it off. Everyone had their own work schedules and she didn't really care when he worked, as long as he did his job. But this?

When your new boss schedules a meeting with you, you don't blow it off, she thought angrily.

That's 10 pm for me, she wrote. *I'm unavailable at that time.*

His status changed to Out of Office.

By ten o'clock, Douglas still hadn't responded to her message and Susana was furious. Enrique kissed her cheek as he and the Obregons went out for an evening stroll on the plaza, leaving her to stew at the kitchen table, her laptop open.

I should just fire his ass, she thought, as she opened the call, then waited nearly five minutes before he joined.

"Hey, Susana," he said, his tone casual. "How's it going?"

She glared at him. "It's not going well, Douglas," she snapped. "It is ten o'clock in the evening for me and I told you I wasn't available. I'd like to know why you ignored my message."

He looked down at his phone and ran a hand through his hair. "Oh, wow. Guess I missed that."

Susana took a deep breath. *This kid is not going to get the better of me. He's barely more than an intern.*

"What was so important that you had to delay this meeting for six hours? You know how critical the Liscia account is."

"Last minute golf game with another client. Pete couldn't make it, so he asked me to fill in for him."

Pete? Susana ground her teeth. "By 'Pete,' I suppose you mean Peter Gelbarr?"

"Yeah. Sounds funny to hear him called that." Doug chuckled. "He's just Pete to me. Anyway, he said you wouldn't mind. Said you're basically on vacation so it wasn't a big deal for you to take a late call."

She steadied her breathing. She wasn't about to argue with this…*boy.* She would deal with Peter later.

"Let's make this quick. I want all your notes on the Liscia account. I haven't decided which account you'll move to just yet, but I'll let you know this week. Until then, spend your time getting all your files together—I want them in my inbox by end of day tomorrow." She looked at him, her face stern. "This isn't a suggestion, Doug. This account is in crisis thanks to your behavior and I will not accept excuses or delays. Am I clear?"

"Yeah, you're clear." He tilted his head, inquiring. "So this is all because of Tiffany? You know that was completely consensual. I didn't do anything wrong. In fact, she pretty much started the whole thing." He smirked. "She definitely started it."

What are you, ten years old? she wanted to ask.

"We have very clear company guidelines that you agreed to upon employment," she said instead. "We don't have romantic relationships with clients. You violated that rule and it's fortunate that you're not being terminated for it."

"Guess I'm not in the good old *chicas* group, huh?" he muttered.

Susana stared at him, aghast. "What did you say?"

"Never mind."

"Oh, I very much mind," she spat. "What did you just say to me?"

He looked at her, the hint of a smile playing on his lips. "Look, I saw Lauren and that Thompson Toys guy the other night at the Cellar in Daytona and it definitely wasn't an agency/client meeting." He straightened his shoulders. "You're obviously covering for her, so spare me the lecture. I'm guessing Pete and the partners don't know about their little…*romantic relationship*."

Susana burst out laughing. "Are you trying to threaten me?"

He glared at her, and she could imagine that face across the line of scrimmage. *It might work on the football field*, she thought. *Not here, little boy.*

"I'm just saying that I'm sure you can put me on a good account and none of this needs to go any further."

"So that's where you're wrong, Douglas. Lauren and Mr. Rivera decided they would like to explore a personal relationship. They each told their respective companies and it was decided that Lauren would leave the account and move to another team." Her voice was razor sharp. "That's how *adults* manage their professional lives. And it has already gone to our HR department, because that's how I manage my teams."

Which is where this conversation is going, too, she decided.

"Get those files to me, Douglas." She closed the call without saying goodbye and messaged Christian Beran, MPG's HR director.

Hey, I need to talk with you about an employee. Do you have some time tomorrow morning?

Hi Susana! Yup, I'm free between 8 and 9.

Great—I'll send an invite.

She closed her laptop and rubbed her temples. Her relationship with Peter was already fraught and this situation could only make things worse, she was sure. *The kid has some* cojones *to threaten me.* She wondered what it must be like to feel so privileged, so entitled. She couldn't imagine ever speaking to a supervisor like that.

But she'd never been a nepotism hire. She'd worked her way up through talent and grit, excelling at every role, every rung on the career ladder. And as angry as she was, she knew this situation required careful handling.

Peter wouldn't miss an opportunity to oppose her at every turn.

An hour later, her friends and Enrique returned to the flat and she was still fuming. She gave her husband the long version of the conversation while they readied themselves for bed, emphasizing Douglas' pompous disrespect. He listened without a word, responding only with nods and frowns. At last, she pulled the covers over her lap and sat propped up against her pillows. "Can you believe that? I keep trying to imagine ever talking to one of my managers like that. Or can you picture my *abuela* sassing any of the people she cleaned for? Even if she couldn't stand someone, she would never have spoken to them that way." Susana glanced at Enrique. "You're awfully quiet."

"I didn't want to interrupt you. It sounded like you needed to get that out."

"I guess I did. Easier that punching something." She smiled and patted the bed beside her. "Thanks for listening. It always makes things better when I can share them with you."

Enrique turned out the light and got into bed. Susana snuggled up next to him, draping her arm across his chest.

"At the risk of being a broken record, is this the sort of thing you want to deal with? I know you love the work, but this isn't what you went into marketing for. It's like adult daycare for brats."

Susana pulled away and lay on her back, staring into the darkness. "You're right. You do sound like a broken record." She rolled over to her edge of the bed, all thoughts of sleep gone in her anger. Her voice was terse. "No, I do not want to deal with Douglas. But if I don't want to go backwards twenty years and make my living writing social media posts, then it's part of the job. You don't like everyone you manage, do you? But I haven't once asked you to second guess your career track." She waited for his response, but he said nothing.

8

Over the next week, the four friends settled into a comfortable routine. They'd walk to the square for breakfast at La Rosa de Barcelona, Esteban's first café, for breakfast, sitting outdoors, sipping *cafecitos* and enjoying *pan dulce* and *tortillas*, the traditional Spanish dish of eggs, onions, and potatoes cooked in a deep skillet. After their leisurely meal, Esteban would remain at the café to work while the others spent an hour shopping at the neighborhood market or simply looking in store windows and watching people. Everywhere people bustled, calling out *"Buenos días"* as they stopped along the boulevard to embrace and chat with friends.

The entire neighborhood thrummed with energy as locals purchased their daily supplies. In the market, brightly colored vegetables filled baskets next to stalls with fresh meats and cheeses. The aroma of fresh bread wafted across the kiosks as the bakers unloaded their wares. Each morning Enrique helped Azalea with her Spanish as they strolled, always patient and encouraging, and Susana marveled at the tranquility that filled her soul. *He's a born teacher*, she mused.

And then they'd return to the flat.

Azalea had set up the dining area as a work station for the three of them. Each had a spot at the table for a laptop, and if one of them had to take a call and needed quiet or privacy, the others would move to their respective bedrooms. It was a well-choreographed dance they managed throughout the day. In the afternoons, often it was Enrique on the video calls, working with his team in Florida as they collaborated on a new museum project in Tampa.

On one such call, Azalea stopped Susana before she entered the spare bedroom. "Got a minute?" she asked.

Susana nodded, and Azalea beckoned her. They walked down the hall to Azalea and Esteban's room and sat on the bed. "You okay?" asked Azalea.

"I'm fine—why?" Susana knew she couldn't hide anything from her friend. It was pointless to try. At Azalea's knowing look, Susana gave in. "Okay. I'm not fine. Things at work are a mess. It's not just client stuff—it's office politics. One of the partners is a complete dick and we keep butting heads." She took a deep breath. "And then there's Kique…. *We're* not fine. This was supposed to be a great trip for our anniversary and we're hardly even talking, much less anything romantic." She scowled. "He hates my new job and he's pushing me to stop giving so much time to work."

Azalea raised one eyebrow. "Kique's pushing you? Since when?"

Susana relented. "Okay, that was an exaggeration. He's not pushing, but it's clear he's not happy with me."

Her friend took her hand. "Suze…c'mon. It's not you he's not happy with. That man adores you. It was obvious thirty years ago and it's obvious today."

"I just wish he were more understanding. He's been through this grind—shouldn't he be completely in my corner? I would expect him to get it more than anyone. Every single day is like running a gauntlet at work, like I have to prove myself over and over. I want to show them they didn't make a mistake when they promoted me. SVP is no joke, *'mana*. I have so much more responsibility and I know that two of the three partners are hoping I choke." She frowned. "I'm not just a diversity hire to check the HR box. I'm good at what I do. Damn good."

Azalea nodded and squeezed Susana's hand. "I know that, Suze. I do. And I'm rooting for you—we all are. You have a team back in

Florida—what are they doing? I talked to Lauren yesterday and I know she's eager to take on more responsibility."

Susana nodded. "Yeah, she asked me about that before I left. She's doing a great job and I know I can count on her. The whole team is really talented…except this new kid who got dumped on me. He's the reason I got stuck with the Liscia account." She grimaced. "He's buddies with one of the partners and tries to leverage that to get what he wants." She laughed harshly. "You'll love this: He tried to bully me into putting him on a good account by threatening to tell the partners about Lauren and Jayson."

Azalea gaped at her friend. "You're kidding. What a moron."

"Right? I'd love to just fire him, but it's not gonna happen. And so this premier account is in trouble and the partners are on my back. It's why they want me to go to California. They're relentless."

Azalea frowned. "And now you know why I started my own consulting firm. I got sick to death of working for people who couldn't care less about me or my family or anything apart from their personal goals. Just be sure you don't give those jerks all your time and energy. Remember, my friend: They aren't the ones who've been around for thirty years."

Ouch.

The two hugged and Susana went back to her bedroom where once again she reviewed the agency history with Liscia. The company's designers were all located in California, creating their high end clothing in the States with production in Bangladesh. They were a tier one client, probably MPG's top customer, with lots of upside opportunity. Why they'd given it to Douglas was beyond her. He was pretentious and utterly full of himself. She didn't see him as exceptionally talented, but his claim to an important MPG role was obvious: He had played football at Florida State where he roomed with Peter Gelbarr's son Preston. Peter was an FSU alum and an enthusiastic booster for their football team, so when Preston and Douglas graduated, he insisted the boy was a perfect account manager. Maybe so, but for the top client? There were plenty of other smaller accounts he could have cut his teeth on. She had never thought Peter was stupid, but his decision had put the agency in a precarious position.

And now she was stuck with the mess he'd made. Even Christian had cautioned her to tread lightly.

Thanks for documenting your conversation with Doug, the HR director had written after their call. *Just know that Peter is backing this hire 100% and has specifically told me that he'll handle any "warranted disciplinary action."*

Which means none, Susana thought. *Fabulous.*

She was deep into her emails when she heard the knock on the door.

"I'm done if you want to come back out," said Enrique as he entered.

Susana stood and stretched, then dove for her laptop as it slid off the bed and nearly hit the floor. Enrique reached it just as she did, their fingertips meeting under the silver metal. Both of them were on their knees, their faces inches apart. She looked at him, noticing the faint lines around his gold-flecked brown eyes, the silver threads at his temples. Enrique had aged beautifully—he was still her Kique, the handsome, quiet architect she'd met so many years before, and her heart still warmed at the sight of him.

She raised a hand to stroke his face, but he pushed himself up and stood before she could complete the gesture. He took the laptop, put it safely back on the bed, and reached down to help her up.

"Good teamwork," he said, his voice bland. "Anyway, the table's free if you want it."

"So you're done for the day?"

"Yeah, I just needed to give the team a little more direction on the museum project. I'm gonna go outside for some fresh air. Need anything?"

I need you, she thought. *I need us.*

She reached for her laptop and walked to the bedroom door. "I'm good. Have a nice walk."

That night after dinner, the four friends sat in the living room sipping wine and chatting. Susana sat back on the loveseat she shared with Enrique, then leaned into him, her head against his shoulder. She was finished for the day, she decided. After hours of review, she reluctantly agreed with Peter—her involvement was essential to salvaging the relationship with Liscia. She knew he'd complain, but she assigned Douglas more junior work with a far less important client and pulled Lauren onto the Liscia team. *She may be my friend*, Susana mused, *but she has a strong fashion and retail background that will help.* The account needed bold ideas and Susana was eager to prove her worth to both the client and the partners. She emailed her initial thoughts to Steven, then shut down her laptop. *Let him deal with Peter*, she decided.

For now, she was going to enjoy the evening with her friends and her husband, and hoped she and Enrique could regain some connection. They hadn't made love in over a week, and she longed to feel his body against hers.

Enrique set his glass down and put his arm around her. She snuggled closer, wishing it were late enough to say goodnight to Azalea and Esteban. It was Friday night and they were discussing plans for the weekend.

"Cadaqués is a little over two hours away," Esteban said. "If we leave around ten o'clock, that gives me time to check on La Rosa first. I assume you three have work to do as well, so does that give everyone enough time?" When everyone nodded, he continued. "*Bueno*…we'll be at our café Rosita Del Mar by lunch and have time for a swim." He smiled at his wife. "*La bahía es muy especial para nosotros. Muy romantica.*"

"It is special," Azalea agreed, then patted her husband's hand. "I don't think I told you, but Esteban writes poetry and he read some to me for the first time on that beach. It's so picturesque and the water is gorgeous."

"Dalí painted there, too, no? He's one of my favorite artists," said Enrique.

"*Sí*," answered Esteban. "He lived and painted there for many years."

Enrique looked down at Susana and hugged her tightly. "It sounds wonderful," he answered. "I'm looking forward to it."

Susana leaned forward, her elbows on her knees. "I'm not a huge Dalí fan, but I do want to hear all about that romantic poetry on the beach," she said, her voice mischievous. "Tell us, 'mana. Describe it… *in Spanish*."

Azalea's eyes narrowed. "You're a brat, Susana, but I am up for the challenge." She cleared her throat and began. "*Esteban y yo…estabamos? Estuvieron?* Argh…." She put her head in her hands. "Why does conjugating verbs always mess me up?"

Susana laughed. "You think too hard about it. You were right the first time. *Estabamos* means we were." She smiled encouragement at her friend. "*Sigue, chica. Recuerde: Tienes que practicar. No tienes que ser perfecta.*" Remember: You have to practice. You don't have to be perfect.

Azalea sighed. "I know, I know. Okay. *Estabamos en la playa cuando el sol…*was setting." The friends laughed.

"*El sol se ponía,*" suggested Esteban.

His wife looked at her watch. "I hope you have plenty of time, because this could take a while."

Just then, Susana's phone vibrated on the table. She felt Enrique stiffen next to her and the lighthearted banter ceased.

It's ten o'clock on a Friday night. I shouldn't pick this up.

She waited…then picked up the phone.

9

"…yes, but that's not accurate, Steven, and you know it." Susana gritted her teeth and tried to lower her voice. Taking the call from the bedroom only blocked some of the noise, she was certain. She closed her eyes and breathed deeply. *I have got to get this under control,* she thought fiercely.

Enrique walked in, his face clouded. She couldn't tell if he were angry or disappointed, but she was certain he was displeased. She tilted her head and mouthed *I'm sorry,* but he shook his head and held up a hand to forestall her.

"Steven, it's Friday night. I don't care if it's still afternoon in California. I'm not getting on a call with them now—" She looked down at at Enrique's phone where he typed on his notepad and held the screen up for her to read.

Do what you need to do. I don't like it, but I understand and I'm trying to support you. We're going out for a drink and we'll leave you some privacy.

Her eyes widened and she stared at him. *Are you sure?* she whispered.

He nodded, a slight frown creasing his forehead. He leaned down to kiss her cheek, then left the room.

"No, I know *you're* sure," Susana said, responding to Steven's irritated tone. "I was talking to Enrique." She grimaced. "Okay, I'll join a call. Send me the link but this is the last time, Steven. I know they're important but aren't you the one who taught me to set good boundaries with clients?"

She hung up the phone and took her laptop into the dining area where she settled, notebook and pencil ready. She clicked onto the video call link and forced a smile as both the new Liscia CEO and Chief Marketing Officer joined the call, quickly followed by Steven.

"Hi, Geneva, Desirée," she said, her tone bright. "Great to see you both." She dug her fingernails into her palms, loathing herself for the insincerity. The two women looked grim although they both nodded and greeted her.

Steven began. "Thanks for taking the time to meet, everyone. I know we're all eager to get to our weekend and get this difficult week behind us." The Liscia executives nodded, and Geneva sat back, folding her arms across her chest as Steven continued. "I want you to know we've removed Douglas from the account and Susana will handle all communications and projects with Liscia from here on out."

Susana kept her face impassive but anger bubbled up and she wondered *What does that mean? That isn't what we discussed. I'm a senior vice president, not an account executive.*

Desirée answered, her tone harsh. "I have no idea why you put someone so junior on our account, Steven. The first time he showed up late for a meeting was bad enough. The fact that he hit on one of our employees was completely over the top. You're lucky she doesn't sue him—and MPG. And his utter ignorance of the luxury women's clothing market is insulting. That kid can't even spell sustainability, much less define it. We have enough issues internally without having to deal with your incompetence. Frankly, I don't know why we're keeping MPG. My vote was to fire you, but what do I know? I'm just the CMO." She folded her hands in front of her. "It's Geneva's decision and I'll follow it." She stared into her camera. "I sincerely hope you know what you're doing, Susana."

Geneva's eyes darted to what Susana assumed was Desirée's Zoom window before she spoke. "We've worked with MPG for three years and we know their work, Desirée. We've been through all this." She steepled her fingers, then dropped her hands. "But yes, Susana, we're expecting big things from you. Steven speaks very highly of you and your attention to clients. I expect we'll be having these calls regularly to ensure we get back on track. The Fall season is around the corner and it's huge for us with the new line."

Regularly? What the hell does that mean?

The CEO looked down and tapped her pen to her lips. "I can clear my calendar for meetings at this time for the next couple of weeks. Desirée will manage the day to day, but I'll want an update on progress, so let's say Monday, Wednesday, and Friday at this time?"

Susana cleared her throat. "Actually, I'm in Bar—"

"That works perfectly for us," interrupted Steven.

Her phone lit up with his message: *Do NOT say anything about Spain. Make this your 1 priority!*

"Good," said Geneva. "I'll leave you to it, then. I'm off for a quick jaunt to Napa this weekend, but I'll expect progress when we talk Monday." She left the call without further comment, but Desirée wasn't finished.

"I need an entirely new creative strategy by Monday," she said. "The one Douglas sent over is garbage. This is a huge evolution for Liscia and changing the color scheme and website navigation doesn't come close to what this launch should entail. This is a luxury brand, not an eco-friendly line of clothes you pick up at Target. The messaging has to appeal to our traditional customers while bringing in new ones. That boy didn't even come close." Her eyebrows drew together in a scornful look. "I'll expect it in my inbox Monday morning when I walk in the door and I'll need you to be available throughout the morning for comments so we can be ready for the afternoon meeting with Geneva."

Afternoon for you, thought Susana. *One more late night for me.*

Again, Steven interjected. "That won't be a problem. Susana will handle everything to your satisfaction. You can count on MPG."

Susana dug her fingernails further into her palms, deepening the grooves to keep herself from screaming. She smiled. "Right! Not a problem." *So much for a measured approach.*

Kique is gonna just love this.

Enrique pulled her close and whispered in her hair. "*Calmate, cardito. Es un sueño.*" She snuggled back into him, grateful for his closeness. It *was* just a dream, but it was real enough to wake her fully. The knot in her stomach hadn't loosened since her call with Steven and the Liscia executives. Would MPG claim both her days and her nights?

After a few short minutes, her husband's slow breathing told her he had fallen back asleep, his hand resting lightly on her hip. But now she was restless, her mind whirring with plans and ideas. The fashion industry moved so fast—Liscia's Fall line would be in stores in less than a year. She needed a new strategy for the company, but she needed a full team to support it. She'd already moved Lauren over—maybe Timothy, too? He was great with messaging.

She stopped herself. *No. Not tonight*, she decided. *It's the middle of the night, I'm in bed with my wonderful husband, in a beautiful city far from home. I am not giving one more minute of time to my job or my boss or this stupid client.* She rolled over to face Enrique and he sighed in his sleep. The moonlight fell on his face and she gently traced the stubble on his chin, noticing the silver interspersed with the black. She lightly brushed his lower lip with her finger, then leaned forward to kiss him. She stroked his shoulder, then his arm, letting her hand slide down his hip. She felt his smile under her lips and then he pulled her close, kissing her as his body responded to her touch.

They slipped into a familiar rhythm, their bodies knowing each other intimately and well. "I have missed you, *querida*," he whispered, his hands gripping her hips as he rolled to his back. Her long braid trailed across his chest as they came together in a harmony only decades of love could evoke.

"Oh, Kique…." Susana forgot that they were in Azalea's home, forgot her work, forgot everything but the man she adored. Their lovemaking was slow and sweet and everything she needed to reconnect. They melded into one and her body shuddered with their shared pleasure.

At last they quieted and she moved to lie next to him. "No, no," he whispered, holding her on top of him. "*Quédate aquí.*"

She sighed into him, content to remain still, and settled her head against his chest. "I love you," she whispered. "I love you so much."

Enrique squeezed her tightly, then loosened his embrace, his fingertips light on her back. He was quiet, and Susana asked, "What are you thinking?"

"I'm thinking that I love you," he said simply. She nuzzled into his shoulder as he continued. "I'm thinking that we have fewer days in front of us than behind us, and I'm thankful we can spend them together. Who else do we know who's still married after thirty years? Much less still in love? We can't waste a single moment, *querida*." His tone was serious, almost plaintive. *That's not Kique*, she thought.

"Babe, I'll do my best to get this work stuff under control. I know it's ridiculous what they're asking of me—I do. Please trust me that I'm not just rolling over for MPG because of the promotion."

She felt his chuckle as he rolled her to her back, still holding her tight. Though they'd finished only minutes before, she felt him harden against her and she eagerly wrapped her legs around his hips. "The only one I want you rolling over for is me," he said, a boyish grin on his face.

And then the man returned and their slow, sweet joining was a thing of the past as he held her tightly, his strong hands in her hair, his lips and tongue on her collarbone. *Thirty years*, she marveled, and then was swept away in desire, passion, and love.

10

The next morning, the couples returned to La Rosa de Barcelona for breakfast. Intimacy with Kique did more than sate her physically. Susana felt more hopeful than she had since arriving a week ago, and she sat with a contented smile. Esteban and Enrique were chattering about the unusual bread pudding Esteban's son had put on the menu before he'd met Azalea. *They're like two old women*, she thought lazily. *Viejas lindas.*

"Let me show you the kitchen," said Esteban. He and Enrique rose and he asked, "Susana? Would you like to come, too?"

Azalea reached out a hand before Susana could answer. "You two go—we have some catching up to do." She smiled sweetly at the two men.

Susana looked askance at her friend but nodded to the men. "I'll see it another time. I'm enjoying just sitting here with my coffee."

Esteban nodded and he and Enrique walked toward the kitchen. Azalea looked at her friend with a knowing smile. "Okay. I don't need details, but things seem better. You kinda have that post…ya know, glow."

Susana barked out a laugh—there was no pretending with Azalea. Over thirty years of friendship meant they read each other without words. She shook her head fondly and smiled. "Yes, things are better." She gazed unseeing out the window. "You know, I envy you, Azalea. I watch you and Esteban and I'm honestly jealous of you." She looked back at her friend. "It's like Kique and I have had this storybook life. We've been in sync about our careers and kids and where we live…pretty much everything. It's not like it's been perfect, but all of a sudden it's not easy. We're at this point where we have to work hard to stay connected and we aren't used to it. I look at you and it seems effortless for you guys. I know you're still newlyweds, but you're not twenty years old and this isn't the first time for either of you. You're mature adults and I'm sure you have your disagreements. But all I see is love and respect." She looked down, suddenly embarrassed. "Sorry for getting so mushy, but you have a beautiful marriage and I'm really happy for you, my friend. You deserve it."

Azalea touched her friend's arm and Susana looked up. "You have a beautiful marriage, too, Suze," she said quietly. "Esteban and I just treat ours differently." She spread her hands, taking in the café. "It's so different here. Even owning a business in two locations doesn't mean working the kind of hours you do. We don't allow those demands in our lives. I miss Tomás and Landon, and of course I miss Amelia. Having a grandchild changes everything. But if I didn't have them, I'm not sure I'd want to leave Spain at all." She tapped a finger to her mouth, evidently considering her words. "I'm not judging you, Suze, honestly. It's just that I've never seen you so stressed out or so out of touch with what's important."

Susana sat back, her face thoughtful. She knew Azalea supported her completely. She didn't like her friend's words, but she knew they came from a place of love. She leaned forward, her eyes intense. "When you first started Mora Communications, you worked a lot of hours. You were constantly with clients, trying to build your consulting business. I don't think you slept a lot and I know you were stressed out. Just because you've changed your lifestyle doesn't make my choices wrong. I'm quite clear on what's important." She sat back again, confident she'd won her point. *Doesn't anyone get what I'm trying to do?*

Azalea shook her head, sorrow plain on her face. "You're right—I've been there before. And yes, I've made some significant changes to my life. But that doesn't mean I can't worry about you. You know as well as I do that the stress I felt in those days was more from the divorce than building the business. You can't compare this." Susana opened her mouth to speak, but her friend cut her off. "What you've accomplished at MPG is admirable and there's nothing wrong with ambition. And I get that the demands at this level are much higher than anything either of us has dealt with before." She reached out again, then dropped her hand. "But I've never seen you let anyone push you around like this or be so worried about what people think. You've always been my inspiration when it comes to sticking up for myself. What's going on with you?"

Everything in her wanted to react, but Susana forced herself to think carefully. *What is going on with me?* she wondered. "I guess I'm just worried they'll think they made a mistake," she finally confessed. "Like I'm just some diversity promotion and I'm not up to the challenge." She slumped, suddenly fatigued. "And what if I'm not? What if this is one job too much?"

Azalea stared wide eyed at her friend. "You're kidding me, right? Susana—you are the most capable person in that agency. You're brilliant and you have to know that. They should have given this promotion to you a long time ago."

"I'm not thirty years old anymore, *'mana*." She pushed her hair behind her ears, then rubbed her hands across her face. "Hell, I'm not even fifty anymore. Some of these kids who work for me are barely out of college and they are whip smart and so hungry." She looked at Azalea, worry contorting her face. Her words came out as a whisper. "This Liscia account is an absolute disaster. What if I can't fix it and they decide they can't count on me? What if they suddenly care I had a 2.8 GPA in college and my grandmother was a Mexican housekeeper? *What if I'm not as good as I think I am?*"

"I can't believe—" Azalea's stunned retort was cut short by Esteban and Enrique returning to the table.

"You have to check this out, Susana," enthused Enrique. "This place is fantastic. I think we should just quit our jobs and open a café."

Esteban laughed. "And become my competitor? No, no!" The men sat and the women composed their faces after their fraught conversation. "I think you should open a wine bar—that way *we* can have the morning crowd and *you* can have them at night."

Enrique looked at Susana. "What do you think, *mi amor?* How about a wine bar for our next career?"

"That sounds intriguing," she answered. Determined to put her conversation with Azalea behind her, she made herself smile.

What is wrong with me?

The following week settled into a predictable rhythm. On Monday, Wednesday, and Friday night, Susana sat at the dining room table on a video call with the Liscia executives while the others went out for late night drinks in the nearby plaza. Steven, she noticed, didn't feel the need to join the meeting after the first evening. Susana and Geneva developed a respectful relationship as Susana proved her skill and tact, demonstrating her increasingly strong understanding of the market and Liscia's moves to differentiate itself in creative ways. The company had been one of MPG's key clients for years and Susana took pains to smooth over the rift Douglas caused. And she grudgingly agreed with Peter's assessment of the CEO, however crude. Geneva was clearly keen to put her stamp on the company.

Nevertheless, Peter still expected Liscia to sell. Susana wasn't so sure. The shift to sustainable luxury wear was revolutionary, not a move for a company expecting M&A activity. Playing it safe in their popular niche would have made more sense. She felt she was beginning to understand Geneva—a woman who'd paid her dues and was now in the top spot, trying to make a name for herself and her company in a notoriously challenging industry.

Desirée was another story, however.

One night, Azalea, Esteban, and Enrique left the house and Susana joined the Liscia call. She was determined to finish early so she could run down and meet her friends—Friday at ten o'clock was only the start of the party on the plaza and she loved the energy of the crowds. Her team had done great work throughout the week and she felt confident. *Surely we can get through this quickly,* she thought as the women appeared onscreen.

Without any preface or small talk, Desirée began, a biting note to her voice. "Before we commence with the 'Let's review the week' blather, can we just admit that these conversations aren't going anywhere and MPG doesn't have the chops to take Liscia forward? I can't really see us signing this contract."

Susana blinked, her heart dropping. She thought the week's calls had been productive. Douglas' notes had been virtually useless, with everything needing to be redone. Yet Lauren and Timothy had galvanized the team in Florida—they were thrilled with the opportunity to create the new branding campaign and dove into the project with enthusiasm. Geneva loved the creative approach, and Susana assumed the contract was simply a formality. The MPG team was fired up to begin the work, just awaiting the CEO's signature. She scrambled for a response when Geneva intervened, her face hard, her voice clipped.

"Susana, I've reviewed the plan and Liscia is ready to proceed with a limited 60-day project. That gives us enough time to ensure you can deliver but allows us to bring another agency up to speed if you can't." Even on the video call, it was clear she was avoiding Desirée's glare. "Your finance department will have it in a few moments—" She glanced away, as if at another screen. "There. It's done."

Susana breathed again. Had it really been that close? Stupid Peter and his nepotism—they could have lost this deal over patronage? Sixty days wasn't anywhere near ideal, not even a full quarter, but it was better than nothing and gave her time to win over the CEO.

"...so perhaps you should drop and we'll continue." With a start, she realized Geneva was still speaking.

"Fine." Desirée spat her response. Her window disappeared and Geneva and Susana looked at each other onscreen.

What did I just miss?

Geneva drew a breath. "Well, that was unpleasant," she said, a wry smile on her face. "I apologize you had to see that. Things aren't terribly harmonious over here."

Susana adopted a business-like tone. "I'm sorry—it can't be easy with all the changes Liscia is going through—"

"Oh, cut the crap, Susana," said Geneva. She seemed angry, and Susana's heart began racing again. "Look, let's be honest. Desirée wanted this job when the board canned Joanna. She didn't get it and now she's trying to sabotage everything I want to do." She looked thoughtful and Susana remained quiet, unsure what to say. After a few awkward moments, the CEO continued, her tone calmer. "Look, I know this is completely unprofessional and I'm probably going to regret it on Monday. But I'm betting I'm going to need a new CMO next week and, at the risk of infuriating Steven Mills, I'm considering you for the job."

What?

11

Susana walked to the open air café in the plaza, her thoughts awhirl. Amidst the crowds, she saw Enrique sitting at a table with Azalea and Esteban, then waved when they noticed her.

"Hey, you got done early!" exclaimed Azalea. "Just in time—we ordered tapas."

Susana smiled and pulled up a chair next to her husband. Enrique studied her and asked, "What's wrong, *querida*? Did something happen?"

She looked at him, then at her friends. "Liscia just basically offered me a job." When she spoke, her words came out slowly, almost questioningly. She glanced sideways at Enrique, wondering what his reaction would be. Truth was, she was still in shock and she wondered how he would take the news. "Turns out the new leadership is in a bit of chaos and they're going to hire a new chief marketing officer. The CEO wants me to consider taking the job."

"That's a good thing, isn't it?" asked Esteban. "I mean, if your client is so happy they want you to come work for them, that says a lot." He glanced at Azalea. "I don't know too much about your world, though." He chuckled. "I suppose if Esteban Junior started making *posteles* for a customer and they tried to hire him, I might not be so free with my compliments."

The women nodded. "Poaching someone from another company is done all the time," said Azalea. "But it's not going to look good." She frowned, then asked, "Would Liscia keep MPG as their agency if you took the job?"

Susana shook her head. "No idea. I don't have the faintest idea what she's thinking. It was sort of a throwaway line at the end of our call. But that would have to be part of the deal. There's no way I'd take the job if they fired MPG. But then I guess I'd have to wonder if she'd fire us if I didn't take it." She looked up as the waiter returned with their tapas, then glared at Enrique. "I should have stayed in the flat," she groused. "Are you having more food? You know I love *patatas bravas!*"

Her husband grinned. "I wasn't expecting you to meet us so soon. I thought we'd have finished them before you got here." He looked up at the waiter, then his wife. "Sangria?"

"*Sí,*" she said. "*Roja, por favor.*"

The four friends dug into the tapas and the waiter returned quickly with Susana's red wine, slices of fruit floating lazily in the large glass.

"So would you consider it?" asked Azalea. "Big change from MPG."

Susana shook her head, her mouth full of the savory potatoes. Before she could answer, Enrique reached up with his napkin to dab the corner of her mouth. "Little bit of sauce, *amor,*" he said. His touch was gentle and he winked at her as he put his napkin into his lap.

"That's me," she said, an impish look in her eyes. "A little bit saucy."

Azalea laughed and shook a finger at them. "That's enough, you two. Keep it family-friendly!"

Enrique burst out laughing and nodded his acquiescence. "Yes, ma'am," he said gravely, leaning over to kiss his wife on the cheek. "Strictly G-rated."

Esteban glanced back and forth, clearly confused. "Ignore them," advised Susana. "They're just being silly." She glowered at Azalea. "Stupid American humor."

Later that night, Enrique and Susana lay in bed, his arm around her, her leg across his thighs. "Any chance we can forego the G-rating now?" he asked, his hand lightly stroking her cheek.

"You don't want to talk about the work thing?" she asked innocently.

"Absolutely not," answered her husband. "I'd rather talk about why on earth you're still wearing a nightgown." He leaned forward and kissed her hard, his hand sliding down her back and gripping her backside.

"Easily remedied," she answered with a laugh. She pushed him away and sat up, pulling her nightgown over her head, then wriggling out of her panties. She slid back into place beside him, draping her leg and arm over his warm body. "Better?"

Enrique buried his face in her breasts, kissing and stroking her. "So much better," he whispered.

So much better.

The next morning, Azalea and Esteban were eager to show off their other café. The trip would take less than three hours, so they'd arrive in time for lunch and a swim. The drive to Cadaqués was beautiful. Impossibly blue skies and bright white cotton ball clouds attended the entire trip, and the sun warmed Susana's skin once they parked and walked to the restaurant. She was entranced by the boats bobbing on the crystal clear water, the sailors tossing nets and calling to each other. The entire harbor looked like something from a postcard, its beauty simple yet potent. She felt a palpable sense of calm—she couldn't quite put her finger on it, but allowed herself to bathe in it.

"This feels so good," she murmured to Enrique as they walked.

He squeezed her hand and smiled. "They really know how to live, don't they?" he asked, nodding at Azalea and Esteban, who walked ahead of them.

Susana nodded, silent as she pondered her friend's new life, so different from before her marriage to Esteban.

So different from mine.

After strolling along the harbor, Esteban stopped the group at a quayside restaurant. "Everything here is good," he told them as they looked over the menu, "but this is our favorite spot for *paella*." He approached the host and the two men embraced fondly. They spoke rapidly in Spanish and then the man directed them to a table under a bright blue awning..

"*Mucho gusto, amigos,*" said the proprietor. "*Bienvenidos a Cadaqués! Que queréis beber?*"

"He's asking—" began Enrique, looking at Azalea.

"Oh, I've got this one," she laughed. "You can't be around the cafés without learning how to order something wonderful to drink." She looked at the owner and smiled. "*Una jarra de sangria, por favor, Sergio.*"

"*Sí, señora,*" grinned Sergio. "*Cualquier cosa para la bella esposa de mi amigo.*"

Esteban chuckled. "She is beautiful but you need to stop flirting with my wife, *guasón.*"

Sergio shrugged and laughed as he walked into the restaurant. "I have to try, *amigo,*" he called over his shoulder.

An hour later, the friends were finishing the last of the delicious *paella*, the pan scraped nearly clean, the mussel shells piled into a bowl. They looked out at the water, and laughed at their collective sigh of contentment.

"You both seem so happy," said Enrique. "This life suits you, Azalea."

Azalea nodded, then reached for Esteban's hand. "You're right. I never imagined this—" she waved a hand to encompass the entire harbor, "would be my life, not just a vacation." She smiled at her husband, then continued. "It took me a little bit of time to acclimate to it, for sure. This is a different pace than I'm used to." She cocked her head toward Susana. "And definitely different from the grind you live with."

"But you like it now?" asked Susana, her voice hushed.

Azalea looked long at her friend. "I love it."

Esteban looked expectantly at Azalea and she nodded. He said, "There's an even more peaceful place we'd like to take you." At Susana and Enrique's questioning looks, he continued. "I hope it isn't — hmm, how would you say it? Presumptuous? We have booked four nights in France—it's our anniversary gift to you. There's a beautiful château in the Cevennes—it's in a little village called Saint-Félix-de-Pallières. It's very remote and *very* romantic."

Azalea put a hand up to forestall Susana's reaction. "We debated asking you ahead of time but we wanted it to be a surprise." Her eyes implored her friend. "I know you're knee deep in work, Suze, but you could work from the car there and back and they do have wifi at the château in a pinch. Most of the stuff we want to do is on the weekend anyway."

Susana sat back, looking from her friends to her husband. Three sets of eyes looked at her, waiting for her response. *This is all up to me*, she realized. *Lovely.*

Enrique took her hand but looked at Esteban. "When is the reservation?"

"We would leave on Thursday. It's about a four hour drive from Barcelona. We'd stay Thursday through Sunday night, then drive back on Monday."

"If you work from the car Thursday and Monday, could you get Friday off and have a three-day weekend?" Azalea leaned forward, looking directly at Susana. "I really think you would love it."

Susana's thoughts bounced wildly in her head. Maybe she could skip the Liscia meeting on Friday if she checked in with Geneva on Thursday instead. What would Steven say? And what was she going to do about Geneva's proposition?

Through her agitation, one thought percolated to the top of her mind: *Thirty years.*

She looked at Enrique, the love of her life, her partner for three decades. She knew he wouldn't push her, but she felt the weight of his entreaty nevertheless. She softened at the sight of his warm brown eyes, the eyes she knew as well as her own.

Mi corazón.

"Okay. I think there's only about a fifty percent chance I can get Friday off, but I'll try." She took a deep breath. "Let's go to— where did you say?"

Azalea smiled. "The Cevennes."

12

"I realize it's last minute, Steven." Susana strove to keep her voice steady. "There won't be any downside to me taking a couple of days off. I am on top of everything with Liscia and all the other accounts under my org. Timothy and Lauren are up to speed on everything and they can handle any issues that might come up on Friday. Otherwise, I'm easily accessible."

"Susana, 'easily accessible' means I can walk down the hallway to your office. Look, I understand that you're in Europe and you want to take some time to enjoy it," huffed her boss. "But now isn't a great time. I think there's more going on at Liscia than just a shake up in the C suite. This account is key for us and you have to know the partners are watching this very carefully." He glared at her on the video call. "I went to bat for you—"

"I do realize that, Steven. You've reminded me on several occasions." Her voice came out harsher than she intended and she took a deep breath to calm herself. Now wasn't the time to be prickly. "Look, I'm not some junior employee who doesn't understand the importance of a top tier account. I've never let you down in the past twenty years and I have no intention of starting now. Geneva is very happy with the work we're doing—she signed a preliminary contract and we're moving forward. I don't care what Peter says—I'm convinced Liscia isn't selling. This is a great opportunity for us." She briefly considered her next words, then threw caution to the wind. "I'm sorry that Peter's boy almost lost it, but my team and I have completely rehabilitated this account. We have sixty days to win this business long term and I'm not going to throw it away now just so I can enjoy a long weekend."

Steven looked away. "Peter's on the warpath over this, Susana. He heard from their CMO that things aren't as rosy as you paint them. And a sixty-day contract isn't what we need."

Her eyes flared but she bit her tongue. It also wasn't the time to tell tales on the client, despite what she knew of their internal feud. "I recommend you speak directly with Geneva," she said, her tone even. "The CEO is making the important decisions, not Desirée."

"I have a call with Geneva on Monday," said Steven. "I'll get a better sense of what's going on—I hate to think this is Peter trying to cover his mistake. I just don't know."

Susana fumed. Having her integrity questioned infuriated her, but she knew there was nothing to be gained by arguing. She composed herself and began again, her voice taut. "I would like to take a few days off, Steven. You know I haven't taken a vacation in ages and I don't see how this creates any problems for MPG. I'll be available on Thursday and Monday by phone. I'm basically asking for Friday off and I'm sure you can reach me over the weekend—in an emergency." It was all she could do to keep from shouting.

The MPG partner waited several heartbeats before responding. "All right, Susana. Take your days off. But keep your phone on hand Thursday *and* Friday. If things go south I want to be able to reach you."

She knew she shouldn't agree to it, but she was certain it was the only way to get his support. "Fine," she said. "Thanks."

She waited until the screen was dark before cursing and flipping off her boss.

Susana walked into the living room where everyone sat. "Okay," she said brightly. "I got the time off." Enrique's smile made all the angst worth it—she knew he'd been concerned that MPG might have refused her vacation request. She stifled a yawn and asked, "So what's on the agenda for tomorrow?"

The four had driven back to Barcelona after a long day in Cadaqués where, after lunch, they swam in the bay and visited Esteban and Azalea's café. Unlike the Barcelona restaurant, this one was small and only open until noon. They had coffee and pastries before driving home and now sat cozily, too tired to go out for their usual Saturday night on the square.

"We were thinking about going to Aire tomorrow," said Azalea. "Remember the Roman baths I told you about?"

Azalea had raved about the underground baths and massage she had first experienced when working in Barcelona. She and Esteban went once a month when they were in Spain and Susana had been eager to try them. "That sounds amazing," she said, yawning again. "But right now, this old lady just wants to go to sleep."

The other three nodded—the travel and day in the sun had worn them all out. "I'll book us online right now," said Azalea. "I'll make it for later in the day so we can all sleep in."

The friends said goodnight and went off to their respective bedrooms. After she slipped into bed, Susana snuggled close to her husband, her head on his shoulder.

"Thank you for making this happen," he said, his voice drowsy. "I can't wait to get away and be completely cut off from everything— just time with you, *querida*."

"Kique," she began, but his soft breathing told her he was already asleep. She sighed and kissed his cheek.

How do I tell him it's not exactly 'cut off'? she wondered. She hoped MPG could live without her for a couple of days and it wouldn't be an issue. *Surely I can have a little time to enjoy this trip?*

She felt the brush of Enrique's fingers on her cheek and smelled the coffee. She smiled and slowly opened her eyes. "What time is it?" she asked, her voice groggy.

"Already nine o'clock," he answered. "We've been up for an hour but I wanted you to sleep." He leaned down and kissed her forehead. "Azalea made us reservations at Aire for three o'clock, so we were thinking maybe we'd get up and go to La Sagrada Familia this morning, then have lunch."

She stretched and sat up, taking the mug from him. "That sounds great," she said. "How much time do I have before you guys want to go?"

A knock interrupted his response and Azalea poked her head in the open door. "Is the princess awake?" she teased.

"I'm awake," said Susana, making a face. "Not my fault you guys keep these crazy late hours in Spain."

"Oh, so it's my fault you're still in bed?" Azalea laughed and plopped onto the bed next to her friend, nearly causing Susana to spill her coffee.

"Hey, watch it!"

"Get up and let's go." Azalea grinned. "I bet it's been a minute since you've been inside a church."

Susana nodded—church services weren't part of her regular life, although she and Enrique were both raised in the Catholic faith. Azalea always teased her about being part of the "EC Club"—those who attended services only on Easter and Christmas. She found she was eager to see the great cathedral. It had been years since the last time she'd visited, and she knew there had been significant improvements in the never-ending construction of the edifice. She could only imagine the excitement her architect husband felt.

She finished her coffee and handed Enrique the cup. "Okay, give me ten minutes to get ready and we can go." She looked quizzically at Azalea. "Don't we need reservations? And can we get up into the towers yet?" The last time she'd been in Barcelona, the towers were under construction and didn't allow visitors.

"Done and done," said Azalea, dusting her hands together. "The towers are open." She leaned against Susana, putting her head on her friend's shoulder. "I know I'm probably being totally obnoxious, like a little kid showing off," she confessed. "I just love sharing my new home with you guys."

Susana reached up to pat Azalea's arm. "You are obnoxious, but I love you."

Enrique leaned down to kiss the top of his wife's head, then stood. "Okay, *princesa, mover la culita!*"

Azalea burst out laughing. "Even I know what that means. Move your butt, princess!"

Susana smirked. "It's actually *Move your ass*, Miss Priss."

Enrique shot a fond look at his wife and grinned at Azalea. "She's awake now."

75

13

"It never fails to astonish me," said Azalea, her voice hushed. Susana stood and gazed at the cathedral's immense stained glass windows, their light refracting into a rainbow on the floor of the sanctuary. She reached for Enrique's hand without looking at him, awestruck at the sight.

"So beautiful," whispered Enrique. They stood quietly for several moments before he looked at Susana and asked, "What do you want to see? Shall we just walk around or is there something special you want to look at before we go up to the tower?" The four had spent several minutes outside admiring the intricate carvings of the Nativity façade and had a reservation in an hour to take the tiny elevator. It was Enrique's first trip to the cathedral and Susana knew he looked at it from a unique perspective—his architect brain was firing on all cylinders, she was certain.

"I know you're dying to look around at everything," she said, squeezing his hand. "I think I'm going to just sit in a pew for a bit. You go ahead."

He smiled and kissed her cheek. "I'll be back in a few minutes."

"Take your time."

As Enrique headed across the immense marble floor, Susana glanced over at Azalea and Esteban and motioned to the quiet reflection area in the nave. "I'm gonna sit for a few minutes," she said. Azalea nodded and smiled, and she and her husband moved away to look around the basilica. Susana walked up the center aisle, found an empty pew and sat, looking up at the immense statue of Jesus hanging over the altar.

"Well, it's been a while, hasn't it?" she whispered. While tourists roamed the sanctuary chatting and taking photos, people of all nationalities sat on the wooden benches. She noted the flash of rosary beads as some prayed while others sat silent. *Mami and Papi would love this*, she thought. *I should bring them to Spain one day.* She made a mental note to buy them a rosary from the gift shop before she left.

After a moment, she closed her eyes and folded her hands. *I don't really feel like praying*, she thought. *I just want to sit here and…*
And what?

She was surprised to find herself so emotional. Tears pricked her eyes and she fought the urge to brush them away. *Why does life have to be so confusing?* she wondered. All the anxiety that had dogged her for weeks seemed to coalesce behind her eyes and the tears began to fall.

I love my job, but I hate the way it's turning out. I love my husband, but I need him to understand what I'm trying to do. I love Spain and I'm eager to go to France, but I'm terrified to take time off.

Then she considered the job at Liscia. After finally reaching the MPG position she'd worked so hard for, what was the allure of Geneva's offer? At her agency, she ran teams staffed by the smartest marketers in the business, teams that respected and admired her. She had the opportunity to mentor young professionals and to shepherd the careers of midlevel people—people like Lauren. She worked with a wide variety of clients, with organizations of every size and industry. It was fascinating, creative, and never dull. Despite the near constant friction with the partners, she loved the work and the people.

But a CMO job….

Adding the C-suite to her résumé held an appeal she couldn't deny. She wondered how her grandmother would feel if she were alive. *Estoy tan orgullosa, mija*, the tiny woman would say. Susana thought about the MPG business cards she'd ordered only months before and imagined her parents' delight to see even newer ones with Chief Marketing Officer beneath her name. Making her family proud had been a part of her motivation since childhood, yet in a moment of honesty she wondered again if she genuinely wanted the job—or just the prestige.

She wondered if she were good enough for it.

Susana fidgeted, her body restless, her thoughts and emotions a chaotic mess. Yet after several minutes, the serenity of the church's reflection area finally overcame her anxiety. She took deep, slow breaths, forcing herself simply to be in the moment, a feat she feared was nearly impossible when she first sat down. The warmth of the air and the soft susurration of prayers around her brought her a slow, but welcome tranquility. At last, she wiped her eyes and looked around. Enrique stood by the pillar at the end of her row, gazing at her with the deepest expression of love she'd ever seen. Her heart swelled with gratitude—*My God*, she thought, *there is no one more dear to me than this man.* She beckoned to him, and he came to sit next to her, his arm sliding across her shoulders to pull her close.

"*Te amo, Susana. Con toda mi corazón.*"

She knew it—she felt it to the core of her being. And she returned that love.

"*Lo mismo, mi amado.*"

Susana leaned into him and closed her eyes. For the moment, at least, all was well.

Across the street from the cathedral, the friends sat on a third-floor patio lingering over their lunch, passing around the traditional *tapas* as they recounted their morning.

"What was your favorite part, Enrique?" asked Esteban. "I think the three of us just marvel at the beauty, but I imagine you look at it differently."

Enrique nodded. "I do see the incredible beauty of the design. The carving on the façades is more spectacular than I imagined. I've seen it in books, but in person it's astonishing." He sipped his sangria, lost in thought. "And the tower! Seeing all of Barcelona laid out below us—I'll never forget that. What an amazing city…." His voice trailed off as he gazed across the street at the edifice. "I'm sorry. It's hard to put into words all the things I'm thinking and feeling." Then he warmed to the topic, looking around the table, his face animated. "But what really amazed me was the *structure* of the place—the way there are no right angles, the fact that every side is different, the materials used…." He laughed. "I'm sorry—I get kind of carried away with this stuff. It's remarkable."

"It's a gift to see it through someone else's eyes," said Esteban, his deep voice serious. "If you live here, it's easy for something so magnificent to become merely a part of the backdrop of life. I appreciate your point of view, *amigo.*"

Susana sat quietly listening to the men talk. She felt a swell of pride at Enrique's passionate description. *He is so good at what he does,* she thought. *And he loves it.*

Then he looked at her, eyes shining. "Enough from the architect. What about the rest of you? Does it lose its lustre when you see it every day?"

Esteban nodded. "It is a little different here, I think. We are used to it and don't get so excited by it, yes. But we are very proud of Gaudi's work and love to show it off." He kissed Azalea's hand. "And our new Spaniards are even more proud." He looked at Susana. "How did you like it? You've been here before, I think?"

Susana considered her time in the chapel and the beautiful view from the tower. "I've actually been here a few times, but it never fails to amaze. It's astonishing to think it's been under construction for over one hundred years and it's still not done. There's a serenity here that sort of sinks into you." She smiled at her friends, sensing Azalea's pleasure at her response. "It's hard to explain."

Azalea smiled, then looked at her watch. "Oh! It's two thirty already. We need to go."

Susana smirked. "*Que hora es? Diganos in español, chica.*"

Her friend grimaced. "Okay, okay…*son las dos y media y tenemos que irnos a la spa!*" She grinned widely. "How was that? I meant to say it's two-thirty and we have to go to the spa."

"*Perfecto, mi amor,*" said Esteban. "*Estamos listos—vamos!*"

Azalea smiled and shook her head. "I probably sound like a kindergartner and it's ridiculous for me to be so pleased when I get it right."

As they stood, Susana put her arm around her friend and hugged her. "Don't think that way. Everyone has to start somewhere, and you didn't grow up speaking Spanish like we all did. None of us judges you for trying to learn." She squeezed again. "We love it when you try and I'm sorry for teasing you."

The friends walked two-by-two down the plaza toward the baths and Azalea glanced behind them at Enrique. "I noticed those looks between you, Suze. I'm so happy to see you guys looking at each other like that again." Her face grew pensive and she added, "I was jealous of you guys, you know. Your marriage has always been the model for me. When David and I were struggling and finally fell apart, I looked at you guys and dreamed of a marriage like yours." She looked back at Esteban, a soft smile on her face. "And now I have it and I don't want you to lose yours."

Susana nodded. "It takes work. A lot of work." She looked at her dearest friend and saw compassion. "I need to put in as much work with Kique as I do with my job—no, *more* work. Thanks for the reminder, *'mana*." She bumped her shoulder against Azalea. "You always were the smart one in the group."

"Well, straight A's in school clearly don't translate into real life." She smiled over her shoulder at her husband. "But I'm learning."

"Aren't we all?"

14

Susana slipped on her swimsuit and put her clothes in the locker. She and Azalea put on their robes and sandals and walked out to the candlelit area where Enrique and Esteban waited. The four of them walked to the largest pool and hung their robes on hooks.

"Just wander around however you like," said Azalea in a hushed voice. Trancelike music surrounded them and the other patrons whispered when they spoke. "Next to this pool is the cold one—" she pointed to a much smaller pool where only two people sat. She indicated the larger pool next to them. "This is warm water and down there is the hot pool and the salt pool." She smiled. "That's my favorite, but go wherever you like. There's also a jetted pool and a sauna." She took Esteban's hand. "We have an hour before our massages, so relax and enjoy." She pointed to a dark walkway, lit only by candles. "You can sit there and have cold water or tea. Just enjoy yourselves."

Susana looked around and decided. "I'd like to start in the warm pool. Kique? Where do you want to go?"

Her husband smiled and slid his arm around her waist. "Warm water and my hot wife? Easy decision." He took her hand and walked to the pool where several couples lounged. They stepped down into the water and Susana moaned. "This is fabulous," she whispered as

Enrique followed her across the pool to an open area. They leaned against the wall and she closed her eyes.

Enrique leaned into her, their shoulders and arms touching. "Azalea wasn't exaggerating," he murmured.

She opened her eyes and leaned her head on his shoulder. The candles flickered, their shadows dancing on the stone walls. The music was soft and ethereal and the couple relaxed into each other.

After several minutes, Susana turned to her husband. "Shall we try some of the others? I feel like I could fall asleep here and I want to see what else there is."

Enrique smiled and leaned down to kiss her. "Wherever you want to go, I am all yours, *mi amor.*"

She kissed him again and reached for him. The back of her hand brushed his swimsuit as she reached for his hand and she startled. "Oh...."

"Yeah," he whispered into her ear. "Walk in front of me, please."

Susana stifled a laugh.

"It's not funny, *querida.* If you only knew how badly I want you right now."

She realized the feeling was very mutual. "I do know, my love," she whispered. "I feel the same way."

They maneuvered their way out of the pool and walked slowly to the hot pool, careful not to slip on the wet stone. They stepped gingerly into the water, which was several degrees hotter than the previous pool.

"Well, this will take care of things," muttered Enrique. "Good thing we aren't trying to get pregnant—this is hot enough to kill every sperm in my body."

Susana burst out a laugh, then quickly covered her mouth with her hand. "Shh…" she said. "You'll get us kicked out of here." Alone in the hot bath, the couple lleaned against the wall and looked around. The steam rose all around them and they could only vaguely make out people walking around, voices soft and low.

At last, Enrique stood. "This is a bit too much for me, love. Let's go try the salt pool Azalea likes. She said you can actually fall asleep floating."

Susana agreed—the hot water was nice, but not for too long. They climbed the steps and walked to the salt bath where the water was pleasantly heated. Along the walls were rails and they found a spot and leaned back, their shoulders touching while their bodies floated.

"Oh," sighed Enrique. "This is perfect." He lay quietly with his eyes closed, his arms floating at his sides.

Susana looked at her husband and watched his breathing slow. He seemed to be falling asleep and she smiled. *I could just float here and look at you forever*, she thought. She remembered the first time they skinny dipped in their backyard pool. *That was what, 25 years ago?* It had been midnight shortly after they moved in, and the young couple had giggled themselves silly as they reveled in the purchase of their first home. They made love under the Florida stars, her legs wrapped tightly around him, their lips pressed so hard together neither of them could breathe.

My Kique. Mi único amor verdadero.

My one true love.

"Susana? Enrique?" A soft voice woke them, and they simultaneously pushed themselves to standing. An attendant stood at the side of the pool. Smiling, she said, *"Es hora de tus masajes."*

The two blinked, trying to wake up. "How long did I sleep?" mumbled Enrique.

"No idea—I was dozing, too," answered Susana.

They walked out of the pool and followed the attendant to their robes, then up the stairs to the massage areas where they were directed where to remove their swimsuits. After putting their robes back on, they emerged from the dressing rooms and were shown to the couples massage area.

"Me llamo Juan Carlos," a young man told Susana. She vaguely heard someone else speaking to Enrique, but didn't catch the name. She turned to her table and her massage therapist removed her robe. She glanced over at Enrique as his therapist took his robe and she admired his strong back and broad shoulders. Then he lay on his table and she lay on hers.

At some point, Juan Carlos whispered to her to turn over. She was groggy but understood enough to comply—then promptly fell asleep again. After an hour, the massage was over and she was awakened. "Take your time, *señora*," whispered her therapist. "There is water, wine, and chocolates for you when you are ready. I hope that was enjoyable?"

Susana sighed. "It was amazing," she said, her voice thick with sleep. "I'm so sorry to have slept through it."

Juan Carlos chuckled. "No, no—that is the best compliment you can give me, *señora*." He smiled. "Take your time," he repeated, then walked out of the room.

Susana looked over at the table where Enrique lay. "How was it, Kique?" she asked softly.

Her husband made an indecipherable noise.

"That good, huh?"

"I may never leave this place," he said.

After several minutes, the couple arose from their beds to put on their robes. As she slipped one arm into hers, Enrique walked quickly from his bed to stand before her. He glanced around but there was no one in the room with them. He slid his hands along her shoulders and arms, still silky from the massage oil, then down her waist to her hips.

"Kique…" she whispered, half excited, half embarrassed.

"Just one second, *querida*," he whispered into her ear. He leaned forward to kiss her, one hand gripping the small of her back and one sliding between her thighs.

She reached for him, pulling him toward her, feeling his hardness against her. She moaned as he leaned forward to take one nipple into his mouth, his warm tongue drawing circles around her. "I cannot wait to get you home," she whispered as she grasped him, her fingers stroking him lightly.

They broke apart reluctantly, and Susana's breath came quicker as she looked at her lover, his oiled body shimmering, his longing evident. He reached for her once again and smoothed her hair from her face.

"I love you, Susana," he said, his voice strong despite the quiet surrounding them. "I love you."

The four friends emerged from the spa into the sunshine, blinking and disoriented. "I know in my head it's only six o'clock," said Enrique. "But it feels like it should be nighttime." After over two hours in the near dark of the Roman baths, they felt oddly out of sync with the late afternoon.

"This always happens to us when we go at this time of the day," said Azalea. "I actually prefer the evening appointments, but there wasn't anything available today." She rolled her shoulders back and stretched her neck. "I'm ready for a siesta. How about you?"

The other three nodded. "I feel like I just got poured out on the sidewalk," said Susana, stifling a yawn. "I'm very ready for a nap."

Enrique pinched her butt and winked.

"*Claro—vamos a la casa*," said Esteban, and the couples walked home in contented silence.

15

Susana slipped into the cool sheets and heard Enrique's slow breathing. "Are you asleep already?" she asked softly.

He reached for her hand and slid it down his body. "Does it feel like I'm asleep?"

She laughed and lightly ran her fingers across him. "If you're too tired…" she began.

Enrique stopped her with a kiss, his hands tight in her hair. She gasped at his intensity, but then matched his ardor, pulling him to her…and in her.

Their coupling was almost frantic, as if they hadn't made love in months. Her fingernails raked across his back and she gripped him hard with every thrust. Their breath came fast and Enrique moaned into her neck as she pulled him deeper and deeper.

She wanted all of him. She wanted them to meld into one—to pour every ounce of her love into their union, to erase every argument over the past weeks. "Yes, my love…yes," she panted.

His breath grew ragged. "Susana—I can't—"

"Don't stop, don't stop," she pleaded, her own breath quickening, her body reaching its crescendo.

His climax came a moment before her own, their bodies a tangle of passion and heat. Susana lost every thought, her entire existence rapt with the wonder that was their love.

This *is all that matters. We* are *all that matters.*

They lay still for some time, Enrique's arm around her shoulders. Susana's body snugged against his, and she felt the sense of peace and belonging she'd longed for all week. "This is my favorite spot in the whole world," she said.

He squeezed her but was quiet for several moments. At last he spoke. "How did I ever get so lucky to have you in my life?"

She sighed. "Baby, what we have is beyond luck. I don't know what it is, but we're that one in a million couple." She stroked the hair on his chest. "How many couples our age still even like each other, much less have crazy wild sex like that?"

He turned to face her, brushing back her hair with a light touch. "It's so much more than sex," he said. "I love you as much as when we first got married. No," he corrected himself. "I love you more. You're everything to me, Susana. Everything."

He seemed so serious that she felt a flicker of concern. "Is something going on, Kique? You aren't normally this, I don't know… subdued? What is it?"

He closed his eyes for a moment, then began, his words slow and tentative. "I guess I've been feeling like we're drifting apart a little. We've always been ride-or-die, like nothing could hurt us. But these last few months have felt like there's a wedge between us— between what we want and need." He ran his finger along her lip, then leaned forward to lightly kiss her. "I don't want us to jeopardize what we have."

"What we want and need?" she asked. She felt a sick feeling in her stomach. *This is about my job,* she thought, suddenly annoyed. *Are we seriously going to make this a thing between us?* She tried to keep her voice level as she pushed herself a little apart from him. "What exactly is it that you want and need that you aren't getting?"

His hurt look crushed her. "I'm not trying to start an argument. I just hoped maybe we could talk about the future. What are we going to do with the next thirty years? I look at Azalea and

Esteban and their lives are so different from ours." He held up a hand to forestall her rebuttal. "I don't mean we should be like them. I'm just realizing that life can be different—that we don't always have to grind. They seem to find time to enjoy life and each other, even though they're busy with the cafés. And they have kids—and now a granddaughter."

She knew she was being unreasonable, but she spoke anyway. "Oh, so is this about us not having children? Now you're regretting the decision we made—*together*, by the way?"

He scooted toward her, reclaiming the closeness she'd abandoned in her irritation. "Whoa—of course not. We made that decision a long time ago and I've never regretted it. Not once. I wasn't making a point about them having kids like it was better. I just meant they're busy and have a lot of things going on in their lives but they still make it a priority to slow down."

"So what would you like me to do, Kique? Do you want me to quit working? Abandon my job so we can 'slow down' when you get home from your big important career?"

He stared at her, his eyes intent. "I don't think I deserved that. But since we're on the subject, let's talk about my job.

"I actually have been thinking about maybe retiring."

Susana gaped at him. "Retiring?"

He quirked his face in an embarrassed grin. "I've been there for 25 years, babe. I've been a partner for three. There's nothing I really have left to accomplish." Enrique took her hand and stroked her fingers. "I was thinking maybe I'd teach a couple of classes? You know, give back a little? Or get involved in a mentoring program? Not many Latinos going into architecture and I might be able to make a difference with some high school kids?" His voice questioned every thought, but she could tell he'd been considering this plan.

Since her promotion, she'd been so busy with her own career, she hadn't paid much attention to his. Susana let out a deep breath. "I didn't see that coming. I've been so consumed with my job and I just thought you were upset that I wasn't around as much." She frowned. "And I obviously haven't been there for you while you're sorting through the options." She put her arm around his waist and pulled them closer together. He looked at her, his face thoughtful, and she kissed him lightly. "Can we start this conversation over?"

Enrique nodded. "*Sí, querida.*"

"You asked what we're gonna do with the next thirty years. That's easy. We're gonna keep being that one in a million couple—and if that means you're at home or out teaching and mentoring while I find a way to meet my career goals for the next few years, then we'll figure it out." She hoped she was right. "Because, my love, *we* are what truly matters."

She smiled as Enrique relaxed. "Thank you, *querida,*" he whispered. They held each other tenderly, their kisses gentle and soft.

We are what truly matters.

At eight o'clock, the friends rose and met in the living room, ready for the traditional Spanish evening dinner. "Did you get some sleep?" asked Azalea.

"We did," answered Enrique. "I could have slept for two days after that massage." He smiled at his wife. "I could get used to this siesta lifestyle."

"What would you like to do for dinner?" asked Esteban. "We can find a restaurant or we can go back to the plaza and eat outdoors again if you aren't bored of it."

Susana shook her head. "I love being outside and watching people but it might be fun to go inside someplace—especially if we can get more good *paella.*"

Azalea and Esteban looked at each other and simultaneously said, "Colom." They laughed and Esteban explained. "Colom is one of our favorite restaurants in Barcelona. The ambience is fantastic and the food is even better." He picked up his mobile and began to scroll. "*Momentito,*" he said. "I will see if I can get us a table."

Esteban stepped away from the others and Susana asked, "So what's the dress code?"

"Nice casual is fine," answered Azalea. "It's getting a little cool in the evening now, so I'll wear jeans and a light sweater."

Esteban returned with a smile. "They are very booked but we can get in if we're there by eight thirty. It's a quick drive, but we should leave in about ten minutes."

Everyone nodded and went to their respective bedrooms to prepare. As they walked into their room, Susana swatted Enrique. "So you like siestas, huh?"

"Well, I liked the sex and the making up part. Not so much the argument." He grinned and pulled her in for a kiss. "We have ten minutes, if you're ready for round two."

She laughed and pulled away. "If we keep at it like that, I won't be able to walk tomorrow. We're not twenty-five anymore, you know."

He made a face. "Thank God. Who wants to be young and stupid like that ever again?"

They got ready quickly and Enrique stopped her before she put on her lipstick. "Let me kiss you before I mess up your makeup," he said.

Susana set down the tube and put her arms around him and the two kissed, their embrace lingering until she pulled slightly away. "Let's go, lover boy. One more kiss like that and I won't be able to turn you away."

"Promises, promises…" muttered Enrique with a chuckle.

16

"…that *paella* might have been better than the one in Cadaqués." Susana patted her stomach. "They're gonna need a crowbar to get me out the front door."

The waiter returned to take their dessert order and the four continued their leisurely chatting. "So tomorrow we thought we'd just relax," said Esteban. "We can go for a late breakfast and then lounge at the beach or just stay at the house. We'll leave on Thursday afternoon about one o'clock once I finish with the lunch crowd at the café. My son will be here to handle the days we're gone. We'll get to Saint-Félix in time to unpack and look around the château before we have dinner." He looked at Susana. "You'll be able to work from the flat until we leave. I hope that helps?"

Susana smiled. Esteban was kind, trying hard to make the weekend easy on her. *But he doesn't understand my team is on Eastern Standard time*, she thought. *I'd be working while they're asleep.* "That's very helpful, Esteban. Thank you."

Enrique said, "So tell us more about this château. It sounds fantastic—I'm eager to see the building." He glanced at Susana and hurried to add, "And spend quality time with my wife for our anniversary."

Susana rolled her eyes. "And you guys think I'm obsessed with work. Wait until you see him around the château. He'll be like, 'Susana who?'"

Esteban smiled. "Then I'll apologize in advance. The castle dates from the twelfth century and the grounds are magnificent. There are sheep and goats and deer everywhere. We've also planned a few outings in the nearby area—we want to show you some of the villages in the Cevennes where we especially love to go. And of course the Pont du Gard—we thought we'd visit there on Saturday afternoon."

Enrique's mouth dropped open. "I studied the Pont du Gard in college but I've never been there." He looked at Susana, excitement lighting up his face. "It's one of UNESCO's World Heritage Sites. It would have been absolutely incredible if it were built ten years ago. The fact that it was built *two thousand* years ago is miraculous."

He's like a little boy, she thought and her heart swelled to see his excitement. "I can't wait to see it."

"I'm interested in your profession, *amigo,*" said Esteban. "I know a little about marketing—" he nodded at Azalea, "but I know nothing about architecture. What made you choose it? What kinds of projects do you work on?"

Enrique glanced at Susana, hesitation showing on his face. She nodded, then nudged him with her knee.

"Well, I guess I didn't choose architecture so much as it chose me. I've been building things since I was a boy. My brother and I turned everything into a fort or a castle and I just kept going with it in college." He smiled. "It's turned out pretty well, I suppose. I still love it and I'm learning all the time, especially from the younger architects in my firm. They think they're learning from the old guy, but they don't realize I'm getting as much from them—new ideas, new energy."

Esteban was nodding. "I feel the same way with the bakery. I was very set in my ways for a while, but then my son pushed me to think about new approaches. I was reluctant, but I'm glad I gave in. He's made some very good changes that improved both bakeries." He smiled at his wife. "Azalea has helped me see the value of letting him take more responsibility. I could barely get him out of bed in the morning for school when he was a boy, but now he is up before sunrise in the kitchen and stays late at night." Esteban shook his head in wonder. "I am very proud of him."

Susana couldn't help herself. "That's what it takes to be the best," she said. "Long hours and creativity."

"True, but having a good balance makes a happier life," said Azalea. "And Junior is choosing his hours. We don't demand them of him."

"A bakery is a bit different from a marketing agency," retorted Susana just as the server brought their desserts.

"Ah, you'll love this," Esteban interjected smoothly. "This *tarta* is a specialty of the restaurant."

The four friends tucked into their treats, but Susana snuck a glance at Enrique. His face was thoughtful, but he concentrated on his dessert.

As they drove back to the house, Susana sat in the backseat of the car, Enrique's arm draped around her shoulders. She was pleasantly languid, the wine and heavy dinner making her drowsy. She thought back over their conversation, wondering if she'd overreacted. No, she decided. Azalea's comment was uncalled for, but she knew her friend hadn't intended to hurt her. They'd been friends too long to let things fester and she was sure they'd hash it out soon. All four of them were professionals—they had to understand and appreciate what she was going through. This relaxed lifestyle wasn't the way Azalea and Esteban lived every day—they were business owners, and Susana knew they worked hard. But Saturday and Sunday were just that: *el fin de semana*, the end of the week. Azalea wasn't trying to cram in phone calls with clients. Esteban hired a baker to come in early on Saturdays to bake for the weekend. They set firm guardrails around their private life and they were reaping the benefits.

Could I do that, too? Or was this the life you only got if you lived in Europe?

It's the life you get when you're retired, she thought, a tendril of jealousy snaking into her mind. If Enrique retired, she could imagine him having this perfect life while she'd still be working insane hours.

They'd always been in sync but this was new territory. Was their love strong enough to weather a division like this?

Of course it is.

She didn't feel tired anymore. Just worried.

Sunday morning found the friends lazing about the house, drinking coffee. The weather was cool but the forecast was for a warm afternoon. It was the season of change in Spain—cool nights gradually overtook the warmth of the summer days.

Susana sat on the sofa with her laptop reviewing the latest report from the MPG/Liscia account team. She was pleased with their creativity and looked forward to seeing them present their work to Geneva later that week before she left for France. She wondered if Desirée would still be there. If she were, Susana was sure the contentious chief marketing officer would find something to complain about. She knew the creative assets and plan were solid and hoped Geneva would simply override any complaints. Why couldn't Desirée just accept that she didn't get the top job and stop trying to derail their progress? She wondered if Geneva would fire the CMO or if Desirée would just quit. *What a mess. No matter what happens, I have to get them to sign the full annual contract.*

She looked through her emails from the day before, pleased with herself that she'd stayed out of her inbox for the entire day. She stopped abruptly when she saw a meeting request for Monday. Geneva scheduled a one-on-one with her for six o'clock, an hour before their regular update call. Unusually, it was scheduled as a phone call, unlike their three-times-a-week video meetings. Susana sat back and frowned. This had all the hallmarks of a difficult conversation. Either Geneva had reconsidered her position on the CMO job or she'd given in to Desirée's badgering and was going to fire MPG. Or maybe she fired Desirée and would just offer Susana the role.

Stop being so dramatic, she thought crossly. *It could be anything. Maybe she'll be driving and just needs to talk in the car.*

She accepted the meeting and moved on to the rest of her emails. She found a terse note from Peter Gelbarr asking for yet another a status report on Liscia.

I assume you're working this weekend since I understand you're tak-ing time off later this week, read the email. *I expect your comprehensive report tomorrow morning when I arrive at the office. WE CANNOT LOSE THIS ACCOUNT.*

Susana knew from experience that Peter would start emails at home by five o'clock in the morning, then get to the office by six. She could push off the report until tomorrow morning her time, but decided to use her Sunday afternoon to pull together all the information he could possibly want. She was annoyed that Steven evidently hadn't updated Peter—the partners met nearly daily, especially about the top tier clients. She assumed he'd kept Peter and Jonathan apprised of the account status. After all, Steven was techni-cally her supervisor and therefore *au fait* with all the progress they'd made with Liscia.

Except the possible job offer.

17

After an hour working with her laptop on the sofa, Susana stretched her neck, needing to move. Enrique and Esteban were chatting in the kitchen over *pan dulce* from the café; Azalea was reading on the loveseat. "Aren't we just the *perezosos*?" asked Susana with a grin.

"Speak for yourself, *mi cardito*," answered Enrique. "Esteban and I aren't lazy—we're going for a run. It's too beautiful a day to waste inside."

Esteban bent to kiss his wife. "We'll check in at the café and then run on the beach. We'll be back in a couple of hours."

Azalea smiled. "Enjoy yourselves. We may go out for a bit, too, if I can pry Suze from her laptop." She grinned at her friend. "I know, I know...you have a lot to do and I'm gonna be patient because we get you for five whole days later this week."

The men went to change into running clothes and Susana stood and arched her back. "I have a big report due to Peter by morning," she said, grimacing. "I'm gonna be stuck inside most of the day, but I'd love to walk a bit while it's nice out." She smiled fondly at her best friend. "Plus it will be fun to have some time just the two of us. We don't get that so much anymore."

"Okay," said Azalea. "Let's go and maybe grab a snack and then get you home in time to finish your report."

The two friends followed minutes after the men left. Susana was glad she'd worn a light sweater as the late morning brought a brisk breeze. They walked along the plaza, glancing into windows and chatting idly, enjoying their time together.

"So how are things?" asked Susana. "How are the boys? Tomás must love being a dad."

Azalea smiled. "He does. I love to hear him talk about his wife and daughter. He's super traditional—such a protector and a provider. And Emily is happy being a stay at home mom." She chuckled and shook her head. "The really funny one is Landon. He takes his uncle duties very seriously. He loves that little girl to pieces."

"And Esteban Junior?"

"He's got a new girlfriend, so we don't see him much. It's only been a couple of months, so who knows if it's serious. She'll have to be all in on the café to stick around. He's really serious about taking over."

"And what about your work? How's Mora Communications doing?"

"I've scaled back a fair amount," answered Azalea. "I'm mostly doing writing for clients—a lot of blog posts and articles. I don't have clients in Spain, so I do everything online. When we're in the States, I'll visit a few in Orlando, but I'm pretty content not to be full time consulting anymore."

The women walked quietly for a few minutes before Susana asked, "Do you miss it? Being the superstar marketing genius like you were before Jeremy screwed it all up?"

Azalea looked at Susana, her face thoughtful. "I guess so… sometimes. It's a heady feeling to work that hard and have great success. But when I compare it with what I have now, it just doesn't motivate me the same way. Like it's another chapter in my life—an early chapter that I've read and loved and now I'm on to the next chapters, eager to see how the story unfolds."

Susana stared at her friend. "Damn, girl…that's pretty philosophical."

Azalea laughed aloud. "That did sound kinda pretentious, didn't it?"

The friends walked a few blocks down the main thoroughfare before Azalea asked, "So what's going on with you? I know you said things are better with Kique, but it's obvious something's bothering you." She looked at her friend with concern.

Susana was silent for a moment, then snapped, "It's this fucking job." She glanced around and then spoke more quietly, the words tumbling out. "I get this fabulous promotion and then they treat me like crap. I'm cleaning up after one of the partners who made a colossal mistake with Liscia. He hired this dumb kid who completely screwed things up and somehow now it's my job to fix it. Lauren and the rest of the team are doing a great job, but the partners just won't let up on me." She sucked in a breath and continued, her emotions boiling after being tamped down for too long. "And I have a front row seat to watch a power struggle between these two executives at Liscia—it's absurd."

Azalea gaped at her friend. "That's a lot—no wonder you're stressed. So do you think she's gonna formally offer the job?"

Susana shook her head. "I don't know. And I don't even know if I want it. I've lived the agency life for more than twenty-five years. I've been at MPG for twenty. As much as I hate what's going on there, at least I know the players and the game." She scowled. "And then there's the little wrench Kique threw in this week. He says he wants to retire."

She glanced sideways at Azalea and was gratified to see her friend's shocked expression.

"Oh. Wow."

"Yeah."

"How do you feel about that?"

Susana made a face. "I'm all over the place. I'm mad. I'm jealous. I'm happy for him. I'm stunned that we're old enough to even think about it." She stopped walking and threw her arms out in frustration. "Can you imagine retiring? I mean, I know you've slowed down a lot since you got married, but you're still the boss lady with your clients, right? You wouldn't just buy a rocking chair and give it all up, would you?"

Her friend burst out laughing. "Is that how you see retirement? *Kique in a rocking chair?*"

Susana had to laugh. "Okay, so I'm sure that's not what he means. He talked about teaching some classes or doing some mentoring. I'm sure he'll stay busy."

The women resumed their walk, each considering their conversation. "So what are you really worried about, Suze?"

Susana hesitated before answering. "We don't have a perfect marriage, but we've never been out of sync," she said finally. "I'm not ready to slow down. I'm still grinding, *'mana*. I haven't achieved everything I want yet. I just barely got the SVP gig and now I want to make partner." She stopped abruptly. "Holy shit, I just said that, didn't I?" She looked at Azalea and repeated herself. "I want to be a partner."

The friends looked at each other for a moment. "You know you can do it—you know you'd be great at it," said Azalea, a bit of hesitation in her voice.

"But?"

"I just wonder if it would turn out to be what you really want. I wonder if you might realize there's something else in life to conquer, some other goal. Another chapter to write." Azalea's eyes gleamed. "Something that fills you with so much joy you want to explode."

Susana frowned. "Please don't start talking to me about being an *abuela*. I'm thrilled for you, but you know that's not ever gonna be my life." The thought of bouncing a grandchild on her lap felt even more confining than sitting in a rocking chair, but she held back the sentiment.

"I know that's not your thing," agreed Azalea. "I just think there's something like that for you—something that brings you joy you can't even imagine right now. And I honestly don't think it's working at MPG. Even as a partner."

Susana didn't respond, waiting for Azalea to say more. At last, her friend continued.

"Remember when we were in college? You were lousy at doing the actual work but you loved the research—and you had better ideas than a lot of the professors. Once we figured out how we meshed, you and I were a great team on all the projects we did. Have you ever thought about going out on your own and hiring people to do the stuff you don't want to do? And having the luxury of being your own boss? Then if Kique does retire, your time is your own—you're not bound to how many vacation days you have or how annoying your management team is." She chuckled. "And CEO and founder sounds even more impressive than senior vice president."

Susana considered her friend's words. "I don't know," she said, her tone measured. "I've never really thought about it. Working in an agency always gave me new challenges and new opportunities for promotions. I haven't ever had that drive to be my own boss."

Azalea looked long at her friend. "Maybe you're just addicted to the next promotion, Suze. Maybe it has nothing to do with the work."

Susana finished her report and attached it to an email to Peter. "And now I've finished ruining my entire Sunday," she muttered as she pressed Send. She pushed back her chair and looked across at the empty living room. The other three had left an hour earlier and the flat was quiet and dull.

I just love my life, she thought sullenly, remembering Azalea's conviction earlier. *Isn't this everything I dreamed of?*

She walked back to her bedroom and sat on the bed, unsure what to do next. Go out to the plaza and look for Kique and her friends? Take a shower and go to bed?

Or just sit here and feel sorry for myself.

She undressed and got into the shower, unwilling to leave the flat in her morose state. The hot water ran down her body and she lathered her dark hair. The day had been long and draining. Her conversation with Azalea nagged at her, and she was mentally exhausted by the work she'd done all afternoon and evening. *I just need to get through these next few days*, she told herself. *Give myself the chance to really enjoy this weekend with Kique.* She sighed, remembering she hadn't bought him anything yet. *I should have looked while we were out today*, she chided herself.

She wished he were with her—she loved showering with her husband. He'd wash her hair as she rubbed bath gel all over his body and they'd be making love within minutes, the scented bubbles sliding across their skin. They rarely made it out of the shower before the water turned cold, but the heat of their passion warmed them. They'd take turns drying each other with thick towels before tumbling into bed, only to find themselves once again wrapped in each other's arms.

She turned the cold tap on high to dispel her fantasy. She was torn between desire and confusion and anger. She and Enrique had weathered difficult times before. His father died early in their marriage, leaving him to care for his mother. Although she wasn't old, she was a very traditional *mami*--she had never paid attention to their finances and had spent her entire life raising the family. Enrique had to step in and ensure her bills were paid, including the university fees for his younger brother, Antonio.

Susana hadn't always been patient with her husband as he spent hours with his mother, helping her through grief and loss, all while building a career for himself as an architect. She regretted her sharp tongue when her young husband would either come home late or spend the weekend at his mother's house. She would occasionally join him, but she chafed at the old school Mexican ways he'd been raised with. Señora Guerrero didn't like the fact that her daughter-in-law wanted a career instead of children and she never missed an opportunity to remind her son.

"*Ay, mijo,*" she would say to Enrique, "You are such a good man to come here to take care of your poor old *mami*." She'd glance sideways at Susana before adding, "But who will take care of *you* when you're old? You won't have anyone to love you."

Susana stifled her response time after time. "One of these days I'm going to stop being so polite," she groused at Enrique. "I guess I don't count as someone to love you when you're old. Why is it always my fault we don't have kids? Doesn't she know this is the decision we made together?"

The unwelcome memories provoked her even more and Susana stomped hard on the tile as she stepped out of the shower. Her foot slipped and she fell forward, cracking her cheekbone on the counter before she could stop herself. She landed hard on the floor and lay there stunned before reaching up to touch the swelling on her face.

"Dammit, dammit, dammit," she cursed. Her cheek was tender to the touch, but she didn't feel any blood. She stood and looked at herself in the mirror. Her cheek was red and swollen and she could see the exhaustion in her eyes. Part of her wanted to collapse on the floor in tears.

"*Estupida*," she growled at her image, refusing to cry. "Get. It. Together."

18

Susana lay in bed reading when she heard the three friends come into the flat. Their voices became hushed—she supposed they quieted when they didn't see her. She heard their soft *"Buenas noches,"* and then Enrique entered their bedroom.

When he saw the nightstand light on, he smiled. "Ah, you're still awake! Did you get everything finished? I wish you'd come down to meet us. You won't believe what—" He broke off suddenly and he rushed to her side. "Susana! What the hell happened?"

She pushed herself up to sitting. She knew she must look a mess. Her face had surely bruised in the hour since her fall. "I'm okay. I slipped getting out of the shower." She offered a weak grin. "It was your mother's fault."

At Enrique's puzzled look, she added, "Sorry. Bad joke. I was thinking about your mom and how she'd always blame me for us not having kids. I was mad and I wasn't paying attention when I got out of the shower and the next thing I knew I smashed my face."

"Maybe we need to get you to the hospital," he said, pulling out his phone. "You could have a concussion, or a fracture, or—"

"I'm fine, babe. I just have this lovely goose egg that's gonna turn all kinds of pretty colors in the next week. I guess we can't take any fancy anniversary pictures."

He shook his head and lifted her hand to his lips. He kissed it softly, then said, "It's not funny, Susana. You could have really injured yourself."

"But I didn't," she said firmly. "Honestly, I'm fine. It just looks awful. So tell me about your evening."

Enrique stared at her for a long while, then stood and began undressing for bed. "We were just sitting there talking and this couple walks by. I'm not really paying attention—you know how many people are down on Las Ramblas at night." He slipped on a t-shirt and pajama pants and slid into bed next to her. "But I had this funny feeling that I knew the guy." They turned to face each other and he grimaced. "That looks so painful."

"It hurts like hell," she admitted. "But talking about it doesn't make it any better. Tell me—did you know the guy?"

"I did. Turns out it was Hayden Grant—remember him? He was with CDG before I became a partner. We worked on that big tower down in Fort Myers a few years ago."

Susana remembered him. She'd met him and his wife at a Cooper Dallas & Guerrero function but didn't recall any specifics. "So what's he up to in Barcelona?"

"Turns out he lives here now. Got divorced and remarried—his wife is Spanish and they live about ten minutes from here." He shook his head in wonderment. "What a small world."

She took a steadying breath before casually asking, "So…what does he do now?" *Please say he's working sixty hours a week as a busy architect.*

Enrique laid back against the pillow. "That's the funny thing," he said. "He's semi-retired, just working as a consultant about twenty hours a week. His wife is a travel agent, so they spend a lot of time traveling all over the world. His kids are already out of college—one's even married. Cristina doesn't have kids, so they're just living the good life." He turned back to her and gently kissed her good cheek. "I'm gonna brush my teeth and hit the sack, love," he said. "But wake me if you need anything." He got up and walked to the bathroom and Susana turned out the light.

Semi-retired with a jet-setting new Spanish wife. *Living the good life?*

She lay back and tried to sleep in spite of the throbbing of her cheek and the ache in her heart.

Don't we have the good life?

Monday morning came far too early.

Susana groaned and hit the snooze button on her phone. Her cheek was hot to the touch and painful. She lay on her back try-ing to convince herself to get out of bed, but couldn't muster the energy. Enrique's breathing was steady and deep and she longed to stay under the covers next to him.

But no. If she were going to take time off later in the week, she needed to get up and get busy. *Liscia's not our only client*, she thought. She'd been so focused on saving their account, she had left the rest of her portfolio to others to her team. Today she'd check in with her account executives to ensure no one else was going off the rails.

Wouldn't that be fantastic? I save Liscia and something else falls apart.

She slid out of bed and walked to the bathroom where she splashed water on her face. Just dabbing at it with a washcloth hurt, and she wondered again how bad the bruising would be. Azalea was a genius with makeup and Susana knew she'd probably have to ask for help covering up the purple she knew was coming.

Enrique was still asleep when she finished dressing and walked to the kitchen. Azalea was at the table sipping coffee and reading a book when she entered.

"*Buenos días*," said her friend brightly. Then she scowled. "Suze! What happened to your face?" She stood and moved to look more closely.

Susana attempted a smile. "Ask me in Spanish."

Azalea frowned. "Not funny, Susana. What happened?"

"I slipped getting out of the shower last night and face planted on the counter. Do you have some ibuprofen or something?"

After a cup of coffee and some pain meds, Susana was ready to work. She knew Azalea would have preferred to sit and delve into a conversation, but that would have to wait. There was too much to do.

She opened her laptop and began scrolling through emails. Predictably, Peter had sent her three more since the previous evening. *Does the man ever sleep?* she wondered crossly. She looked over her to-do list for Liscia—there was nothing more to do until that evening's meeting with Geneva and Desirée. Even Peter would have to be happy with the progress. The last email from him, however, gave her pause.

Susana,

I'm sure I don't need to explain to you the expectations MPG has of the SVP role. Not only are you an ambassador to our top tier clients, you are a role model for the company. The notion of "work-life balance" is nonsense. MPG is your priority and retaining clients is simply table stakes—particularly tier 1 accounts.

I am sure you know I was not in favor of your promotion nor was I in support of this jaunt to Europe. Your portfolio is in jeopardy and being halfway across the world doesn't align to our objectives. Jonathan agrees with me; however, Steven assures me you are up to the challenge and I am reserving judgment until you prove either him or me wrong.

Liscia is key to MPG's ongoing success but they are not the only client that deserves your attention. I expect you to manage your teams on every account in your portfolio and I want a full update on their progress no later than Thursday before you take this little vacation from your already less than optimal work schedule.

Peter

She sat back, furious. Peter had been a pain in the ass for a long time, but this was harsh even for him. One part of her wanted to send a two-word response: I quit. *Or maybe just 'fuck you,'* she thought. Another part of her wanted to succeed beyond everyone's wildest dreams, proving him utterly and unequivocally wrong.

And then say fuck you.

But no. She couldn't afford to lose her temper, no matter how much the man goaded her. She opted to ignore the email and began a list of items to discuss with Timothy and Lauren. The pair was proving to be exceptionally capable, and she was once again thankful Lauren had returned to MPG. Between the two account execs, she was sure every account was in order. They weren't just good with clients; they were turning out to be exceptional leaders and the team loved them. She'd toyed with putting Douglas on one of Lauren's accounts just out of spite, but she knew it wasn't a good idea. She didn't need any more drama. Instead, she put him on one of Timothy's teams and the young man hadn't created any problems. *Pretty low bar*, she groused, but knew she had few options when it came to Douglas…and Peter.

One issue she hadn't solved yet was the BD team. Based on their competitive and market research, the business development department never stopped complaining there was more work to be secured. *They're probably right*, she admitted, *but it's not like selling groceries.* The account teams continually built trust with their clients, knowing that success would breed more work…over time. It took patience and consistency, traits she'd learned the hard way over decades in the business. She knew Steven understood that, but why Jonathan and Peter didn't get it was beyond her. *No one is going to force me out of this job*, she vowed—although she suspected that was Peter's intent. Get her to fix his screw up and then pressure her so much she'd resign, letting him claim he knew she wasn't up to the role.

Good luck with that, cabrón.

Unless she took the Liscia job.

Enrique emerged from their bedroom an hour later, going straight to his wife to take her face in his hands.

"How does it feel this morning, my love?" he asked quietly.

Susana grimaced. "Probably the way it looks."

"I still wonder if you shouldn't see a doctor." He sat next to her and frowned. "What if you fractured your cheekbone?"

"It's not like they can put a cast on it," she snapped, looking up from her laptop. Then she attempted a smile. "I'll just have to be careful not to smash my face on anything else for a while."

Enrique looked askance at her, then shook his head. "All right, I'll stop bugging you about it." He smiled as he sat, clearly ready to change the subject. "So have you thought more about the Liscia job?"

"You aren't going to let me work, are you?" she complained.

He grinned. "Nope."

Susana sighed, closing her laptop to face her husband. "Fine. I still don't know what to think. Geneva might not even be serious. I know she's pretty much done with Desirée, but she could have just been venting." She shrugged. "I'm so torn. It would be a huge difference to leave the agency and go in house, but maybe now is a good time to try something new?"

"Big jump to go to CMO," he said. "Looks good on a résumé and adds a new layer to your experience." His voice dropped and he took her hand. "You'd be wonderful at it, *querida*. But you're right—it's a huge difference and a big decision. You know I'm happy to talk it through or just be a sounding board."

The words came out before she could stop them. "Are you sure you wouldn't rather I became a travel agent?"

Enrique frowned and looked about to say something more, but then stopped as Azalea walked back into the dining room.

"Good morning!" she said. "*Quieres café?*"

"*Sí, gracias,*" he replied.

Azalea made a *Take that!* face at Susana who rolled her eyes and remarked, "Show off."

She reopened her laptop, avoiding Enrique's gaze.

I can be such a bitch.

19

That evening, the three friends left Susana to take her phone call in private. She answered on the second ring.

"Hi Geneva," she said.

"Hey, Susana. Thanks for taking the extra call. I wanted to follow up with you on our conversation from last week."

Susana nodded. "No problem."

Geneva's tone was brusque. "Look, it's no secret that Desirée is unhappy with the way things have turned out at Liscia. She's decided to…pursue other opportunities."

Susana snickered at the stereotypical phrase, then composed herself. "I see."

"I need a new CMO pretty quickly and I'm not interested in a lengthy executive search. I don't have anyone here I trust to step into the role—Desirée hasn't developed a terribly strong bench, quite frankly."

Susana listened, then realized Geneva was awaiting a response. "That's not great," she said, her voice hesitant.

"That's an understatement. Let me cut to the chase: I want you to take the role, Susana. We work well together and I trust you." She stopped for a moment, then continued. "Are you interested?"

Susana took a minute to gather her thoughts. She'd known what the call was about before it came, but she still wasn't certain how she wanted to respond. "I'm interested," she answered at last. "I need a lot more information, but I'm interested."

"That's great," Geneva responded. "I'll get you a brief later today so you can see what I'm thinking. I know it's a crazy request, but do you think you can let me know this week?"

Susana considered her next words carefully, then abandoned caution. "I guess I should tell you something that MPG didn't want me to share," she began. *This is so unprofessional,* she thought, then plowed ahead. "I've been working remotely for the past couple of weeks and I'm gonna be offline for a few days starting on Friday. I'll be back to work on Monday, but I won't be back in the US until next month."

Geneva laughed. "You've been this productive and responsive and you're not even in the country? Where the hell are you?"

"Barcelona. And leaving for France on Thursday." Just saying the words felt good, and Susana knew she'd made the right decision telling Geneva the truth. "Steven was worried that you'd object to me being so many hours away from Pacific Time."

"I might have," admitted Geneva. "But now that I know after the fact and we've had this much success, I couldn't care less if I tried. I can only imagine how fabulous you'd be in California."

California? thought Susana. *That's a hard no.*

She was glad she wasn't on video to betray her feelings. "So I'd have to move to California?"

"Well, that would be the best, but I'm willing to talk about a hybrid situation to get you on my team," answered the Liscia CEO. "Let me get you the brief and we'll talk about how often you'll need to be out here."

"Sounds good," answered Susana. "I'll look forward to seeing it."

Sounds good? she thought. *So much for telling the truth.*

The next two days flew by as the friends prepared for their long weekend in the Cévennes. True to her word, Geneva sent the comprehensive job description on Tuesday. Susana shared the brief with

Enrique, who repeated his contention that she was perfect for the job and his support for her decision. After her Wednesday night Liscia call, the first without Desirée, the couple finished their packing and prepared for bed.

"I need to give Geneva an answer tomorrow," said Susana.

"And what do you think it will be?" asked Enrique.

"I feel like I can argue both sides," she answered. "It's a fabulous opportunity. I don't want to miss out on something great just because I have to be in California every six weeks." She slid under the covers and looked up at her husband. "But I want to make Peter eat every single negative word he said about my promotion. I want to be the best damn SVP they've ever had and I want to be the first woman partner."

Enrique lay down next to her. He reached tentatively to stroke her bruised cheek, then pulled away when she winced. "I'm sorry—I didn't mean to hurt you."

She shook her head. "It's okay. It's probably gonna be tender for a few more days." She smiled wryly. "It'll stop hurting by the time it's green and yellow instead of purple."

He leaned forward to kiss her lightly. "So can you take any more time to decide or do you absolutely need to tell her tomorrow?"

"I could probably get a few more days if I asked," she replied, "but I'd rather get it over with so we can enjoy our weekend. I don't want to think about it while we're gone. I've been distracted enough since we got here. When I'm supposed to be enjoying time with you, I'm worried about work. And when I'm working, I'm worried about neglecting our time together." She frowned. "I'm sick of feeling torn about everything."

Enrique slid his arm around her and pulled her close. She lay her head on his chest and snugged herself to his side. "How can I help?" he asked quietly. "We always make big decisions together. I feel like you've been pulling away from me when it comes to your career."

Susana stiffened. "Well, I guess I could say the same for you. It's not like you came to me to talk about retiring."

He blew out a breath. "Susana, come on. I thought about it and then I told you. That's as far as it's gone. The idea occurred to me, I spent a day thinking about it, and then I shared it with my wife…my *partner*. When it comes to your job, I feel like I get the same quick updates you give Azalea. You know we've never made decisions like that."

He was right, Susana knew. They always shared their hopes, their dreams, and their plans, deciding things together since before they were married. *What had changed?*

Before she could answer, he kissed the top of her head and rolled away. "Good night, my love."

She lay awake for a long time. She thought about her parents. Their marriage was incredibly traditional but both her mother and father had encouraged her to be strong and independent. She'd found the ideal match in Enrique Guerrero—a man who shared her culture yet delighted in his strong-willed wife. Their union combined Latin flavor with a thoroughly modern partnership that supported them both. Her grandmother had especially loved her husband. *Ay, abuelita. I miss you so much.* She wished she could talk with the diminutive woman. They'd been close until the day she died and Susana missed her down to earth advice. "He's a good man, *mija*," she had told her granddaughter, a twinkle in her eyes. "*Y tan guapo!*"

He is a good man…and handsome. So why am I pulling away? she wondered. She rolled closer to her husband and lay her good cheek against his back. The happiest she felt was when they were aligned, encouraging and cheering each other on. Something was pulling them apart and it was making her miserable.

Susana thought back over the past weeks, noting all the small but significant differences in her husband. He said all the right things but she often sensed he didn't completely believe his words. His admiration for what he called 'the good life' grated on her. The good life meant striving and achieving and winning, didn't it? She frowned. *Great time to turn into a traditional Mexicano.*

Susana slept fitfully and finally got up at five-thirty to keep from waking Enrique. She dressed quietly and went to the dining room where she was relieved to see she was alone. She opened her emails and, predictably, there were several from her team. Each email had an attachment with detailed account information and she smiled at the thorough updates. She remembered Geneva's comment about Desirée's lack of a bench. That certainly wasn't a problem MPG faced with Susana's team.

Everything was in order on every account. *Peter will be furious,* she thought with a wicked grin. Then she pulled up a note from Steven.

Susana,

I suspect you've heard from Peter—perhaps several times. He has ratcheted up his complaints about you and I'm finding it difficult to counter them. I know you are on top of the Liscia debacle and, between you and me, I do recognize where and why the account went awry. But that is neither here nor there—the bottom line is you are now responsible for its success. For better or worse, Liscia represents a sizable (admittedly unhealthy) percentage of our revenue and losing this account would create significant challenges for us, perhaps leading to a RIF or other difficult business decisions.

I know you will do your best to not only salvage but to enhance our relationship with this key client. **We need that full year contract signed.**

I've spoken to Geneva and she seems very pleased with your work. There are, however, continuing internal challenges at Liscia that we must navigate with tact and skill. I assume she's discussed these with you?

Enjoy your vacation but please remain available should the need arise. I hope we don't have to call you while you're in France.

Steven

Susana blew out a breath. She hadn't realized that losing the Liscia account could force the partners to initiate a reduction-in-force. The thought of laying off any MPG employees was awful.

After twenty years with the firm, she'd built close relationships with employees and colleagues alike. She thought about Lauren. She was at a middle management level and could very well be on the chopping block of a RIF. *But that won't happen,* she assured herself. She was convinced the Liscia account was in good shape, especially since Desirée was leaving and wouldn't undermine her anymore.

But what if I take the CMO job? Susana wasn't sure Liscia would keep MPG as their agency. *And if I don't?* Who would Geneva hire and would they bring their own agency?

As if I didn't have enough to worry about already. What am I going to tell Geneva tonight?

20

The final presentation was on its way to Peter's inbox and Susana felt a surge of elation. Her teams continued to perform well, scoring 4.8 out of 5.0 on the most recent client satisfaction surveys. Despite the constant irritant that was Peter Gelbarr, she knew she and her entire organization were at the top of their game, more than capable of managing a sizable portfolio of business.

And she loved the work.

Would she feel the same way if she took the Liscia job? Moving into a CMO role would stretch her skills—she was certain she'd learn a great deal. At MPG, she'd never been bored a day in twenty years. She worked with clients from industries as varied as consumer goods, banking, tech, and hospitality. What would it be like to work in one business sector day after day? She loved fashion and could easily imagine the allure of marketing such a posh brand. She'd have the opportunity to go far deeper into the business end of things, becoming the face of the company to the media and analyst community. Would she have to wear only Liscia clothing? She laughed at the thought of showing up for an analyst interview wearing another designer's dress. *I'd never make that mistake*, she thought. The travel did concern her a bit. Thankfully, Geneva only wanted her in California one week out of six, but would that much become a burden? And what about attending the various fashion weeks around the world? London, New York, Milan…. It sounded glamorous, but she knew business travel was anything but after a while. She wondered if she could take her retired architect with her and giggled at the thought of Enrique sitting next to Donatella Versace or Kim Kardashian along a catwalk.

She pulled up Liscia's website and scrolled through the fall collection. "Gorgeous," she murmured, admiring the signature pleating on the silk blouses and chic dresses. This time next year, all these elegant pieces would be made from sustainable fabrics using environmentally sound production techniques. It was a heady thought, being at the cutting edge of fashion and production.

And I could be the CMO.

Susana glanced at her watch—only seven o'clock in the morning. Back home in Florida, she wasn't even out of bed at this hour, but in Spain she couldn't seem to sleep with her thoughts racing. Making a monumental decision about her career was the least important priority, she realized. She hated the increasing tension with Enrique. No matter what happened in her life, her relationship to her husband never failed to sustain her. They were the two who fell in love in college and were still crazy about each other thirty years later. Susana recognized the treasure they'd uncovered all those decades ago and she vowed to fight ferociously to hang onto it. She'd been unfair to him last night, she admitted. He didn't deserve her anger.

She looked up as Azalea came in. Her friend looked at her with surprise and a yawn. "You're up early. Want some coffee?"

"That would be great," said Susana. "I've been working since five thirty and I'm beat. A little caffeine would help."

"Come with me," said Azalea, walking toward the small kitchen.

Susana rose and stretched, then followed her friend. She leaned against the counter as Azalea turned on the kettle and then poured boiling water into the French press. The aroma of rich freshly ground beans soon filled the room. "Mmm…that smells fantastic."

"Esteban's signature roast," said Azalea, her voice filled with pride. They waited quietly until the brew was ready. Azalea poured two cups of coffee and handed one to Susana. "I know I've been a nag," she began, "but I can't seem to stop myself." Her lips lifted in a wan smile. "I probably pushed too hard on our walk and I'm sorry. I even talked to Lauren about it—tried to get another perspective."

Susana bit back a hasty response. She knew Azalea loved her and she didn't want to derail their conversation with a spiteful retort. She already regretted her comments to Enrique and it wouldn't help to alienate her best friend, too.

But this was too much and she couldn't keep the bite from her response. "You talked to Lauren? C'mon, Azalea. We're all friends, *but she works for me.* And what do you mean by 'help'? What makes you think I need help?"

Azalea looked askance at her. "You know exactly what I mean. And yeah, I probably shouldn't have called Lauren. I'm sorry about that but you don't have anything to worry about. She's your biggest fan over there—she pretty much hates the way they've treated you." She looked long at her friend before continuing. "I've looked up to you since college, Suze. Did you know that? You don't take crap from anyone—ever. You've been super weird about work since before we left Florida." She shook her head, clearly frustrated, but then laughed quietly. "And you and Kique aren't normal either. One day you guys are like teenagers and the next you barely speak. I'm just worried."

Susana made a face and sipped her coffee. "Super weird and abnormal. Thanks."

Azalea sighed. "I'm not saying—"

"I think you're the one who's changed," interrupted Susana. "Your life is completely different now and it's like you don't even remember the old you. Maybe you weren't ever as ambitious as I am, but you worked like hell to get Mora Communications off the ground and you busted your ass in Barcelona for Seaside Tech." She glared at her friend. "Don't tell me you didn't want to be the best back then, Azalea. I know you did."

"You're right. I did. And I had a lot of success—and a lot of heartache, as you well know." She frowned. "I wouldn't have met Esteban if I hadn't been here in Barcelona grinding away at my career. And I wouldn't have the clients I still have if I hadn't pushed myself so hard after the Jeremy debacle. You guys helped me through all that. You're a big reason why I have the life I have now."

"We just nudged you. It didn't fall in your lap. You had to work for it. Hard."

Azalea didn't answer and Susana squirmed under her compassionate gaze. "Don't feel sorry for me," she finally managed. "I'm just in a little bit of a rough patch but I'm doing what I love. Kique and I will be fine." She turned back to the dining room. "I need to get back to work."

"I'm here if you want to talk," said Azalea.

I don't need to talk. I'm fine.

That evening, Susana finished her update with Geneva and Steven. Both executives were smiling and Steven looked relieved. They were wrapping up the call when Susana glanced at her phone and saw a text from Steven.

Great job, Susana. I'm very pleased.

Thanks, she responded, trying to keep from looking down instead of at her computer screen. *The team is doing great work.*

Yes, but this is your win. Well done. Still waiting on the contract but I'm feeling more positive.

She smiled as she told herself, *It is my win, dammit. I busted my ass to fix this.* Then a private chat message from Geneva came onscreen.

Stay on the line when he drops.

OK.

The three said their goodbyes and Steven's window disappeared from the screen.

"So?" asked Geneva without preamble. "What's your decision?"

Susana took a deep breath. *Here we go.*

"Will you keep MPG as your agency if I take the job?"

Liscia's CEO laughed. "Didn't I just sign a big fucking contract with you guys?"

"Actually, you signed a sixty-day agreement. You haven't signed the annual contract yet. I don't want to be responsible for people losing their jobs if I take this one."

Geneva steepled her fingers and looked long at Susana. "I like that you care about your people. That's just one more argument in your favor."

Susana wanted to press the exec on an answer but held her tongue.

Geneva raised an eyebrow. "Do you have confidence in whoever steps in when you leave?"

"I do. I always build a solid bench on every team I lead."

"Then yes. I will sign the annual contract with MPG if you take the job."

Susana grinned. "Then I accept."

"About damn time. You're lucky I like you so much." Geneva smiled back. "When can you start? I know you need to give them a reasonable notice, but I'll send you over some things to read this weekend. It will probably mean you're doing two jobs for the next couple of weeks while you wrap things up over there, but I get the feeling you can handle the challenge."

Susana's heart sank. *Two jobs? Have I just jumped into a bigger shit show than MPG?* "Well, remember I do have plans this—"

"Oh, damn—gotta run," said Geneva, looking at her phone. "Send me your private email address and I'll get the stuff to you along with the formal offer letter. HR will get with you on the details. Shouldn't be more than a few hours and we'll figure out how to manage those MPG boys when you let them know. *Ciao!*"

Susana sat back in her chair, spent. She stared at the screen where Geneva's face had been and wondered if she'd made the right decision. The thought of trying to explain to Enrique and Azalea why she had to work this weekend nauseated her. The excitement of the new job warred with exhaustion over making the decision and she realized that more than anything she wanted to talk to her husband. Enrique had gone out for his usual Wednesday night stroll with Esteban and Azalea so she could take her call with Liscia in quiet, but now she wanted him with her. She grabbed a sweater and her purse and headed out to the plaza.

Even midweek, Las Ramblas was packed with people. She scanned the crowd, looking over the various tables at the cafés that ran the length of the boulevard. It seemed that every seat for blocks was taken. She knew she could text Enrique but was surprised to find herself enjoying the stroll as she searched for her husband and friends. The evening brought a cool breeze and she was thankful she'd grabbed a sweater before heading outdoors.

At last she saw them. They were sitting at a round table with two others, a man and a woman. As she walked down the block toward them, she noticed Kique's relaxed posture, his genuine smile. He and Esteban exchanged some words and they both laughed. A waiter approached the table with a large pitcher of sangria, and Esteban poured glasses for everyone.

Azalea was the first to notice her and waved. Kique looked up and beamed when he saw his wife walking toward them, then stood to pull an extra chair over between him and the unknown man. Susana glanced at the two additions to their party as her husband pulled her in for a hug.

"I'm so glad you made it, *querida*," he said. He held out a hand. "You remember Hayden, don't you? And this is his wife, Cristina."

Susana smiled and tried not to wince at the pain in her cheekbone. She reached out a hand to Hayden. "Of course. It's nice to see you again." She turned to the gorgeous wife—*Dios mío, how young is she?* "*Mucho gusto*," she said.

Cristina stood and reached across her husband to air kiss Susana's cheeks. "*Encantada de conocerte*," she breathed. "*Lamento mucho tu cara.*"

"*Gracias*," said Susana, a bit put off by the familiarity. She would never have mentioned the bruise if it had been on the other woman's face. *Settle down—she's just being polite*, she told herself.

"You're done early tonight," said Azalea. "I'm so glad you could join us." She smiled at Esteban. "We were just talking about the Château—Cristina's been there before."

"It's fabulous," the travel agent beauty broke in. Her Spanish accent was lush and Susana wondered how often she had to speak English. "You are going to love it." She reached across her husband to clasp Susana's hand. "*Muy romantico, amiga.*"

Susana forced herself to smile and not pull her hand away. She wasn't sure why, but she felt an unwelcome annoyance—*I'm not your friend*, she thought. She purposely spoke English. "We're looking forward to it," she said, pulling her hand away at last and leaning into Enrique's shoulder.

Her husband put his arm around her and squeezed. "Thirty years is a special anniversary," he said, glancing around the table. "It sounds like this place just might be special enough for this beauty." He looked at his wife, love plain in his eyes.

Esteban raised his glass. "To Enrique and Susana. *A treinta años más de felicidad.*"

The six of them clinked their glasses and smiled. Susana leaned into Enrique and tipped her head back for a kiss.

To thirty more years of happiness.

21

"So…did you make a decision?" Enrique stood by their bed, his tone and face neutral.

They hadn't discussed her job offer when they were on the plaza, instead talking about their trip to France while the four friends visited with Hayden and Cristina. Enrique waited until they returned to the flat, but Susana could tell he was eager to broach the subject.

"I did," she answered. Susana sat cross-legged on the bed brushing her long hair, then plaiting it into a thick braid. "I told Geneva I'd take the job."

Enrique nodded, then sat next to his wife. She finished her braiding and turned to him. "I know it means being apart pretty frequently, but—"

"But it also means no more ridiculous demands on your time," he finished. "I'm not under any illusions that you won't have to work long hours. A C-suite job is no joke, but if it means no more Peter Gelbarr, I'm pretty happy. I don't even mind you being gone for a week—I may come with you once in a while and visit family." Enrique had cousins who lived in San José and the couple enjoyed the Bay Area. "It'll be nice to know the day is over when it's over and you aren't constantly having to look at your phone to be sure the place hasn't fallen apart in the thirty minutes we've been eating dinner."

She scowled. "MPG isn't that bad—"

Enrique looked askance at his wife. "What do you consider 'that bad'?" he asked.

Susana stopped before answering. He was right. She'd always worked a lot of hours, but the promotion to senior vice president had been brutal. It was as if the partners looked at her as a machine with no life outside the firm.

And she had let them.

"Okay," she conceded. "It's been rough and they haven't been the best leaders." She sighed and decided to stop hedging. "And I haven't exactly stood up to them."

Enrique sat back, a look of surprise on his face.

"What?" she asked.

"That's a pretty big admission, *mi cardito*," he answered, his voice quiet.

She bristled, but knew he was right. Susana was self-aware enough to recognize she wasn't great at admitting her weaknesses. She was thankful Enrique knew and understood when she got defensive. He had a way of wearing her down—*No*, she corrected herself. *He's great at giving me the time and space to swallow my pride and let down my guard.*

Susana lay down on her side, her head in Enrique's lap. He stroked her shoulder and she knew he was waiting for her response. "I don't ever want to fall into that trap again," she began. "But I need to tell you something." She turned her face up to look at him. "Geneva is sending me some documents I need to read this weekend. I don't know how many or how long it will take, but I need to get through whatever it is. I'll try to get it done while we're driving."

Enrique exhaled heavily and Susana knew he was trying not to get frustrated with her. "There's no other time to do it?" he asked at last. "You aren't even working there yet—I assume you have to give a pretty lengthy notice to MPG?"

"I'm not sure," she answered. "I'll talk to Steven tomorrow and see what he's willing to accept. I hope he doesn't throw a fit, but I'm sure Peter is going to be awful about the whole thing. And he'll take it out on Steven with all his 'I told you so's.'"

"You know that's not your problem, right?"

Susana frowned. "Well, he did fight hard to give me the promotion. He went to bat for me against Peter for weeks before they gave me the job."

A flash of annoyance crossed her husband's face. "Nobody gave you the job, Susana. *You earned it.* You should have had it a long time ago." He shrugged, then sighed. "I'm sorry. I just hate the way they've treated you and made you feel like you owe them."

Susana rolled to her side, looking away from him. She knew he was right—she was damn good at her job and no one had done her a favor by promoting her. She was irritated with herself. *When did I turn into this…this…?* She didn't know what "this" was, but she didn't like it. Not a bit. She wondered what her grandmother would think of her headstrong granddaughter now.

Enrique continued. "You don't need me telling you how to do your job, *querida*, I know. But please—set some boundaries with Liscia from the start. Don't let them suck you into the same morass you've been in with MPG."

Susana sat up and tossed her braid over her shoulder, feeling defiant. "It's different with Geneva," she asserted. "She wants me up to speed quickly so when I start with Liscia I can jump right into the role. I've never been a CMO before, Kique. There are things I need to learn and I need to learn them right away if I'm going to be successful."

He stood and nodded, looking long at her before responding. "I agree."

Susana grimaced at his double meaning. She watched as he picked up a book from the nightstand and headed for the living room. "You're not coming to bed?" she asked.

"No. I think I'll read for a while." He didn't look at her as he left the room.

She stared at the closed door, anger rising. *Fine. Go pout. I'm going to sleep.*

The next morning, Susana awoke to find that Enrique was already up. She made the bed and dressed for the day, feeling sullen. *Why can't he understand?* They should be celebrating, not fighting. She dressed and went to the kitchen where she found Azalea making coffee. Her friend moved about humming and putting away dishes as the Moka pot bubbled on the stove.

"You're awfully cheerful this morning," she said, trying to keep the edge from her voice.

Azalea looked up and smiled. "Oh, no! Did I wake you?"

"Nah. I was up." She looked around. "Where are the guys?"

"Esteban had to go to the café early this morning to help Junior with a catering gig. Kique went with him. I think they'll be home in a couple of hours." Azalea poured cups of coffee and motioned to the table. "Wanna sit for a minute before you start work?"

Susana nodded and Azalea set the cups on the table before returning to the kitchen for a small basket of *pan dulce*. "Might as well have breakfast," she grinned.

The two friends sipped their coffee, dipping the pastries in the aromatic brew. Azalea looked concerned as she began. "So…you don't look so hot this morning, Suze. Wanna talk about it?"

Susana looked at her friend and sighed. There was no hiding from Azalea. "I took the Liscia job," she said flatly.

Azalea's eyebrows drew together in confusion. "Isn't that a good thing?"

"I thought so. But Kique and I fought about it last night and haven't talked since."

"I'm confused. I thought he wanted you to leave MPG."

"He did. He does." Susana described her conversation with Geneva and then with Enrique. "He doesn't trust me to set any boundaries," she finished angrily, glaring at Azalea. "I suppose you agree with him."

Azalea leaned back in her chair, her face impassive. "Are you gonna keep pushing everyone away, Suze?"

Susana stared at her friend. *Is that what I'm doing?*

Azalea continued. "Nobody loves you more than Kique. And you know I've had your back for more than 30 years. Steven and Geneva may like you, but you're a tool in their toolbox. They're gonna use you until they use you up or you're not valuable to them anymore." She shook her head and frowned. "You've been in business long enough to know what's going on. They want you because they need you. You're the best at what you do and they will drain the life out of you if you let them."

Susana squirmed under her friend's scrutiny. "Thanks for the backhanded compliment, I guess."

Azalea's smile was sad. "I've never seen you like this before, my friend. Don't forget what's really important." She reached for Susana's hand and squeezed. "You once reminded me of that and it's the reason Esteban and I are married. Don't let that go."

Susana thought back to the time she'd confronted Azalea over her decision to break things off with Esteban. She and Enrique had essentially kidnapped her for the day, pulling no punches with their friend. Azalea had taken their advice and reconciled with Esteban.

And now look at their life.

Susana grinned. "I called you an idiot," she remembered.

Azalea laughed. "You did. Because I was." She sipped her coffee, looking thoughtful. "You're kinda being an idiot now."

Feelings warred inside her. She knew Azalea was right—her marriage was struggling and she wasn't fighting hard enough to put it back on track. Her career wasn't what she'd dreamed it would be and she wasn't sure how to align her ambition with the rest of her life. She loved Kique and she knew he loved her. But his new interest in retirement and his lukewarm support for her professional aspirations grated on her.

And her cheek throbbed with pain.

She drained her cup and stood. "I gotta get to work," she said, leaving Azalea at the table.

"You have got to be kidding me, Susana," sputtered Steven. His face was a mask of confusion on the laptop screen. "Do you know what I went through to get you this job?"

Susana gritted her teeth as she considered her words. "I'm sure you had a difficult time convincing the other partners," she said, her voice taut. "But you know I earned this job, Steven. I've been loyal to MPG for twenty years and I have consistently delivered." She thought back to her conversation with Kique the night before. "You didn't do me a favor by promoting me."

"Bullshit. I actually did do you a pretty damned big favor," he snapped. "I put my reputation on the line and I fought with the partners for a month."

Susana's eyes widened. Steven never used foul language and it was a bit unnerving to have him curse at her. She softened her gaze. "I'm sorry, Steven. I really am thankful—I know you advocated for me. But this job with Liscia is too good to turn down—and I got Geneva to promise to keep MPG as their agency of record before I accepted the role."

Steven ran a hand through his short graying hair. "That's sort of the least you could do," he muttered. Then he spread his hands in a conciliatory gesture. "As your friend, I'm happy for you," he said at last. "As your boss, I'm furious."

"What do you need from me during the transition?" she asked, relieved the storm had passed. "I'd like to give MPG a month before I leave. I have great people in place across the organization—you can easily promote in-house. They aren't SVP level, but I have excellent leaders who will happily take on more responsibility."

The two spoke for another half hour, mapping out the next month's transition. When they finished, Susana attempted a smile.

"I've enjoyed these twenty years, Steven. I've learned a lot from you and I'm grateful for the opportunities you've opened up for me."

He looked long at her before answering. "Be prepared for the backlash, Susana. It won't go well." He shook his head. "I really hope I'm wrong, but I know I'm right. Just be prepared.

"And what on earth happened to your face?"

22

Thursday morning dawned bright, yet Susana rose with a mild sense of dread. After she told Steven she was resigning, she'd been on high alert the remainder of the day, waiting to see how the other partners would react.

But the two men were conspicuously silent. She was particularly surprised not to hear anything from Peter—she'd been certain he'd waste no time in castigating her, either by email or on the phone, but there'd been nothing all day.

Instead, that afternoon she'd called Lauren.

"Hey, *chica*!" answered her friend. "Wazzup? You're calling me from Spain?"

"I am." She took a long breath. "Hey, are you alone?"

There was a beat before Lauren responded. "I'm working from home today—no one's here. Susana, what's wrong?"

"Nothing's wrong, but I do have some news and I need you to keep it to yourself. This isn't a business call—it's a friends call."

"Okay." Lauren's voice was subdued. "*Qué pasó?* Do I need to punch somebody?"

Susana laughed. Lauren was a combination younger sister, friend, and employee, but in every role she was as fiery as Susana.

"Nah—no violence required." She took a deep breath. "So…I gave MPG my notice. Liscia offered me the CMO job and I start in a month."

Her friend was quiet and Susana asked, "You still there?"

"Yeah, yeah. Just processing." Lauren chuckled. "And trying to decide if I'll hit you up for a job."

"Well, you know I'd love to bring you with me, but there are two reasons it might not be the best idea. First, I shouldn't poach from the agency—the partners would have my head. And second, I'm recommending you for a more senior role when I leave. It could be a great career opportunity for you."

"Hmm." Susana could almost hear Lauren's mental gears grinding over the phone. "I appreciate that. But I do love their clothes.…"

Susana barked a laugh. She was familiar with Lauren's penchant for beautiful clothing. She and Azalea were two of the best dressed women she knew. "Well, I'm not in any position to hire you at Liscia right now anyway, so slow your roll, *amiga*."

"*Sí, jefa*," smirked Lauren.

"And as your boss," continued Susana, "I need you to keep this absolutely quiet. I'll tell the whole team next week when I get back to Spain and you'll have to act like it's news to you."

"When you get back? Where are you going?

"Oh, I forgot to tell you: Azalea and Esteban are taking us for a long weekend in France to celebrate our anniversary."

"Damn, rough life," she laughed. "But honestly, congratulations. You guys deserve every good thing. Give Kique a hug from me!" She paused. "And I'm not supposed to mention anything about this either, but Sara will probably be calling you and Azalea this weekend. She has some news, too."

Susana smiled. She could guess what that news would be and her heart swelled for her young friend. She wondered if Liscia would ever carry a children's line.

The next morning, she and Enrique finished packing for the weekend and took their bags to the living room where Esteban and Azalea sat talking quietly. Their friends looked up and smiled, and Esteban stood.

"*Estaís listos?*" he asked.

"*Si*," replied Susana and Enrique in unison.

But am I ready? wondered Susana.

"*Ahora, vamos a Francia!*" answered Esteban, his Catalan accent softening the word with what Susana likened to a lisp.

The four took their bags outside and Esteban loaded the car. When Azalea opened the back door to sit with Susana, Enrique shook his head. "No, no…take the front seat with Esteban," he said.

Always the gentleman, thought Susana. She smiled as she considered his courtly ways. So many women balked at a man opening a door or pulling out a chair, fearing it put them in a subordinate role, but she loved his traditional manners. She never saw them as archaic or demeaning. "I haven't opened a door for myself since I met Kique," she told friends. "Does that make me weak? Hell, no." She'd laughed. "It makes me a princess."

"I'd actually rather sit back here with Susana, if that's okay," answered Azalea.

Esteban finished loading the overnight bags, then opened the door for his wife, kissing her before she slid into the back seat. Enrique opened the door for Susana and she slid in her laptop bag, then turned back to face him. She reached up to kiss his cheek and was astonished when her husband swept her down in a perfectly executed flamenco move, her long hair grazing the ground. As he kissed her lips, his mouth hard on hers, Susana's heart pounded with the passion she felt emanating from him. She was still breathless when he smoothly stood her up and held the door open. "*Señora*," he said quietly, his gaze penetrating.

Susana looked questioningly at him, but he didn't answer and she slid into the seat next to her friend.

After a quick stop at the Obregons' café for coffee and *pan dulce*, the four settled into a comfortable ride, the men chatting in Spanish while Azalea and Susana spoke English. "You're going to love this place," enthused Azalea—*For the hundredth time*, thought Susana. "It's ancient and elegant and just gorgeous. There are so many things we want to do but it would be perfect even if we never left the grounds."

"I did remember my swimsuit," said Susana. "The sauna and a swim in the morning sounds great."

"It's nice to get out there before breakfast even if it's raining." She smiled at her friend. "I hope you'll get to relax this weekend and enjoy your anniversary."

Just then Susana's phone buzzed and a shadow crossed Azalea's face. She pulled out a book and nodded to her friend. "I know you have to take that. Go ahead."

Susana glanced at the screen and grimaced. Peter Gelbarr was calling.

You have got to be kidding.

"It's four o'clock in the morning in Florida," she muttered before answering. "Hello, Peter."

"Sor-sorry to interrupt your vacation, Su-su-su...." The partner's slurred voice betrayed him.

He's drunk, Susana realized with a start. *The perfectly controlled partner was drunk?*

She grit her teeth and tried to control her annoyance. "It's fine, Peter. I told you I'd be available today if you needed me. What can I do for you?"

"How mush...money is Geneva throwing at you?" His tone was contemptuous.

Sloppy and angry drunk, Susana corrected herself.

"I don't think it's appropriate for us to have this conversation right now," she said, willing herself to stay calm. "It's the middle of the night for you, Peter. Perhaps we can talk in the morning?"

"You think you're so much better than everyone, dontchu?" He continued as if he hadn't heard her. "You think you can just wal... wal...*waltz* in and sweet talk our biggest client because you're a woman and you're Mexican, or whatever the hell you are—"

Susana's eyebrows nearly reached her hairline as she exploded. "We are *finished* with this conversation, Peter. Go sleep it off and when you wake up I suggest you call our HR department *and* your lawyer, you bigoted bastard!" She hung up and stared out the window, her heart pounding. She was taut with fury, longing to throw her phone or, as Lauren suggested, punch someone. She wasn't sure which.

Enrique turned in his seat, his face a mask of concern. "*Querida? Qué ocurrió?*"

Susana took a deep breath before recounting her brief conversation. Repeating the words made her even angrier and she found her hands were shaking.

"Would you like me to pull over?" Esteban asked. "We can stop just a couple of kilometers ahead if you need to get out of the car."

Susana shook her head as Enrique twisted in his seat to reach back for her hand.

"I'll be fine," she said. "The sooner we get to France the better." She squeezed Enrique's fingers and struggled to control her shaking voice. "I'll be fine. I'm sure the French have some nice strong wine and that sauna is sounding better every minute."

Enrique lifted her hand to his lips and kissed it, then looked questioningly at his wife.

"Really," she insisted. "I'm fine."

If she had any doubts about taking the Liscia job, they vanished. *Steven wasn't joking about a backlash.*

Azalea sat reading while Susana spent the next hour answering email. She used her phone as a hotspot for her laptop so she could work online the entire drive. As they traversed the Pyrenees, she was only vaguely aware of the majestic landscape, and instead concentrated on answering the numerous notes in her inbox. When she reached one from Samantha Roberts, she opened it and found a pleasant welcome to Liscia from the company's HR director.

We're delighted to have you join Liscia as our Chief Marketing Officer, the email read. *Please read and complete the Docusign agreements setting forth your compensation package and associated legal documents. We look forward to seeing you in California next month!*

Susana looked at the Docusign button in the middle of her screen and clicked it.

Here we go.

She spent the next thirty minutes reviewing the offer letter, the nondisclosure agreement, and various other documents appropriate to her new C-suite role. Everything seemed in order and she was pleasantly surprised by the bonus structure. While her salary was only marginally higher than her MPG role, with the bonus she'd be well beyond anything she'd ever earned. She wished she were alone with Enrique—it would be awkward to share financial information in front of Azalea and Esteban. She'd just have to wait until they arrived at the château.

For the next two hours, Susana worked on the transition plan for her departure. She kept her messaging app open and wasn't surprised when Steven popped up in her feed.

No chance you've changed your mind, right?

She smiled. *Good morning to you, too. And no—I haven't changed my mind.*

Didn't expect so but I had to ask.

Have you spoken to Peter? She wondered how much to share with her soon-to-be former boss.

No, why? Did you?

She sat for a moment, considering. *He called me a few hours ago.*

The ringing of her phone startled her and she answered. It was Steven.

"A few hours ago?" His voice was concerned.

"Yeah. It was four o'clock in the morning for you."

Steven's sigh was heavy. "What did he say?"

Susana recounted the conversation, deciding to share every word with Steven. "It was…unpleasant," she finished. Steven would draw his own conclusions. She didn't need to embellish or rant about Peter's off the rails call. "But I do think I want to reduce that one month we discussed and get out in two weeks."

When Steven began sputtering his disapproval, she interrupted. "Steven, he's lucky I don't sue him. The only reason I don't leave today is because I care about you and my team. I'm not interested in subjecting myself to his abuse for the next thirty days."

An email popped up, this time from Geneva. Susana tuned Steven out as she opened the mail on her laptop and did the math. In California, it was four o'clock in the morning.

What is wrong with these people?

"…so I can agree to the two weeks but I need that transition plan in my inbox this morning, Susana," finished Steven.

"It's nearly done," she answered, now training her attention back on the MPG partner. "I just need to amend the timeline."

They said their goodbyes and hung up. Susana scanned the email, still astonished that the Liscia CEO was up and working in the middle of the night. *I sure hope she doesn't expect that of her executives*, she thought. She began to read.

Susana,

My EA Annie will call you later this morning to work on your travel arrangements for your trip to California next month. I know you're committed to a month-long transition with MPG and I respect that—but if you can cut it short at all, it would go a long way toward getting you up to speed before our big analyst event in January. I'm pretty sure I mentioned that, but if I didn't, it's January 10-12 in NYC. You'll be there all week, though, since we'll schedule customer calls while we're in town. Our investor relations team will send you briefing materials for the analysts. I like to be prepared well in advance, so you can expect those this week. We can talk on Monday if you have questions.

We also need to draft the press release announcing your hire. I'll have the agency work on that but you'll need to review it, too.

As far as your time in California, I'd appreciate you arriving and departing to give yourself as much time as possible here in the office. There's a lot to do to get you ready for Q1.

You should already have heard from HR. Get your paperwork done as soon as possible and we'll get your laptop and mobile phone shipped to your home. I assume this Barcelona trip is just a short vacation?

Talk soon,
Geneva

Susana leaned back, closed her eyes, and stretched her neck from side to side. She hadn't realized how tightly she'd held her shoulders while she was typing. Working on the transition plan was easy—she knew what needed to be done and she had the right people on the team. But an analyst event in three months? She'd never done one before and felt unexpectedly nervous. Liscia was publicly traded and she knew these events were significant. She'd need every minute of the next several weeks to feel prepared.

And what did Geneva mean by "short vacation"? *Didn't she hear a word I said about my travel?*

The four friends stopped for petrol in Narbonne and to stretch their legs.

"I could use some water," said Enrique. "Anyone else?" When they all agreed, he reached a hand out to Susana. "Come with me?"

She nodded and took his hand. The two walked into the station and Enrique spoke quietly. "You okay? You've been very quiet the past couple of hours."

Susana grimaced. "I'm just trying to get things done so we can enjoy our time at the château." She realized her tone was sharper than she intended and squeezed his hand. "I'm sorry. I didn't mean to bite your head off. I'm still irritated by Peter's call, I guess." They took four waters and the couple paid at the counter.

As they walked back to the car, Enrique said, "You know you don't have to do this alone, Susana." His eyes were gentle. "It's kinda why people get married. So you have someone to share your life— good times *and* bad. Like we always have."

Susana bristled at the rebuke, then shook her head. *Why am I so irritable?* Part of her longed to tell Kique everything—the middle of the night email from Geneva, her concerns about the New York trip, her anger over Peter. She forced a smile. "You're right. We can talk when we get to the château."

Azalea was looking at her phone when Susana returned to the car. "Did you see the note from Sara? She wants to talk to us this weekend. Wonder what's up."

Susana smiled. "Ten bucks says she's pregnant."

Azalea's brow furrowed. "So soon after the miscarriage?"

"It's been almost a year. How long are you supposed to wait?" Susana had no experience with pregnancy and was unsure of the protocol.

"Hmm, I'm not sure. I think after a normal one you don't have to wait too long, but hers was so bad…." Her voice trailed off as the women remembered the terrible hemorrhaging that landed Sara in the emergency room. "And she's forty now. I think that puts her in a higher risk category all by itself."

Susana looked at her phone and saw Sara's message:

Hope you guys are having a wonderful time! I'd love to talk with you this weekend for a few minutes—I have some news! xoxo

"I'm sure she's okay," she muttered, her thoughts already returning to her own problems. She opened her laptop and began searching for Liscia's last quarter financials and press release.

She didn't need to look up to feel Azalea's disappointment.

23

"And here is your room," the woman said, opening the door for Susana and Enrique. Her French-accented English made the simplest sentence sound elegant. The suite was sumptuous, complete with a king sized bed covered in a rich midnight blue comforter and several throw pillows. A dark, heavy wood wardrobe stood open on one wall, with thick cotton robes hung inside. Lush rugs lay on the tiled floor and Susana had a sudden urge to dig her bare toes into them. The early evening light streamed through the windows, casting a warm glow on a small writing desk and chair. The woman led them through the room to the expansive bathroom. It had a deep tub, fully long enough for Susana to lie in, and she began to fantasize about a luxurious hot bath after dinner.

The couple thanked the woman and Enrique wheeled in their overnight cases. Susana sat down on the bed, then lay down on the pillows. "This is glorious," she murmured, closing her eyes.

Enrique sat next to her and she felt his kiss on her forehead. "Don't fall asleep, *querida*," he said softly. "We have to meet for dinner in half an hour."

Susana pulled him to her. "Half an hour? Plenty of time." She was tired from the drive, worn out from the mental stress of her calls with Peter and Steven and the demands of her new role—a job she hadn't even officially started yet. Everything in her longed for a respite, no matter how brief. She ran her hands through her husband's thick hair and looked at the face she loved. *This is what's important*, she reminded herself. *We are what counts.*

And I want you now.

She stood and undressed, never taking her eyes off Enrique who lay quiet and unmoving on the bed. When she was finished, she unzipped his pants and slipped them over his hips, not bothering to remove them before she slid onto him, hard. She needed him—his strength, his love, his steadiness.

But right now she needed his body and without a word, she took him.

Fifteen minutes later, she lay atop him, still breathing hard, sweat beading between her breasts. Her hair splayed across his chest and he smoothed it back, then slid his hands along her hips. She nuzzled his neck, running her tongue along his jaw and she felt him begin to harden again.

"Susana," he whispered, his voice a question.

"Shhh…" she answered, as she rolled to her back, bringing him with her and wrapping her legs tightly around him. "Don't stop, Kique. Don't stop."

The lovers were giggling as they crossed the patio to the dining room. They didn't speak, but Enrique squeezed her hand as they stepped through the door and saw their friends.

"Welcome!" said Esteban. "How is your room?"

"Magnificent," answered Enrique.

"Just perfect," said Susana. "How's yours?"

"I think every room in the entire place is gorgeous," answered Azalea. "They all have a distinct personality." She motioned for the two to join them at the table. "You're just in time." Susana and Enrique sat across from the Obregons as their host brought out two bottles of wine.

"Welcome," said the slight blonde woman. "My name is Céline. I'll be here all weekend to serve you." She smiled. "I hope the rooms are to your liking?"

The four friends exclaimed their appreciation, and Céline continued. "Please let me know if there is anything at all that we can do for you to make your stay perfect." She motioned to the bottles. "These wines are from the vineyard next door. And everything you will eat this weekend comes from local farms." She smiled at a young man who entered the dining room with a large salad bowl. "These greens and tomatoes are grown here at the château, and the goat cheese is from a farm just up the road." The young man opened the wine as Céline returned to the kitchen, coming back moments later with a basket of fresh bread. "*Bon appetit!*"

The meal was spectacular and Susana found herself relaxing and laughing in a way she hadn't in months. *Guess those sex endorphins are a real thing*, she thought, chuckling to herself. Never shy in bed with Enrique, she had nevertheless surprised them both with her aggressiveness this evening. She found she was already looking forward to more lovemaking that night and her stomach tightened at the thought. *Maybe we'll take a bath together first*, she mused, wondering if Céline had any candles.

"Suze?" Azalea's voice cut through her reverie. "You with us?"

Her best friend's smile was knowing, and Susana grinned back. "Sorry—it's been a long day, and this meal and wine is putting me to sleep." She looked up as Céline returned to take their plates, the young man behind her carrying desserts. "More food?" she asked, astonished.

Céline smiled. "This is *clafoutis*, a traditional French dessert usually made with cherries. In the autumn, we bake it here in the château with apples from the neighborhood instead." She gestured to the young man. "Benoit will bring you coffee if you would like, or we have a nice dessert wine."

The four friends all asked for coffee, and Benoit nodded and stepped out of the dining room. "He is my nephew," explained Céline. "This is his first year working at the château and he is a bit nervous to speak English." When he returned, she added with pride, "He speaks very good English and only needs to practice a little harder."

"*Parlez-vous espagnol?*" Esteban's voice was kind and he smiled at the young man. "*Je parle un peu français mais je peux parler espagnol si c'est plus facile.*"

Benoit's face lit up. "*Si, si! Español es más fácil para mi, señor.*" He glanced at his aunt who looked disapprovingly at him. "I will still practice my English," he told her. "I promise."

Céline shook her head at the boy and then smiled at Esteban. "That is very kind of you to offer. He needs to practice his English, but being able to speak in Spanish will ensure he understands your needs and can provide any help you require."

"It is my pleasure," said Esteban with a slight bow.

Azalea was smiling proudly at her husband as aunt and nephew retreated to the kitchen. "That was thoughtful, Esteban," Susana said. "I didn't know you spoke French."

"Very little," he demurred. "It helps to be able to speak to French customers. We get quite a few in Cadaqués, especially in the summer months."

Enrique looked at Azalea and smiled. "You got a good one here."

Azalea nodded, then took Esteban's hand. "It was about time." Then she laughed. "I got sick of just watching you two."

Enrique leaned over and kissed Susana's cheek. "I hope we keep making you sick for years and years."

The friends finished their dessert and coffee and sat contentedly for several minutes before Susana yawned.

"Sorry," she said. "This week has kicked my butt and it's nice to finally relax." Then she sat up, startled. "I left my phone in our room," she said, her voice filled with concern.

A shadow crossed Enrique's face. "I thought you did it on purpose," he said. "It's been nice having you all to ourselves tonight."

Susana tamped down a flicker of anger. She knew Enrique wanted this weekend to be all about them and their anniversary and she was trying to make it happen. But it was still Thursday and she'd promised both her MPG and Liscia bosses that she'd be available all day. It was nine o'clock in the evening in France, but it was still the middle of the work day in Florida and California. She sighed, knowing she'd likely go back to her room to find several messages. The glow she felt all evening began to evaporate.

"It's just a rough time right now," she hedged, knowing that it had been rough for months with MPG and looked to be that way at Liscia for the foreseeable future. "I did tell Steven I wouldn't be working on Friday or this weekend."

"What about the new job?" asked Azalea, her voice taut. "Do you have to work this weekend for them?"

Susana took a breath, trying to decide how to respond and was surprised when Esteban put a hand on his wife's arm. "*Relájate, mi amor.*"

Azalea didn't seem inclined to relax, but didn't speak as Esteban looked at Susana and Enrique.

"This can't be easy for either of you. Why don't we say good night and let's meet in the morning for breakfast." He laughed quietly. "Though the thought of eating again in twelve hours seems almost impossible."

The four stood and Azalea hugged Susana. "I'm sorry. I keep doing that, don't I? I've just been so excited for this and I'm longing for you to enjoy every minute," she whispered as the women embraced.

Susana looked fondly at her friend. "You're a pain in the ass, but I love you."

"Who's the pain in the ass?" countered Azalea with a grin. "I'll see you in the morning at the pool, okay?"

"Deal. Nine o'clock?"

"Breakfast is at nine. Make it eight, *perezosa.*"

Susana laughed. "Oh, now you learn Spanish just so you can call me lazy?"

Azalea shrugged with a grin. "I guess I needed the right motivation."

The couples went their separate ways, and Enrique reached out to take his wife's hand as they crossed the courtyard to their room. Susana was thankful for his touch. She knew she'd overreacted—*again!*—and longed to recover their closeness.

As they approached the door to their suite, Enrique stopped and took her into his arms. "Listen, I know you're being pulled in a million different directions right now. I don't want to add to your stress. I want to be here for you and help you get through it." He cupped her bruised cheek and tipped up her chin. "But I have needs, too, Susana. I love you with all my heart, more than ever, and I need time with you. Time that isn't held hostage by people who don't matter."

"They matter to me," she said, her brows furrowing. "This isn't a hobby, Kique. It's my career. They have to matter if I want to succeed."

His eyes were sad as he opened the door. "Go find your phone," he said. "I'll be in bed waiting whenever you get there." He kissed her lightly and then smiled. "I'm not done with you yet."

Two hours later, Susana set her phone face down on the writing desk. The wifi worked better at night, their host had told them, and she'd taken advantage of the connection to respond to notes from Steven and from Geneva, then set an Out of Office notice on her email. She leaned her head onto her palm, then winced at the pain in her cheek. *Dios mío*, she thought crossly. *Can't anything be simple right now?*

She looked across the room at her sleeping husband. He was naked under the covers, she knew, waiting for her. She brushed her teeth and braided her hair, then slipped out of her clothes. Enrique mumbled as she slid into bed beside him. She reached up to trace his jaw with her finger. "Are you too tired, my love?" she whispered. "I know it's late—"

He stopped her with a kiss. "*Querida*," he answered, his voice thick with sleep. "*Mi cardito precioso.*" He fingered her braid, then took off the elastic, slowly undoing her hair. His gaze tender, he spoke more clearly. "Roll over, my love."

Susana rolled to her stomach and Enrique kissed the small of her back, his tongue sending shivers up her spine. "Be still," he whispered. She heard him pad quietly to the bathroom and, when he returned, felt him straddle her, his thighs warm against her hips. He rubbed his hands together and then she felt the heat of oil on her back. The smell took her back to their massage in Barcelona and she sighed.

"Is that from—"

"It is," he said simply. "Now relax. Let me love you, Susana. Just let me love you."

His strong hands kneaded her tight shoulders and slid down her back. She felt his fingers along her spine, willing the knotted muscles to release. The citrus aroma filled their bedroom and when his hands began to massage her head, her long hair falling across the pillow, she tried to speak.

"Kique—"

"Shh," he whispered, leaning down to kiss her neck.

She was asleep in minutes.

24

Susana awoke to the quiet music on her phone. She reached over to turn it off, then snuggled back under the covers where Enrique lay. The temptation to stay warm and cocooned against her husband nearly overcame her commitment to meet Azalea. The thought of waking Enrique for sleepy lovemaking was an even stronger pull, especially since she'd fallen asleep while he massaged her aching muscles the night before. Sighing, she decided to let him rest. They'd certainly have more time later. She was determined.

She slid out of bed and stretched, glancing at her phone. It was the middle of the night in the States but it was habit, even if she didn't expect to see any messages from anyone. She was glad to see her phone was blessedly empty of texts or voicemails. She quickly brushed her teeth and got ready to walk to the pool. As she rebraided her hair, she thought about Enrique's hands running through her heavy locks the night before. He loved her hair long and unbound, and the memory nearly persuaded her to stay.

She crossed the courtyard and saw her friend just opening the door to the indoor pool. The crisp air was enough to make her hasten her steps and she wondered again why she hadn't just stayed in bed.

"Some vacation," she grumbled as she followed Azalea through the door. The heated pool let off a light curtain of steam and she hurried inside, stepping out of the morning chill. "Remind me why I agreed to this?"

Azalea smiled and shook her head. "Good morning to you, too, *gruñosa*." She took off her cover up and sandals, then walked into the water. "Coming?"

"I'm not grouchy," muttered Susana. "You're just an overachiever, like always." The two women had been friends since their university days, when Azalea's straight A's and disciplined lifestyle were in stark counterpoint to Susana's less rigid approach. "Why do I always follow your lead?"

"Because you know I'm right," Azalea answered primly, before flicking water at her friend. "It's warm, you big baby. Get in."

Susana rolled her eyes but stepped gingerly onto the top step. "Oh, wow," she said, surprised. "It *is* warm." She walked down the steps, then backed up to the wall, letting the water come up over her shoulders. Azalea gripped the wall, then stretched out her legs and began to flutter kick.

"So this is a workout?" Susana grinned at her best friend. "Not just another ass kicking?"

"I can kick your ass while we work on our glutes," said Azalea, returning the smile.

Susana turned to face the wall and began her own kicks. "Okay, let me have it." Then she stopped. "Wait, no. Let me do it for you." She assumed a stern look. "Suze, you work too hard. You let people take advantage of you. You don't spend enough time with Kique. You're stressed out and it's unhealthy. You smashed your face on the counter, you spent the whole drive to France on your computer, you're not twenty-five anymore.... Is that about the gist of it?"

Azalea stopped kicking and turned toward her friend. "Um, wow. I was actually just going to ask how you were liking your time in Europe."

Susana grimaced. "Right. Sorry." She resumed kicking and answered, "It's been great. You know I love Spain. The energy is so—I don't know, fabulous. I wish I could get out more in the evenings with you guys. I love hanging out in the plaza just watching people and listening to the buzz."

Azalea glanced at her friend. "And there's no way to make that happen?"

"You know I can't. Working for companies in Florida and California make it impossible. I have time in the morning, but that's not the same."

The two women kicked quietly, each lost in their own thoughts. At last, Azalea spoke. "Since you brought it up, I did want to say something."

"I was sure you did."

"What I wanted to say is that it's breaking my heart watching you be so unhappy."

Susana stopped kicking and stared. "I'm not unhappy," she began. "Things are just a little complicated right now—" She stopped herself, then gazed out the glass walls. Then it hit her.

"Shit. I *am* unhappy." She glared at Azalea. "Why on earth would I be unhappy?" Tears pricked her eyes and she angrily brushed them away. *So I'm unhappy and I'm gonna cry? Oh, hell no.*

"You've changed ever since you took the SVP job with MPG," said Azalea. "It's like you celebrated for ten seconds and then you were hell bent on the next goal. It didn't seem like you were really happy about the achievement, like it just opened up a new way for you to push yourself even harder." A forlorn look crossed her face. "Did you even want the job?"

"Did I want the job?" Susana was incredulous. "Are you kidding me? I've been there twenty years, Azalea! I've busted my ass for two decades, doing every single thing they've asked me to do, performing beyond anyone's expectations. I've built the best teams in the company and our clients love me."

"You didn't answer the question, Suze." Azalea's tone was implacable. "Did you want the job? Or did you just want to prove that you deserved it? Who are you trying to impress?"

Damn.

Susana struggled to compose herself. She had worked harder than anyone at MPG and she'd loved every role she'd played in the firm. Senior vice president was the stepping stone to becoming a partner, and she could have been the first woman to do so—if she had stayed the course. That course would have meant dealing with the current partners on a daily basis, though, and that had been miserable. Peter Gelbarr took every opportunity to remind her that he hadn't been in favor of her promotion. Jonathan Porter, the least assertive of the three, typically followed Peter's lead, leaving only Steven Miles to support her. The interaction with the partners was exhausting and often demoralizing. And when they nearly lost the Liscia account because of Peter's nepotism, she'd been thrust into juggling two roles—SVP and account executive—just to salvage the business.

My abuela would be impressed.

The thought gut punched her. This wasn't about her grandmother. It was about her career, her life, her marriage. When would she stop chasing the next thing, the next promotion? When was it enough?

What do I want?

No, she wasn't happy. She wasn't happy at all.

But now I'm free of them, she assured herself. *Just two more weeks until I start the new job with Liscia. I can do anything for two weeks.*

Happy or not.

"It doesn't matter now," she finally answered her friend. "I have two weeks and then I'm the new CMO for Liscia."

Azalea scowled and she gave Susana a piercing look. "You don't have two weeks. You're already working for them."

Susana sighed. *Doesn't anyone understand?* "It's just prep work, Azalea. I'm getting ready so I can hit the ground running on day one." She looked ruefully at her friend. "I've never been a CMO before. There's a lot to learn in a hurry." She flicked some water off her fingertips at Azalea's face. "Enough about me. Are *you* happy? Are you even doing any client work anymore? Or just sitting around being a bougie Spanish beauty while Esteban roasts coffee beans?"

Azalea's chin came up and her eyes flashed. The anger was brief, but Susana knew she'd touched a nerve. "I'm sorry," she said. "I shouldn't have said that."

Azalea took a deep breath before answering. "No, you shouldn't have. But you did—and it's one more thing that's changed about you." She turned back to the wall and began kicking again. "You're right. We've both changed. The difference is, you keep pushing everyone away. You're doing it to Kique and you're doing it to me."

"Kique and I are just fine," she muttered, returning to her own kicks. "I know you love us both, but you don't know what you're talking about. We're fine."

"Glad to hear it," answered Azalea, her eyes flicking to Susana. She looked as if she wanted to say more, but stopped. She let go of the wall and dipped underwater, coming up and wiping her eyes. "Guess I'll get a few laps in before breakfast," she said.

Susana kept kicking, her eyes forward. "Okay."

When she arrived back in her room, the bed was made and Enrique was gone. A note lay on her pillow. *Gone for a quick run, querida. See you soon x*

Susana undressed and took a hot shower, rinsing off the pool water. She wrapped up in one of the huge towels, then set to work blow drying her hair. Once most of the water was out, she piled it atop her head in a messy bun, then slipped on leggings, a cozy oversized sweater, and warm booties. It was still chilly and the comfortable outfit would be perfect for lazing around the château. She wasn't sure what Azalea and Esteban had planned for the day, but she hoped it wouldn't be anything too programmed. She unpacked her laptop, then sat on the bed and leaned against the pillows. It was only nine o'clock and there wouldn't be anything requiring her attention, she reasoned. But she felt compelled to check before breakfast anyway.

The subject line on a private email from Geneva startled her: **CONFIDENTIAL**: Please respond immediately.

She opened the email and scanned it quickly.

Susana,

You will see the news even in France, I'm sure, but I wanted to be the one to tell you first. Desirée went public with accusations that our Bangladesh suppliers are using child labor and forced labor and that we knew about it and lied on our sustainability reports and our mandatory California reporting. Of course this is all absolute bullshit. I know Desirée is furious she didn't get the CEO job but this is low even for her. Investors are already calling and I'm off to a board meeting first thing in the morning.

I know you're on vacation and haven't officially started at Liscia, but it can't be helped. This is going to require all hands on deck and the press will be all over us. How soon can you be back in the States? If you can't get to California, I need you much closer to coordinate our response.

Geneva

Susana leaned back against the pillows, stunned. A million thoughts raced through her head at once. *Child labor violations.* Could there be anything more despicable? Was it true? What did it mean for Liscia? Even if the allegations were false, the repercussions could be catastrophic. Would they go out of business?

Then she bolted upright. *What would this mean for MPG?* Liscia was their biggest client and Steven had already cautioned her about the disaster it would cause the agency to lose their business.

What does this mean for me?

She already quit her job. If Geneva and Liscia were going down in flames, she wanted no part of it. *But there's no way in hell I'd go back to MPG,* she thought. *Not after Peter's drunken rant.* Her stomach knotted and she reread the email. Could it be true? She had no idea how to respond to Geneva. The knot tightened and her thoughts coalesced into one:

I need to go home.

The door opened and Enrique stepped in. He wiped his forehead with his sleeve and smiled. "How was the pool?"

Susana stared blankly at her husband, her mind still aghast at the enormity of what she'd read and the decisions she needed to make.

"Susana? Are you all right?" Enrique moved quickly to sit by her on the bed. "*Que pasó?*"

"I need to go home," she said, her tone blunt. "There's been... something terrible at Liscia. They've been publicly accused of using child labor. The press and the investors are losing their minds. Geneva needs me to come home." She looked at Enrique's face, his expression moving rapidly from shock to anger. At last, he managed to control his features and spoke.

"Susana—"

"I know," she interrupted. "It's terrible timing. But everything is unraveling and I need to be there. I've just quit one job and the other one is about to blow up in my face." She took a steadying breath. "Kique, I can't just sit here and do nothing."

"What exactly do you think you can accomplish by going home to a job that you haven't even started?" His voice was clipped.

She stared at him, her brows narrowing. "I still work for MPG and they'll likely get drawn into this. They'll need me, too."

Enrique shook his head. "So the job you haven't started and the job you're leaving both can't get by without you giving up your vacation to go do...something?" He threw his hands up. "Do you really believe that? Susana, this is crazy."

"Crazy? Well, thank you very much for the support."

His jaw tightened, his eyes narrowed. "That's not fair and you know it. This isn't a normal situation and I don't understand why you can't see that."

"What is going on with you, Kique? Why is my job all of a sudden such a big problem?" Scorn dripped from her words. "I'm sorry that our timelines haven't meshed perfectly so your retirement dreams don't line up with my goals, but that's where we are. You pushed and pushed and you achieved everything you wanted in your career and now you can't back me?"

"Don't twist this around, Susana. This isn't about me retiring. You want to throw away our once-in-a-lifetime trip to celebrate our anniversary and you don't even know what you'd do back in the States. It's not about you working hard versus me winding down. Maybe I've just realized all these years weren't worth the nonstop driving. That maybe all this grinding hasn't gotten us what we really want."

"You mean what *you* really want. Am I supposed to stop what I'm doing and we just ride into the sunset like some old couple?"

"You know that's not—"

"I'm just fine working my ass off to get ahead, Enrique. There's a lot more for me to achieve and I'm not done yet. This CMO job is a big fucking deal and I'm watching it start to unravel."

"Doesn't it matter that our marriage is unraveling?" The hurt in his voice was palpable.

Her eyebrows shot up in surprise. They'd had some challenges lately, but…unraveling? He was being dramatic. They'd be fine. She just needed to figure out how to fix things at Liscia and—

"Susana, I can't go on like this," Enrique said. "I've tried so hard to be supportive and patient with you—you know I love you with everything in my soul." He paused, then looked away. "We've been going in different directions for some time." He looked back, his eyes sorrowful. "Not drifting apart, Susana. *Flying apart.*"

She stared at him, her gut twisting. "What are you saying, Enrique?" she asked, her voice barely above a whisper.

"If you're asking me to give you an ultimatum, I'm not going to do that. We've been honest with each other for over thirty years, Susana. I'm telling you that I cannot go on like this. I want our life back. I want *you* back. And if that isn't what you want, then we need to have a very serious conversation about what that means."

"Are you threatening me with a divorce?" The intensity of her voice surprised her.

"I didn't say that."

"Then what the hell are you saying, Enrique?"

He stared at her, then dropped his eyes. "I don't even know." He walked into the bathroom and closed the door.

Susana stared at the floor, fury warring with fear. *This can't be happening.*

She *was* unraveling. And she didn't know how to stop.

25

Are you guys coming down for breakfast? It's nearly ready.

Azalea's text message lit up Susana's screen and she glanced at Enrique as he emerged from the bathroom, a towel wrapped around his waist. "They want to know if we're coming down for breakfast," she said, her voice low and expressionless. Then tears welled up and she bit her lip. "What should I say?"

Enrique closed his eyes and rolled his shoulders before answering. "I'm hungry. I'll go down." He looked as if he were going to say more, then dressed without a word. At last he asked, "Do you want to come?"

She brushed a lone tear off her cheek and nodded. "Do you mind if I bring my laptop with me? The wifi doesn't work up here and I really need to find out what's going on."

"Do what you need to do, Susana." He walked to the door and she followed, the chasm between them dark and wide.

Azalea and Esteban were sipping coffee at the dining room table when Susana and Enrique arrived. Their friends were chatting and Susana was once again struck by their obvious love for each other. Esteban reached out and touched Azalea's forearm as he spoke and her friend threw back her head to laugh. Susana felt a pang. *When is the last time Kique and I just laughed together?*

She set her laptop bag on the chair next to her and Azalea frowned.

Susana grimaced—would she get even a moment without someone judging her? "There's been a—an event with Liscia," she said, preempting her friend's disapproval. "I need to see what the news is and the wifi doesn't work in our room." She looked at Enrique. "Would you please get me some coffee and I'll be right back?"

Her husband nodded and walked without speaking to the table where a full coffee bar was set up. "Be back in a sec," she said to Azalea, ignoring her friend's concerned look. She walked to the far end of the long dining room where a settee and two comfortable chairs sat in a semi-circle. She opened her laptop on the low table in the middle of the seating area and was thankful to connect to the wireless network. She quickly began searching for Liscia news.

Oh, shit. It's worse than Geneva described. Her hands shook as she scrolled down the feed, each headline worse than the one before.

Liscia Faces Allegations of Child Labor Abuses

New CEO Geneva Townsend Accused of Cover Up During Her Tenure as COO

Garment Industry's Latest Disgrace: Liscia CEO's Disdain for Child Labor Laws

Fast Fashion Putting Profits over Safety: Liscia Covers Up Years of Child Labor Violations

Susana kept scrolling, but the Liscia news covered the screen. She clicked one link to read more but was surprised when the wireless connection simply dropped. She tried hotspotting to her phone, but it didn't work either. She glanced up at the three sitting at the table where they ate their breakfast and talked quietly.

This can't be happening.

They looked up when Susana approached them.

"Do any of you have any internet access? I just got dropped and I can't connect with my phone either."

"We left our phones in the room," answered Azalea.

Because you're on vacation, thought Susana, her voice harsh in her head. *Must be nice.*

Just then, Céline walked out from the kitchen, followed closely by Benoit. "I hope you will like this," she said to the four. "I have made you a very special goat cheese omelette served with a salad from our garden." She set plates in front of Azalea and Esteban, while Benoit walked around the table to serve Susana and Enrique. She walked back to the kitchen and reemerged with a basket loaded with fresh bread. Benoit likewise returned with a small dish of what looked like fruit compote. "*Bon appetit!*" she exclaimed.

Enrique and Esteban smiled and thanked their hosts, but Azalea turned to look at Susana, her brow furrowed in dismay. "What's wrong?" she asked quietly. "You look upset."

"I shouldn't have come," Susana answered, her voice dull. "Everything is falling apart."

The men took to their breakfast with enthusiasm, passing the bread basket and the compote across to each other. Neither seemed to notice the women's somber mood, although Susana was certain Enrique felt every pulse of anguish from her. She took a small bite of the omelette to keep from speaking. The tiniest part of her brain registered how delicious the food was, but it was overcome by her anxiety.

"We were talking about driving over to Anduze this morning," Esteban told her. "It's a charming little village about twenty minutes from here." He chuckled. "I know it's silly to think about eating lunch while we're eating such a big breakfast, but they do have some nice restaurants in the main square. And we love a little café there, too. Good coffee and they have reliable wifi when we need to connect with Esteban Junior or any of Azalea's clients in the US."

Susana's eyebrows shot up. "How reliable?" she asked.

"As good as you're used to at our house," answered Esteban. "And there are tables outdoors in a lovely little courtyard where we sit and have coffee and *dulces*."

Susana looked at Enrique, but he kept his gaze on his plate, spreading compote onto a slice of the thick bread. She looked back at Esteban, avoiding Azalea's eyes. "I know I'm not supposed to be working today but something has come up and I need to be online." Her shoulders slumped. "I may even have to go home."

From the corner of her eye, she saw Enrique's jaw tighten, but he said nothing.

"Go home?" asked Esteban. "What happened?"

She glanced again at Enrique. At last he looked up at her and shrugged. "Might as well tell them," he said.

She sat back in her chair and sighed. The sun shone through the windows and she could hear birdsong on the patio. The aroma of the freshly baked bread lingered in the room, and she wondered how on earth she could consider leaving this magical place—an anniversary gift from their dearest friends.

"So it turns out the company that just hired me may have violated child labor laws in Bangladesh. Apparently one of their suppliers routinely uses children in their production facilities. All those beautiful handmade pleats were done by kids under the age of eighteen. The woman whose job I'm taking is claiming that the new CEO—the woman who hired me—knew about it and covered it up for the past few years." She looked at Azalea's horrified expression. "Geneva says it's not true and she wants me back in the States to help with damage control."

Esteban looked at Susana with compassion. "But you haven't started that job yet, have you?"

"Well, not exactly—"

"It's not 'not exactly,' Suze!" Azalea broke in. "You're still employed by MPG for another two weeks and you don't start at Liscia for a month. How can she expect you to drop everything to come help her? You don't even work there *and* you don't know if she's telling the truth!" Azalea looked appalled. "Child labor? That's horrifying."

Susana looked hard at Azalea. Her best friend was the calmest person she knew, always taking a measured approach to life, giving everyone the benefit of the doubt. The habit hadn't served her well when she was married to her first husband, the serial cheater, but Susana could always count on Azalea's even keel—nearly as much as Enrique's. Susana was far more apt to jump to conclusions and respond passionately. Having the tables turned felt odd, and Susana wasn't keen on either defending Geneva or fighting with her best friend.

And Azalea was right. Susana still worked for MPG, which could get roped into the scandal very easily, being the agency of record—and the team who built the Liscia brand. *Talk about a rock and a hard place*, she thought, her stomach turning.

"You're right," she said softly, looking down at her hands, then at Enrique. "I don't work for Liscia and I'm on my way out at MPG. Geneva has no right to demand my attention and I'm not sure how much I can do for the agency—but I still need information. I can't make any decisions for either company without more information." She looked back and forth between her husband and her friends. "Anduze sounds nice but I do need to bring my laptop and get some work done while we're there." She saw Esteban's quick look at Enrique, then back at Azalea. The Obregons both nodded.

"I'm so sorry, Susana," said Esteban. "*Qué situación tan difícil.*"

Susana at last turned to her husband. "Is that okay with you?"

"Do what you need to do," he answered, his voice resigned.

Susana smiled at the young man bringing her *café au lait*. "*Merci*," she said before opening her laptop. The drive to Anduze had been quiet, the four friends only occasionally speaking as they drove the narrow lanes through the French countryside. Once they'd settled her at Tea Pôtes—"Our favorite little spot in the village," said Azalea—the three friends had left to explore the winding alleys while she worked. Azalea had hugged her before taking Esteban's arm but Enrique had simply nodded and followed their friends.

She knew he was hurting but she couldn't muster the energy to tackle the mess that was her marriage along with the sudden career disaster. *One thing at a time.* If she could just get a handle on the work front, she was sure she and Enrique would work things out. They'd never even come close to splitting up—surely this was no different. *He's just midlife crisis-ing*, she told herself.

But she wasn't so sure.

An hour later, she was no closer to knowing what to do. She'd exchanged increasingly abrupt emails with Geneva who demanded Susana's full attention, despite her reminders that she wasn't yet a

Liscia employee. She'd sent off an email to Steven but hadn't yet received a reply. The coverage of the allegations was brutal. Citing unnamed sources, a reporter outlined the company's overseas violations, but more damning was the assertion that Geneva, in her previous role as Chief Operating Officer, had known about the behavior and covered it up in order to meet revenue and production targets. Desirée may have been the catalyst for the investigation but, if the coverage were to be believed, Geneva had been callously indifferent to the plight of children. It remained to be determined who else was involved.

Susana sipped her coffee and looked around the courtyard. A soft breeze ruffled the leaves of the trees surrounding her, and the ever-present birdsong provided tranquil background music. Across the courtyard a young woman sat at a table with two children—a little boy perched in a chair and an infant in a stroller next to her. She idly pushed the pram back and forth as she spoke to the boy in French. The child bounced his legs while he nibbled on a croissant and chattered to his mother. An orange tabby cat sauntered along the tables before curling up next to a pot of brightly colored flowers to wash itself. The entire tableau looked like something on a postcard, she mused.

And then there's me.

She knew she was the glaring blot on the bucolic allure of this quintessentially French courtyard scene. Her nerves were raw and she was unsure of her next move—or where her loyalties should lie. She looked away from the cat who now lay sunning himself and back to the little family. The infant began to fuss and the boy climbed off his chair to lean over the stroller. The mother smiled fondly as he began to sing to the babe inside, his lilting voice soothing, although Susana didn't understand the French words. The mother joined him in the lullaby and Susana found herself leaning towards them, her heart softening with their simple expression of love. She could imagine Sara in the same tableau. Her friend was a born mother.

And then she imagined other children, the ones in Bangladesh. *Children as young as ten years old were found crammed into tiny alcoves sewing pleats onto Liscia garments for up to 12 hours per day,* said one article. The boy crooning into the stroller looked to be that age, she thought. Her stomach clenched at the thought of a child that young being exploited in such a horrific manner.

She wondered for the thousandth time: *Was it true?* Geneva swore it was simply Desirée retaliating for not getting the CEO job. But that seemed overly simple. The board of directors spent weeks vetting candidates before they appointed Geneva to be the new CEO. Did they know anything? Going public with these accusations did more than tarnish her reputation. It put the entire company at risk, a hundred people who could lose their jobs. Desirée may be petty, but would she put every employee out of work to make a point?

It didn't make sense.

I should call her. The thought came out of nowhere, but once in her head, it stuck. If she wanted information, that was a good place to start.

Do I want to know?

26

An hour later, Steven Mills called.

"We have no comment at this time," he told Susana. "The press are already calling, but we're staying out of this for as long as we can. If they reach out to you, send them to me. Don't give them anything."

"I won't," she assured him. "We don't know anything at this point anyway. Geneva swears it's all a lie, intended to damage her reputation now that she's CEO."

"It could be nothing but politics," answered Steven, but he didn't sound certain. "I hate to think we've partnered with a company that's so internally dysfunctional they'd pull something like this." Susana heard the frustration in his voice. "But it's far worse to think the allegations are true."

"I know it's not proof," she began, "but I do feel confident in Geneva. She's passionate about this new sustainable clothing line—she's betting the company on the notion that customers will love purchasing luxury fashion that prioritizes the environment. I've never gotten the impression she's just greenwashing Liscia's brand. She seems genuine in her concerns. It's almost impossible to imagine her caring about trees and not kids."

"Be careful, Susana," warned her boss. "You still work for MPG, not Liscia. Believe in our *client*, but remember where your loyalties must lie. You can't afford to get tangled up in this mess. It will look very bad for us if you're crossing lines that shouldn't be crossed."

"I understand," she said, wondering how she could possibly perform the balancing act between the two companies. *How did I let myself get into this?*

"I hope you do," he said, his voice hard. "I want to be crystal clear, Susana, and this comes directly from all three partners. *You are to stay out of this mess.* If you make any public comments—if you say anything other than referring the press to me—we will fire you and very likely take legal action."

Susana was quiet, her normally volatile temper stunned. "I understand," she repeated. She briefly considered asking him to make MPG's ultimatum clear to Geneva, but just as quickly abandoned the idea, realizing how weak she would appear to her new boss. *I can handle this myself.*

"Good. Joseph and his team are drafting the crisis communications messaging package today. You should have it this afternoon. Or," he corrected himself, "tonight for you. I suspect it will be a long weekend."

"You're probably right."

They hung up and Susana sat back in her chair, her thoughts harsh and painful. *Did he really just threaten me with a lawsuit?* She may have conflicting loyalties, but she'd never put her company— her friends and colleagues—at risk. After twenty years, did Steven have so little confidence in her he needed to give her such a stark warning?

She looked up at the sound of the little boy calling out. "*Papá!*" A handsome man approached the family's table as the boy dove into his arms. "*Papá ! Tu es de retour plus tôt que prévu !*" The young father spun the boy around before leaning down to kiss the woman's cheek and reach into the stroller to grab a chubby fist.

"*Oui, mon petit prince.*" He ruffled the boy's hair as he set the child down, then grabbed a chair from a nearby table to join his family. He nibbled a corner of his son's croissant and the child laughed.

"*C'est le mien !*"

"*Je t'en achèterai plus*," answered the man. He reached into his pocket and pulled out a handful of euros. His wife's eyes widened and she clapped her hands. "*J'ai vendu le tableau*," he told her, his eyes alight.

Susana had no idea what the couple were saying and was embarrassed to find herself staring. Yet she couldn't turn away when the woman, her lovely smile beaming, reached across the table to kiss her man. Whatever he had done, she was proud of him.

When Enrique and her friends returned to the café, Susana had regained some of her composure. She'd taken advantage of the time to sketch out her approach with Geneva, demonstrating that she could be supportive, yet remain in the background until she formally joined the company. It was the right thing to do, and she was certain Geneva would understand.

At least, she hoped she would.

"We've decided to skip lunch," called out Azalea as the trio approached Susana's table. "It's the perfect day to go to Sauve for dinner. Esteban got us reservations at Au Bon JaJa. It's our favorite place on the plaza but we can only get in at seven o'clock when they open. That's too soon for us to have dinner if we eat lunch, too." She looked at Susana's empty plate. "Did you have something already?"

"Just a croissant and a coffee," answered Susana. "I'll be hungry by seven but I'm fine." She glanced at Enrique, hoping to catch his eye. As before, he looked away, seeming to study the buildings around the square.

Looking anywhere but at me, she thought.

"Anyway," continued Azalea, "are you at a place where you can stop working so we can talk to Sara before we drive back to the château? I want to take advantage of the wifi."

Susana noted that Enrique perked up at the question. He finally looked at her, his expression neutral. She could see the tension in his shoulders, the way he anticipated her answer. She looked back at her laptop and saw another email from Geneva. *URGENT: Need your response immediately* screamed the subject line. She grimaced, then nodded at Azalea.

"Almost done. Can you give me five more minutes?" Enrique turned abruptly, then walked across the square to the café's open door. She sighed, wishing he trusted her. But why should he? Susana knew those five minutes could easily turn into an hour. "Why don't you guys grab a coffee and I'll just finish up?"

Azalea nodded then blew Susana a kiss as she and Esteban followed Enrique to the café.

Susana,

I have a phone interview with the San Francisco Chronicle at 1:00 today. I want you on the call with me. Obviously it would have been far better if you were here, but this is the best we can do at this point. We'll explain that you've been hired to replace Desirée but we haven't announced it yet—they can keep that news under embargo for a couple of weeks. But this will position you as the comms leader and spokesperson for Liscia. Elisa Cavenaugh is a friendly—she's followed us forever—so it should go reasonably well. Make sure you are somewhere quiet and with good mobile coverage and we'll dial you in.

We need to get on top of this today. The bottom line is simple.
- *The allegations are untrue*
- *They stem from a disgruntled employee*
- *Liscia is committed to ethical production, sourcing, and retailing of our products*
- *We have an entirely new line of sustainable fashion coming out in the fall/winter of next year and would never compromise our values by contracting with unethical suppliers*

Let me know if you have questions or any suggestions.

Geneva

Susana glared at the screen. This was getting out of hand. Geneva made no pretense of giving her a choice—the CEO simply dictated and expected compliance. One o'clock California time was ten o'clock in the Cevennes, a time when she had expected to be with her friends…or alone with Enrique. She knew she had to prioritize her husband. Their ugly conversation that morning was fresh on her mind and their supposedly wonderful anniversary trip was turning out to be a complete disaster.

But it was just a phone call. *Probably a half hour long*, she reckoned. *No reporter is gonna stay on the phone more than that.* They'd be back to the château from the restaurant long before then, and she could sit out on the terrace for a quick call while her friends kept Kique company.

But Steven Mills had sworn her to silence. If she agreed to Geneva's demands, she risked being sued by her current company. She was torn between wanting to finish her time at MPG with her head held high and diving into the deep end of crisis management for Liscia. Fighting for recognition at MPG was a daily grind and, if she were honest, being considered so valuable at Liscia was a seductive experience.

She stared at the screen, unable to decide how to respond to the CEO's request. *It's not a request*, she repeated. *It's a demand.*

For a brief moment, she allowed herself to imagine standing outside Liscia's flagship store in Palo Alto, impeccably dressed head to toe in the company's trademark clothing, unflappable in front of a group of reporters and photographers…and then snapped out of her reverie. *Don't be an idiot*, she scolded herself. The allegations were serious and this wasn't a fashion shoot. No, she had to turn Geneva down. She could talk to the press without reservation in two weeks when she completely severed ties with MPG. Geneva's demands were unreasonable—unethical even. She'd keep her word to Steven. What more did she have than her integrity?

She thought back to the look of pride on the young woman's face. She yearned for that look from her husband, her friends, her parents. She imagined talking to her grandmother.

No. It was more important than that.

I want that look in the mirror.

Straightening her shoulders, she began typing her response.

When Azalea and the men stepped out of the café, Susana held one finger up, letting them know she was nearly done. She finished the email to Geneva and closed her laptop. *That's it then*, she thought. She had no idea when the CEO would respond and was under no illusion that it would be positive. But she had taken a stand and, for the first time in weeks, felt content. She looked up at Enrique and smiled. Now she was determined to rejoin the group and enjoy the rest of the day. It wouldn't be a great weekend—she knew she'd hear more from both companies—but at least she'd drawn a boundary.

Now she just needed to keep it.

Enrique looked as if he would speak to her, but instead turned toward Esteban and Azalea. "*Estamos listos?*" he asked. Susana guessed he was putting on a cheerful tone for their friends. *We just need to get through this weekend*, she thought. *Everything will be all right.*

Azalea glanced up from her phone with a smile. "Perfect timing! Sara and Lauren are free for a quick call and we have good wifi." She glanced at the men. "Do you mind if we take a few minutes?"

"We aren't invited?" grinned Esteban. He gestured to Enrique. "Let's grab another table, *amigo.*"

Azalea sat with Susana. "Let's use your laptop so we can see them better."

Within seconds, the four friends were smiling at each other onscreen.

"Oh, it's so good to see you!" said Sara. "I've missed you both."

"We miss you, too," answered Azalea. She nudged her friend with her knee and Susana got the message: *Cheer up.*

"So what's the big news? You have us on pins and needles," said Susana, trying to shake off her mood.

Sara smiled at her friends. "Well…we're having a baby!"

"That's wonderful!" "I'm so happy for you!" The women tripped over each other to congratulate their friend.

"When are you due?" asked Azalea.

"Late May," answered Sara. "I waited to tell you guys until we were pretty sure we're safe." She frowned. "The doctor said there's no reason to expect another miscarriage, but we wanted to get past the first trimester just to be sure."

Susana thought back to the loss of Sara's pregnancy early in the year. She felt a pang of guilt at her self-absorption over the past months. *Other people have much bigger problems*, she thought. *People I love.*

Just then, Terrence appeared onscreen, leaning his chin on Sara's shoulder. "How are the European aunties?"

"Just great," answered Azalea. She beckoned to Esteban and Enrique, and soon all seven of the friends were onscreen and talking. They spent several minutes catching up and promised to visit again soon.

After the call, Susana packed up her laptop and she reflected on the journeys her friends' relationships had taken. Azalea and Esteban split up after Azalea left Spain to return to Florida. Sara and Terrence broke up after the miscarriage and the anguish of her postpartum depression. *But they've reconciled and are stronger than ever*, she told herself. *Kique and I have thirty years of history. We'll be fine.*

We have to be fine.

The four friends walked to the car, Susana only vaguely listening to their conversation. Now that she had responded to Geneva, she finally felt free to look around the village and enjoy the constant birdsong. They strolled along narrow side streets until they arrived at a patisserie across from the parking lot. "I love this place," said Azalea. "Mind if we stop in? I know we won't eat them while we're at the château, but we can bring them home." She quirked a grin at her husband. "You won't be jealous if I bring home French pastries, will you?"

Esteban laughed and hugged her. "*No me importa, querida.* They're different from what we make at the café—it's like a special treat when we are here."

They walked into the bakery and Susana inhaled the aroma of fresh bread. Her mouth watered at the sight of the *pain au chocolat* and fruit tartlets. As her shoulders began to relax, she was surprised that all her senses seemed to relish the quaint village. It was like slowly awakening from a bad dream, remembering where she was.

Remembering *who* she was.

"Do you want anything?" Enrique's voice startled her. "We can take some back to Barcelona."

It wasn't pastries she wanted. *I want you*, she thought. *I want us.*

She smiled at him and took his hand. "I'd love some of the chocolate croissants."

Enrique nodded as he pulled away. He walked to the counter, picking out two chocolate and two plain croissants. The feel of his fingers lingered on her hand and her smile faded. *Two more days until our anniversary*, she reminded herself. *Everything will be okay by then.*

The knot in her stomach returned. She hadn't awakened from a dream. She was still knee deep in the mess and she feared two days wouldn't change anything.

27

The couples returned to the château and went to their respective suites to get ready for the trip to Sauve. Susana dropped her laptop bag on the desk and lay down on the bed. Enrique began looking through the closet, the tension thick between them.

"So I talked to Steven and MPG wants me to stay out of the whole media frenzy." She forced a laugh. "He even threatened to fire me and sue me if I get involved publicly." She waited, but her husband remained silent. "I told Geneva I couldn't help with any of the interviews or—"

"Susana, I really don't want to talk about your job right now. Either of them." Enrique stood at the foot of the bed looking solemn. He shook his head as if dislodging his thoughts. "I know I've been asking you to share more with me and this probably makes me a complete jerk, but I just need a break. I'm sorry."

"I do want to share this with you, but I understand." Her voice softened. "We're a team, Kique."

He nodded. "I know." He headed for the bathroom. "I'm gonna take a quick shower."

She sat up and asked quietly, "Do you want company?"

He didn't turn around. "Not right now."

She couldn't remember a time when her husband hadn't jumped at the chance to share a hot shower with his wife. As she lay back on the pillow, tears trickling down her cheeks, she couldn't pretend any longer.

We're in trouble.

Esteban maneuvered the car into the last spot in the parking lot and the four friends got out. The sun was going down and there was a slight chill to the breeze. They strolled through the village and she noted how Enrique studied the ancient architecture. The medieval city streets were narrow, the stones walls rough and beautiful. A fat tabby cat stood sentry at the entrance to one home, his eyes following them as they passed.

"My favorite things here are the doors," said Azalea. "That probably sounds weird, but the doors in Sauve are gorgeous—so rustic and heavy and, I don't know—just fantastic." She reached up to trail her fingers along the heavy wood portal of a shop now closed. "It's amazing this city has been around for hundreds of years and people still live here." She looked at Susana and shrugged. "A lot of artists find their inspiration in this village."

"I can see why," said Enrique. He looked up at the towering wall. "It's magnificent."

They approached the small plaza and Esteban spoke to the owner of the restaurant. "Our table will be ready in just a moment," he said as he walked back to the group. "We're a few minutes early— would you like to see the view while they finish preparing?"

Enrique and Susana nodded and they walked a few yards to a waist-high wall where they looked down at the dark, slow-moving water. The sun was beginning to set, but they could still see the thick line of trees on the far bank and the placid river below them. The breeze picked up and Susana pulled her sweater closer. She watched as Esteban hugged Azalea to his side and she felt the distance between herself and Enrique as a physical pain. She longed to bridge the gap between them and started to move closer when a waiter from the restaurant approached.

"*Votre table est prête, monsieur.*"

"*Merci*," replied Esteban. "*Vamos a comer*," he said with a smile, leading them to their table.

After two hours, the four friends still sat at the table, sipping espresso and nibbling on their rich desserts. The food had been delicious, Susana thought, and the wine and coffee warmed her from the evening chill. Enrique seemed to relax as the meal progressed, and he and Esteban talked animatedly about the village, still standing after more than a thousand years.

"It's just remarkable," he said. "I'd love to come back here and stay for a week just to explore."

Azalea smiled. "We knew you'd love it."

"But wait until tomorrow, my friend," added Esteban. "One thousand years is nothing compared with the Pont du Gard. It was built in the first century and it defies description—at least for me. I look forward to hearing what your architect mind thinks of it."

Enrique leaned forward, his face alight. "I can't wait. It's the highlight of this trip. We build things in Florida to last for a hundred years. I can't imagine the engineering that went into something that's over two thousand years old." He sat back and sipped his coffee. "Amazing," he muttered.

The highlight of the trip? Susana knew he didn't mean anything by the comment, but it stung nevertheless. She noted Azalea's look across the table, her friend's eyes filled with compassion. *She caught that, too.*

She shook off the hurt and tried to put some life into her voice. "So what time do we leave in the morning? We're going to the market in—where did you say?"

"Uzès," answered Azalea. "You'll love it. It's bustling and crazy and fabulous. We can go right after breakfast, if that's okay with you guys."

Susana glanced at Enrique and he nodded. "Fine with us," she answered.

Enrique paid the check, refusing to let Esteban contribute. "No way," he said, shaking his head. "This is our treat. You've done so much for us already."

"*Muchisimas gracias*," said Azalea, smiling.

They stood and looked around the plaza one last time and Susana heard Enrique say once again, "Amazing," his voice reverential and quiet.

Esteban and Enrique chatted in Spanish as they drove back to the château, while Azalea and Susana sat quietly in the back seat of the car. Susana checked her watch—nine-thirty in France meant it was only half an hour until Geneva would have her interview. She knew she'd done the right thing by declining to help the CEO, but her stomach tightened at the thought of the reporter's questions. Surely Geneva would be fine—she'd been in the public eye for a long time, both at Liscia and previous companies. She was poised and forthright—characteristics that impressed Susana. Once this crisis blew over, she was eager to learn from Geneva and become the mouthpiece for the company.

"Everything all right?" asked Azalea.

"Huh? Oh, sorry." Susana looked up from her phone. "Yeah, nothing else has happened. Geneva has that interview with the Chronicle in half an hour." She grimaced. "I'd love to be a fly on the wall for that call."

"What will you do if you find out these accusations are true?" Azalea's quiet voice was cautious.

Susana scowled. "I'm sure they aren't. I told you—Desirée is trying to sabotage Geneva because she didn't get the CEO job." She realized how defensive she sounded. "I mean, if you'd heard her on our calls, you'd get it. She's been undercutting me and trying to sabotage the MPG relationship ever since I met her, and she constantly disrespects Geneva."

"Maybe so, but that doesn't mean she's making this up," continued Azalea. "What kind of person fabricates something like this from jealousy? It could ruin their reputation. That could take years to recover, if it ever did." She shook her head, her brow furrowed. "People's livelihoods are at stake, Suze. You'd have to be a pretty horrible human to make up a story like this just to get back at the one person who got the job you wanted." She reached for Susana's arm and squeezed. "Don't let the new job blind you. How well do you know either of these women to make a judgment call? This is a mess and you don't even have all the facts."

Susana wondered again if she should call Desirée directly. She sensed Enrique's attention and realized the men had stopped their conversation. Anger bubbled up and she fought to rein in her emotions. "Have I ever given you any reason to think I'd do something unethical just to get a good job?" she asked, biting off her words. "You've known me for thirty-five years, Azalea. I would hope you'd have more trust in me than that." She turned to face the window, shutting out her best friend. She knew she was acting like a petulant teenager, but she couldn't contain herself.

"Of course not! I'm sorry. I didn't mean to imply that. I do trust you, Suze." Azalea touched her shoulder, and Susana turned slightly. "I know you'll do the right thing."

She only wished she knew what that was.

Enrique and Susana got ready for bed without a word. While she lay staring at the ceiling, he fell asleep in minutes. *Typical man*, she groused. *Our marriage is falling apart but he's sound asleep while I'm probably up all night.* She flopped onto her side, grabbing her phone from the nightstand, hoping the wifi would connect and she could while away some time searching for information on Uzès. At least it would distract her from thinking about the interview she knew was going on.

Her phone connected immediately and she scrolled through Instagram photos of the market, her emotions slowly calming. There were tables filled with all sorts of goods, from sausages to cheese, from honey to wine. There were colorful photos of baskets and soaps, and she began to idly check off the items she could buy and fit into their suitcases. One stall featured beautiful woven baskets; another had colorful scarves. She wished they had brought an empty suitcase for all the treats she wanted to purchase, both in France and in Spain. She wondered if there was a vendor for baby clothes. She and Azalea could purchase a few things to take back to the States for Sara's new little one.

A WhatsApp message appeared onscreen and she felt a brief annoyance at the interruption. But then she saw the sender: Geneva.

Just finished my call with the Chron. 20 mins was all she had and it was NOT positive. So much for objective journalism. You should have been there. Lots to clean up. I appreciate your ethical concerns but we need to find a way to get you out of MPG so you can devote your time to Liscia. We don't have the luxury of this lengthy notice. Call me.

Susana looked at the time: ten-thirty. She glanced at her sleeping husband and sighed deeply. She could pretend she hadn't seen the text and respond in the morning. Geneva wasn't her boss yet—it was ridiculous that she was feeling this much pressure to answer.

But Enrique was asleep and she was wide awake. She got up and quietly dressed, slipping on a jacket over her leggings and t-shirt, and then headed out for the courtyard.

28

The night air was colder than she'd expected, and Susana pulled her jacket tight. She walked across the courtyard and decided to head indoors for the salon instead. If she were quiet, she wouldn't bother anyone else in the château. She slowly opened the door, taking care not to make any loud noises, then walked across the foyer to the lounge. The house was quiet and she sat down on the large sofa to call Liscia's CEO.

"Hey," responded Geneva, answering on the first ring. "Thanks for calling."

"It's late here but it sounded like you needed to talk." Susana leaned back on the comfortable couch. "So it wasn't a good call?"

Geneva snorted. "It was a shit call. I don't know why I expected her to be reasonable. I kept trying to explain that this was nothing more than a disgruntled employee but she kept asking me about our production controls and had I ever been out there in person to assess the facility, why did I sign off on compliance docs, blahblahblah." Her voice grew angrier as she spoke. "I don't know how to be more clear, Susana. You have to be on these calls because no one will attack you. You're new and you're pristine. Having you on a call sends a strong message that you joined Liscia because you believe in what we're doing. Your reputation is spotless."

Susana shot up, her grip on the phone tightening. "So I'm just a foil for you?" The words slipped out before she could rein in her anger.

"Don't be an infant, Susana," snapped Geneva. "This is all about messaging and perception. Do I need your skills as a marketing executive? Yes. Do I need someone who is completely untainted by any of this absurd scandal? Again, yes. Is that a problem?"

Susana took a deep breath before answering. *And this is why you don't make calls in the middle of the night.*

"I understand. I do. But I can't be there until I'm finished with MPG. I updated my commitment to them for a two-week transition instead of a month, but that means absolutely no involvement with Liscia and the press until then." She closed her eyes and frowned. "Surely you can appreciate that."

"I can appreciate that Steven Mills is pissed off that you're leaving and he's making this as difficult as possible for me." The Liscia CEO's voice was harsh, her words clipped.

For you? What have I gotten myself into?

"Anyway," continued Geneva, "get your ass back to the States and we'll figure it out. I'm declining any more interviews for the next week until you can be here but we'll need to respond to any coverage this weekend."

Susana shook her head. *It's like she doesn't even hear what I'm saying. Or she hears but doesn't care.* She tried again, her voice firm. "I'm in France all weekend for my thirtieth wedding anniversary, Geneva. I don't even get back to Spain until Monday afternoon and I'm not coming back to Florida for another ten days after that—"

"I don't care about your schedule, Susana," broke in the CEO. "We are talking about the life of this company. I'm paying you a helluva lot of money and you have made a commitment to Liscia—and to me."

Susana stared at the phone, unnerved. *Boundaries, chica*, she cautioned herself. *Set them now.* She knew her next words would set the stage for her ongoing relationship with the mercurial CEO.

She spoke slowly, punctuating each word. "Geneva. You actually aren't paying me anything yet but I'm still involved, aren't I? Look, it's after eleven o'clock at night for me. I'm going on vacation tomorrow but I'll check email or you can text me if there's an emergency." She took a deep breath. "Good night."

She heard muttering and then the connection broke. She wondered if she'd lost cell coverage, then realized Geneva had simply hung up. Torn between anger and confusion, she leaned back against the cushions and closed her eyes. It was just too much.

When she awoke, Susana was cold and stiff. Despite the comfortable cushions, her shoulders and hips were tight and painful. As she stretched, her phone fell to floor and a part of her wanted to leave it there, never to be looked at again. The sky outside was still dark and she longed to be in bed, warm and close to Enrique. *How did things go so wrong so quickly?* she wondered.

She picked up the phone and groaned. It was two o'clock in the morning—far too early to just stay up. She stood and stretched again, making her way to the door in the dark. Walking onto the terrace, she looked up at the cloudless sky. The moon cast an ethereal light over the château, and the air, though still cool, seemed warmer than when she'd first come down from her room. The thought of snuggling up to her husband brought unexpected tears to her eyes. She hadn't cried this much in, what? Years. She wasn't ready to go back to bed with all the anger and hurt between them.

She tucked her phone into her pocket and walked to the edge of the balcony overlooking the broad lawn. The night was quiet, the hush only broken by occasional insect noises. She yearned for quiet in her mind and heart, and she slowly descended the broad stone stairway to the grounds. Now, in the middle of the night, the moon and stars were bright enough to light her way, and she soon found herself on the path that surrounded the ancient building.

The grass glistened with dew and she decided to leave the walkway, her footsteps leaving dark smudges behind her as she headed across the damp field. Now wide awake, she considered her situation. The truth was, she hated every bit of it. She knew she was talented—far more than the MPG leadership deserved. She had worked herself ragged to achieve and now had to face the harsh reality that her so-called success hadn't brought her the contentment she hoped. She loved the work and the people on her teams and was proud of everything she'd accomplished, but she was still chasing some elusive goal she couldn't even define.

But now that chapter of her career was over and the last memories she'd have of her two decades at the agency were a drunken phone call from one partner and a threat of a lawsuit from another.

And then there was the Liscia job. The luxury fashion company, so beloved by its customers, was entering a new and exciting phase. The company's surprising commitment to a line created with sustainable fabrics heralded an entirely new way to experience fashion—a means for wealthy customers to look fabulous while making an environmental statement. Becoming their new CMO was the pinnacle of everything she had sacrificed and worked for her entire career. How fitting that her *abuela* once washed wealthy people's clothes and now her granddaughter would be marketing luxury clothing to that same class of people. Yet now she wondered if Geneva hired her for her talents or if she was simply a convenient foil, a distraction from the accusations.

Susana looked around and realized she'd walked far from the château. Her sneakers and the lower part of her leggings were wet with dew, the damp beginning to chill her. But the thought of walking back was suddenly beyond her and she slumped to the ground. Sitting in the grass, she was cold, wet, exhausted…and very much alone. She began to cry, her sniffles becoming sobs as she at last allowed herself to feel the anguish over her marriage and career. She wept over the wall she'd built between herself and Azalea, her dearest friend in the world. Sobs wracked her as she remembered her harsh words with Enrique and how he'd pulled away from her.

Through every difficulty, they'd been her anchors. Azalea had seen past the party girl Susana had been in college, always pushing her to become her best. She knew a good deal of her early success was due to her friend's belief in her.

And then there was Enrique, the love of her life. The man who adored her, encouraged and supported her over three decades. She thought of his beautiful brown eyes, his sweet smile, the way he lit up when she was in the room. *Who still has that after thirty years?* she wondered. She knew why their friends all admired them. They were a couple for the ages, a duet who harmonized perfectly.

No, not perfectly, she corrected herself. *But beautifully.*

When she could cry no longer, Susana stood, wiping her eyes and her runny nose on her sweatshirt, and attempted to brush the damp grass from her behind. The night air chilled her wet legs and she began the long trudge back to the château, weary and forlorn, and no closer to answers for her life.

A knock on the bedroom door awakened Susana. She glanced over to see Kique's side of the bed empty. She hadn't heard him get up and her mind was foggy after her middle of the night wandering.

"Just a minute," she said, her voice scratchy from crying. She rubbed at her eyes and stood. "Who is it?"

"It's me, Suze," said Azalea. "You okay?"

Susana opened the door. "Yeah. Just had a rough night." She held open the door. "Wanna come in?"

Azalea's face was sorrowful. "I just came to check on you. We wanted to leave for the market in a few minutes and you weren't down for breakfast." She frowned. "You look awful."

Susana grunted. "Yeah, I bet. Give me ten minutes? I'll jump in the shower and get dressed."

Azalea stood quietly. "What can I do?"

Susana sighed, then covered a huge yawn. "Nothing, unfortunately."

"Okay. We'll be in the salon when you're ready."

"Kique's down there?"

Azalea nodded. "He doesn't look much better than you do," she said, her voice thick with sadness. "I think—"

"I'll be quick," interrupted Susana. "See you in ten." She closed the door on her friend and hurried to the shower before the tears began again.

Susana leaned her aching head against the window, hoping to fall asleep for even a few minutes on the interminable drive to Uzès. Everyone was quiet—it seemed her mood had affected the entire party. When they finally arrived, she was startled when Enrique opened her door and held out a hand to help her from the car. She looked at him without a word and then took his hand. As soon as she was standing, he squeezed her hand gently, then pulled away.

"This is one of our favorite markets," said Esteban. "When we stay in France, we usually rent a little cottage and do our own cooking." He chuckled and hugged his wife. "We like to be more informal—we don't always stay at the château, and this market is a great place to buy groceries for a quick trip."

The four walked toward the stalls and Susana could feel the exuberance of the Saturday crowd. In spite of her bleak mood, the sights and smells tugged at her emotions. She smelled the fresh rotisserie chicken and the loaves of bread, and was drawn to a fragrant table laden with French-milled soaps.

She glanced at Enrique and tried to smile. "Do you see those?" she asked. "I'd love to take some home with us."

"Sure," he answered with a shrug. "Whatever you want."

Susana's heart ached with longing. *I want you*, she thought for the millionth time. She wondered again how they'd ended up so far apart. For months, instead of sharing their feelings and talking things out, they'd entrenched and retrenched, staking out positions that collided and clashed. It wasn't like either of them to be so rigid, yet here they were. She wished she'd awakened him last night to tell him about her conversation with Geneva, how she'd set boundaries with the woman. She yearned to hear him tell her that he'd also evolved, that if he retired it didn't mean she needed to slow down yet. They couldn't be at a complete impasse, could they? Surely they could find their way back to each other.

She held out a hand, but her husband had turned and was walking toward another booth. *He probably didn't notice me reaching out*, she told herself, determined not to call to him. She refused to look back at Azalea, knowing her sharp-eyed best friend would have seen…and Susana couldn't bear the pity she knew would be in Azalea's eyes.

Instead, she walked toward the soap vendor. There were dozens of different fragrances, from sweet to citrus, spicy to woodsy. She picked out ten bars and paid the woman. "*Merci*," she said, as she took the fragrant bags. Looking around, she saw that Enrique had moved down the aisle to a stall selling beaded jewelry. She watched as he lifted a bracelet, rolling the beads between his fingers. But then his shoulders slumped and he put the trinket back onto the table.

Susana willed her husband to turn and look at her. She saw him take a few steps, then stop, glancing around but not behind him. Then he straightened and began walking away, soon swallowed up by the throng of shoppers, but separated from her by so much more.

29

"*Estás lista?*" asked Esteban.

Susana startled at his sonorous voice. She'd been looking at some beautiful woven baskets and hadn't noticed him before he spoke.

"I am," she answered, then looked around. "Where are Azalea and Kique?"

"Just over there," he pointed. "Azalea wanted some macarons for our picnic." He held out his arm. "Did you find everything you wanted?"

Susana considered the question. What she wanted couldn't be found in a market stall. She took Esteban's arm and tried to smile. "I got some soaps to take back to the office for my team and some lavender sachets for Sara and Lauren." She held up the bag. "I didn't want to get too much. We don't have a ton of space in our suitcases. Did you guys get everything you were looking for?"

Esteban laughed. "Oh, yes. We've been here so many times, Azalea knows exactly which booths she wants to visit. And we got some nice things for a picnic at the Pont du Gard."

Susana sighed. She'd been so distracted, she'd forgotten all about the rest of the afternoon's excursion. "That sounds nice," she answered lamely. "How far is the drive from here?"

"Very quick," he answered. "Maybe fifteen minutes?"

They maneuvered their way between shoppers and joined Azalea and Enrique at the end of an aisle. Azalea smiled and held up several bags. "Got some delicious food for our picnic," she said. "Ready to head for the Pont du Gard?"

Susana glanced at Enrique and was surprised to see his smile. He'd been quiet on the drive to Uzès and seemed downcast the few times she'd glimpsed him wandering around the market. But now he was animated, his eagerness to see the famous Roman aqueduct overcoming his earlier sadness. He rubbed his hands together and nodded.

He looks like a little boy on Christmas morning, she thought. She longed to have him look at her that way, but was just thankful to see him excited. She pulled her arm from Esteban and reached out to take Enrique's hand. "I can't wait to see it," she told him.

He smiled broadly but then seemed to deflate. She squeezed his hand. "If it's important to you, *querido*, it's important to me," she said softly.

"I know. Thank you." He looked away. "I'm trying, Susana. Please be patient with me."

Half an hour later, Susana stood in awe at the magnificent structure. "How…?" She couldn't even put her question into words. The sight of the massive aqueduct, still standing proudly after two thousand years, rendered her speechless. She looked at Enrique and her heart caught in her throat. Her husband was transfixed—far more even than he'd been at La Sagrada Familia. She could almost hear the wheels whirring in his brain as he stared.

"*Es maravilloso, no?*" asked Esteban, clapping his friend on the shoulder. "*Podrías diseñar algo como esto?*"

Enrique barked a laugh. "Are you kidding? I couldn't—and I don't know anyone who could design something like this today—at least not without using the latest technology." He looked back at the ancient edifice. "This is an engineering marvel. I mean, they didn't have design software or heavy machinery or rebar. This is pure genius." He turned his wide eyes back to Esteban. "Can we get closer?"

"*Por seguro, amigo!* We can get much closer."

"We can have our picnic down by the river," said Azalea. "It's a lovely day."

The four walked toward the aqueduct, Enrique never taking his eyes from the ancient arches. They spent the next hour wandering the grounds, with Esteban asking Enrique questions about the Roman design and construction and Susana reveling in her husband's enthusiasm. When they finally walked down to the rocky shore, she saw that he was still smiling.

While Esteban laid out a large blanket for them to sit on, Azalea opened the bags of food. Besides one of the rotisserie chickens, there were a variety of cheeses, a loaf of crusty bread, grapes, and two bottles of wine.

"This is a feast," exclaimed Susana.

Azalea grinned. "I hope you guys are hungry."

Enrique tore his eyes away from the bridge and nodded. "Famished," he answered. He glanced at the slow moving river and said, "Too bad we didn't bring swimsuits. It's really warm this afternoon. Perfect for a swim."

Esteban opened the first bottle of wine and poured it into plastic cups as Azalea passed out paper plates. "We've gone kayaking here," said Esteban. "Next time you come, we'll have to get on the water."

Susana noticed a pained expression on Enrique's face, but it passed quickly. "That sounds like fun," he said.

They ate their lunch and Azalea peppered Enrique with questions. "So how was this even possible back then? I can't fathom what it would have taken to build this."

Enrique began a lengthy explanation of the engineering principles of compression and tension and before long, Susana stopped listening. Instead, she simply watched her husband, his eyes alight and his hands moving expressively as he described the arcane architecture and building methods. She saw—no, she *felt* his excitement over the experience and the opportunity to share his knowledge and she could easily imagine him regaling a room full of undergrads. *No retirement rocking chair for my Kique*, she mused.

After lunch, the four packed up the remains of their meal and hiked back up to the path to the information center. Azalea said something to Esteban and then turned to Susana and Enrique. "They make the most heavenly limoncello here," she said. "We haven't had it in months—I'm gonna run inside and grab a bottle."

"I'll come with you," said Susana.

The women walked into the gift shop and Susana perused the shelves while Azalea went to find the liqueur. Susana found a large display of notebooks and noticed one in particular. She ran her fingers over the leather-covered journal, embossed with the outline of the aqueduct. The rich cordovan leather was supple and she knew Enrique would treasure it. She met Azalea at the cash register and showed her friend.

"I think he'll love it," she said. "Would you put it in your bag so he doesn't see it until tonight? I want to surprise him."

"Of course," answered Azalea. "What a lovely gift." She looked as if she wanted to say more, but turned when the young man at the register spoke to them.

"*Merci*," she said, then looked back at Susana. "I have no idea what he just said," she whispered.

Susana grinned. "I can't tease you about that because I don't speak a word of French either." Then she shrugged. "Except *merci* and *bonjour*, I mean."

"And *pain au chocolat*," laughed Azalea. "I learned that one the very first time I came to France."

Susana paid for the journal and the two women rejoined their husbands. The air was cooling and the sun began its descent as the friends walked to the car. They shared a companionable silence as they drove back to the château until Enrique leaned back and grinned. "Any more of those macarons left?' he asked.

Azalea nodded and passed the bag of goodies to him in the front seat. He offered one to Esteban and before too long, all four of them were munching on the sweet treats. Susana leaned her head against the window, nearly succumbing to exhaustion when she heard her phone vibrate. She winced, tempted to ignore the call, but instead pulled it out of her purse.

As she expected, it was from Geneva.

Well, Emily Cavanaugh is a bitch, it read. *She did a number on me and Liscia and we need to respond to this garbage article. I have the comms team (who report to you BTW) working on a response and it will be in your inbox in the next 15 minutes. I need your reaction and I want you to reconsider getting your name out there on Liscia's behalf. Everyone will expect me to deny everything but if you send out a formal response people will pay attention. Liscia needs this. Don't let me down.*

Susana sighed heavily. Would this woman never stop pushing? She thought she'd made it abundantly clear that she couldn't—she *wouldn't* get involved until her time with MPG was completed.

She looked at Azalea, but her friend was dozing. Esteban and Enrique were chatting quietly in the front seat. She closed her eyes briefly, then began tapping away on her phone.

I'm sorry to hear that. I'm happy to review the crisis comms and give you my feedback. You know I can't do anything formal for another two weeks. MPG will take legal action if I do.

There, she thought. *Now she knows and that has to be enough.*

She saw the ellipsis—Geneva was responding.

Steven Mills is a dick and you know it. I'll pay whatever legal fees are involved. I'm not sure why this isn't clear. You need to be the spokesperson for me.

Susana stared at her phone, then the back of Enrique's head. She knew what he'd say if she asked his opinion. She knew what she should do, but couldn't make herself respond. She put her phone back in her purse and leaned against the window.

Now what?

"Dinner will be ready at seven thirty," said Céline when they returned to the château. Susana glanced at her watch. They had half an hour and she planned to use it reviewing the Liscia crisis communications plans. The four went off to their rooms to wash and ready themselves for dinner, and Susana followed Enrique up the stairs to their suite.

"I need to do a bit of work before dinner," she said. "I'll grab my laptop and work in the salon. It'll only take a few minutes if the wifi isn't acting up."

Enrique nodded, his face expressionless. "I'm gonna lie down for fifteen minutes," he answered. "I'll see you downstairs." He sat heavily on the bed and removed his shoes, then lay back and closed his eyes.

Susana stood for a moment, wishing she could stay and lie down with her husband. It would feel so good to curl up to his warm body, to lay her head on his chest. She was bone tired and the last thing she wanted was to enmesh herself in Liscia's drama this evening. But she'd taken nearly the entire day off and her new employer was knee deep in a scandal that could bring down the entire company. She slung her backpack onto her shoulder and left the room.

"Get some rest," she said as she opened the door. "I love you."

Enrique's eyes remained closed, but he answered quietly. "I love you, too."

30

Surprisingly, the wifi worked before dinner and Susana took advantage of the connection to look at the latest press coverage.

It was all bad.

She knew she needed to check in with MPG—*After all, I'm still working there*, she chided herself. She scanned her emails and dashed off responses she felt were necessary, but then stopped when she saw the latest from Peter Gelbarr.

> *Susana,*
>
> *I'll make this brief. I regret our conversation Thursday and I apologize.*
>
> *Peter*

She didn't know if she were more angry about the middle of the night, drunken harangue or his pathetic attempt to apologize. She felt certain he hadn't written the email on his own. After she told Steven about the call, he and Jonathan had likely forced Peter to do it. *Maybe they threatened him with legal action, too,* she smirked.

Whatever the catalyst, it didn't matter. Peter had made her life miserable for months and his rant on the phone simply put an exclamation point on how he saw her.

Nothing but a "check the box" diversity hire, she was certain. There was no respect and no gratitude for the way she'd bailed him out after the disaster his son's roommate had caused with Liscia. MPG nearly lost the account and it was no one's fault but his own. Peter's ego and nepotism brought the agency close to disaster, but she and her team saved the day. She reminded herself to check in with Timothy to see how Douglas was fitting in with his new account team. She wondered if she should have fired him. His brazen attempt to blackmail her still grated, but it was one more issue and she just didn't have the energy to worry about it.

She was so tired. Tired of grinding, tired of the demands and the lack of respect. Tired of someone else calling all the shots and ignoring her. She felt wrung out and furious, with the men at MPG and the women at Liscia.

And, if she were honest, with herself.

No one could have taken advantage of her without her own complicity, she admitted. She'd made concessions, sacrifices, and turned the other cheek when she should have stood up for herself. Even Azalea saw it. Her best friend knew her so well and questioned her—when had she turned into this people pleaser? When had she given up her own desires and lost her backbone?

Azalea called to her, letting her know dinner was served. She moved to the table and distractedly began eating, her mind far from the château, her friends, and her meal. Sighing, she stared at her plate, moving the food around idly with her fork.

Forget about all of them. What do I want?

As she finished her dinner and sipped the last of her wine, she made up her mind. It was enough. She may have become someone she didn't even recognize, but she didn't have to stay that way. She would draw the line with them all.

"I'm sorry, but I do have to work tonight," she said to Enrique and her friends, interrupting their conversation. "I'm going to take my laptop into the salon and get some things squared away." She looked at Azalea and took a deep breath. "You were right. I've given in too much and I'm gonna set both companies straight." Then she looked at Enrique. "I'll probably be a couple of hours, but I'll be up as soon as I can."

He nodded, then drained his glass. Azalea and Esteban stood, and Esteban asked Enrique, "How about coffee outdoors?"

Enrique stood and walked to the French doors leading onto the terrace and the Obregons followed. Azalea touched Susana's elbow as she passed. "You okay?" she whispered.

Susana nodded curtly and walked to the salon, determined to take back her life.

She leaned back, pushing her laptop away on the table. She was tired, but pleased with her efforts. She started with an email to Geneva, reiterating her position on maintaining distance with the company until she was officially on board. She sent the Liscia comms team a few comments on the messaging they drafted, rationalizing that it was appropriate in her role as the MPG account executive—not their new boss—to offer consulting advice. Then she focused on MPG, writing brief notes to everyone on her team. At last, she tackled the toughest one and was particularly pleased with her email to the MPG partners, wanting to be certain she left on good terms.

On my terms.

Steven, Jonathan, and Peter,

Just wanted to check in as we approach the end of my tenure at MPG. I have enjoyed the past twenty years and appreciate the opportunities I've had at the company. From my first junior coordinator role to my current role as SVP, I have learned and grown as a marketer and a leader.

I am deeply proud of the work I've done and the teams I've led. Over the past year, the campaigns for Thompson Toys and Terraval Software are particular favorites—it's been a delight to lead both B2C and B2B groups. I believe MPG is well represented by the teams I've built and you will find many employees who are ready to move on to the next level of responsibility.

Specifically, I'd like to call out Timothy Ranier and Lauren Ochoa as candidates for promotion. Timothy is beloved by his clients and his colleagues, and I believe he can take on far more responsibility, particularly in the hospitality space. Likewise, Lauren's clients depend upon her keen market insight and no-nonsense approach. Even though she recently moved from her role on the Thompson Toys account to the business-to-business side of the agency, I strongly recommend her for promotion.

I will be back in Spain in a couple of days and then return to Florida ten days later. I'll see you in the office and will deliver my laptop and keys to IT when I get home.

Wishing you and MPG all the very best,
Susana

She looked at her phone and was startled to see it was past midnight. It was Sunday, her thirtieth wedding anniversary.

Please don't let it be the last.

She was certain Enrique was asleep, but she hoped he might awaken when she came into the room, even though he'd likely be annoyed that she'd taken so long. Yet she had to believe they would find a way back to each other. Surely these past few months had been a mere speed bump, a rough patch like other couples faced. This couldn't be the end of their story. She packed up her laptop bag and stood, rolling the stiffness from her shoulders.

"Just a speed bump," she whispered.

Who am I kidding?

The room was dark when she arrived and Susana tiptoed into the bathroom to brush her teeth. She undressed quietly and slipped into bed, reaching across to touch her husband. She hoped he would respond to her gentle stroking and they could make love before all the hurt flared up between them.

But he wasn't there.

Susana's hand met nothing but a cold sheet where Enrique should have been and her stomach knotted. She sat up, her eyes adjusting to the dark, and she looked around the room. She was alone.

She pulled up the sheet to cover her breasts, feeling suddenly foolish. *Where is he?* she wondered. She turned on the bedside lamp and leaned back against the headboard as her thoughts ran wild. *Calmate, chica.* The château was in the middle of nowhere, she reminded herself. *He has to be here somewhere.*

She got out of bed and dressed. She knew he wasn't in the salon, the dining room, or on the terrace, as she'd been in each of those places. She supposed he could have gone outside; after all, she had wandered the grounds just the night before, but that didn't seem like her Kique. Nevertheless, she decided to braid her hair and go outside to look. She went back into the bathroom to get a hair tie and when she turned on the light, she noticed a slip of paper next to the sink.

I couldn't sleep so I'm going to the pool. Get some rest.

Her eyes narrowed in frustration. *Like hell I'm getting some rest,* she thought. She finished braiding her hair, her fingers angrily flipping the strands back and forth in an uneven plait. She put on her shoes and stomped to the door, all thoughts of intimacy fleeing as she left the room.

Susana ran down the flight of stairs and opened the door to go outside. The evening chill had turned damp, and she realized it had started to drizzle. She slowed her pace and took the stone stairs carefully, holding onto the rail that was already slick with water. Glancing up, Susana saw that heavy clouds covered last night's bright stars. The sky's grayness matched her mood as she crossed the patio to the indoor pool.

She opened the door and saw Enrique swimming. She stood watching as he swam the length of the pool, expertly executing flip turns instead of stopping at the wall. After the fourth lap, he stopped and noticed her, yet said nothing.

Susana's ire melted away and she struggled to find something to say. At last, she offered, "A bit late for a swim, isn't it?"

"A bit late for working, isn't it?" he replied.

Ouch.

His shoulders slumped and he asked, "Why don't you just get some sleep? I'll be up in a while."

Susana looked long at her husband, her heart pounding. "Why don't you come up now?"

Enrique looked away, then dropped his eyes to the water. After a long minute, he looked back at her. "It's easier if I wait until you're asleep. I don't want to fight anymore."

She gazed at him, not knowing what to say. Then she spoke. "It's after midnight. It's our anniversary, Kique."

"I know."

"Thirty years, babe." She felt tears threaten and clenched her jaw. "Thirty years."

Susana watched her husband, knowing he was thinking carefully about his words. In three decades of marriage, Enrique Guerrero had never blown up at her, even when her fiery temper had exploded. Nevertheless, she worried she may have finally exhausted his patience.

His face was sad, his voice resigned. "I don't know if I have thirty-one in me, Susana."

"Kique—"

"No, listen to me. We aren't in the same place anymore. I know I'm holding you back. You have all these dreams about your career and as much as I want to support you, I just can't. We've worked hard for so long and I'm ready to enjoy the fruits of all that work. This trip has made things very clear to me. I want to enjoy time with my wife, Susana. I want to travel and not have to worry about whether we have enough vacation time. We have plenty of money and we're young and healthy. We don't have kids—"

"We decided that together—" she began, her voice heated.

Enrique held up a hand. "I'm not complaining, Susana. Yes, we decided together and that's one more reason we have the freedom that so many of our friends don't have." He rubbed a hand over his face, but the frustration still showed. "Don't you see? Now is the perfect time for us—"

"No!" she snapped. "Now is the perfect time for you. For *you*, Enrique."

His face fell. "Well, that's it then, I suppose."

"Kique, I didn't mean—" Susana's phone rang just as she began to entreat him. Her husband's face hardened and she had a brief vision of flinging the phone into the pool. Instead, she took it out, trying to imagine who would call her in the middle of the night, yet not at all surprised to see Geneva's name on the screen. Scowling, she shoved the phone back into her pocket.

She took a deep breath and started again. "Kique, I don't mean that I want us to split up." She covered her face with her hands, willing herself not to cry. "I'm sorry we're not on the same timeline. But that doesn't mean we can't be, does it?"

Enrique looked at her as her phone began to ring again. Again, she pushed the button to silence it, and stuffed it angrily back into her pocket. "I don't think now is a good time to decide," he said. "Let's just get through the next week and we can figure things out when—"

Susana's phone rang a third time and he angrily splashed at the water. "Answer the damn phone, Susana. Or throw it in the pool. At this point, I just don't care." With that, he pushed off the wall and resumed swimming.

She stood for a moment, staring. She was stunned at his reaction. Surely he didn't mean that divorce was an option? She glared at the phone and turned to the door, taking long angry strides outside. "What is it, Geneva? It's the middle of the night—*Saturday* night. I don't even work for you yet. What do you need that can't wait until morning? Or how about Monday, like a normal job?" *Maybe she'll just fire me before I even start,* she thought.

Geneva's voice was low, her words precise. "I'm calling to tell you that you no longer work for MPG and you can start with Liscia tomorrow. I just got off the phone with Peter Gelbarr and he agreed to release you early."

Susana stopped pacing, shocked into silence.

"Did you hear me? You're free to start now. I decided to take another interview on Monday after all. The LA Times should be more amenable to the truth than the Chronicle was. I know you can't be in California by Monday, but I want you on the call. We can talk more tomorrow to get you ready."

Susana looked up at the dark sky, the rain now falling harder and soaking her. "Did you think about asking me what I want?" she asked quietly. She walked toward an overhang to get out of the rain, her stomach clenching with anger and frustration. "Because Peter sure hasn't." Her mind was reeling and she felt completely out of control. Her marriage, her career—was everyone going to make decisions for her? She gritted her teeth, determined not to lose her temper any more than she already had. "It's not like I'm a professional athlete who's being traded to another team, Geneva. I think I should have some say in where I work."

"I thought you'd be thankful," Geneva retorted. "He's a jack-ass—I can't believe you've been working for him all this time. And MPG doesn't need you. I do."

"Geneva, it's after midnight here. You woke me up," Susana lied. "I can't even think about this right now. I'll call you in the morning. What time will you be up?"

"Call me at five o'clock Pacific. Don't make me wait." Then, surprisingly, her tone changed. "We have a lot to do and you are a big part of how this company is going to be successful," she said, her voice soothing. "We are going to make a great team, Susana. I promise you."

Exhausted, Susana leaned against the wall. "I'll talk to you tomorrow, Geneva."

31

Susana looked across the patio in time to see Enrique emerge from the pool house. Their eyes met across the haze and the rain and, though she longed to run to him, she stood still. He walked to her and held out his towel over their heads. Tears filled his eyes as they walked to the stairs and up to their room.

"You're soaked," he said quietly when they entered the suite. "Why don't you take a hot bath?" *Even in the middle of what might be the end of our marriage, he takes care of me,* she thought.

"Why are you being so nice?" she asked, her voice nearly a whisper.

He tipped his head, his eyes questioning. "Why wouldn't I? I love you, Susana. I will always love you."

She started toward him, but he moved to the bathroom. "I'll just start the bath," he said, avoiding her gaze.

I love you, too, she thought. *I will always love you.*

After a fitful few hours, Susana awoke to find Enrique gone. She felt utterly wrung out. What should have been a glorious celebration morning was a disaster and her heart was in tatters. She considered just pulling the covers over her head and shutting out the world, but instead she got out of bed and dressed, then went to the bathroom to brush her teeth and braid her hair. Weary, red-rimmed eyes stared back from the mirror and she thought idly that she looked like her mother. *More like my abuela.* Except she never remembered her grandmother without a smile.

She glanced at the time and realized everyone would be downstairs having breakfast. Food was the last thing she wanted, but she knew being alone wasn't going to help her mood. She tapped on some concealer and a bit of mascara, then slicked on some lipgloss. It was all she could manage, but it helped a little.

Azalea glanced up as Susana walked into the dining room. "Hey, sleepyhead! I was just about to come up and drag you out of bed." She pointed to the table along the wall. "No one cooks on Sunday morning, but there are some gorgeous cheeses and some muesli." She took a sip of her coffee. "And there is always some delicious compote to have with the fresh bread. Come! Sit and eat."

Susana pulled out the chair next to her husband. "Is this seat taken?" she asked. She meant it as a joke, but somehow the words came out bathed in the hurt she couldn't conceal.

"Just waiting for you," he said with a sad smile. "Would you like me to get you some coffee?"

Her lip quivered but she held back the tears. "Yes, please."

She walked to the side table and served herself a small plate of cheese and bread. The fruit compote looked to be some kind of berry, so she added a dollop to her plate. Enrique slid past her to the coffee station. Everything in her longed to reach for him, but she kept her attention on her food as she walked back to her seat. When he returned with her coffee, she thanked him quietly.

Azalea cast a worried glance at the couple, then turned to her husband. "I can't wait for today. It's my favorite part of coming here." She looked at Susana and Enrique. "I know I keep gushing over the café, but it's so quintessentially the Cevennes. The feeling is unlike anything I've experienced." Her eyes were alight, her smile full of joy. "I can't wait for you guys to see what I mean. It's a wonderful way to celebrate your anniversary."

Susana couldn't imagine celebrating, but she tried to respond without destroying her best friend's mood. "And you, Esteban? How do you like the Sunday café?"

Esteban smiled and hugged his wife. "I have to agree *con mi esposa*," he replied. "There's something very special about it—it's hard to describe. *La comunidad es tan amable—hay una sensación de serenidad y felicidad....*" He chuckled. "We probably sound silly, don't we? After all, it's just a neighborhood luncheon."

Serenity and happiness. Just what I need.

The four finished their breakfast and Azalea asked, "So what do you guys wanna do until noon?"

Susana looked at Enrique, waiting for some cue.

"I think I'm going to take a walk—it's a beautiful day." He paused, then asked, "Esteban? Feel like a hike?"

"*Por seguro, amigo.*"

Susana's shoulders slumped.

"Shall we go sit outside?" Azalea asked. "It's nice to have a lazy morning."

The bread and cheese seemed to turn to concrete in her stomach as Susana answered. "I have a few things to check on if we'll be out all afternoon. I think I'll take my laptop out on the terrace and take advantage of this nice day. It's so fresh after the rain last night." The memory of Enrique holding his towel over her head flashed through her mind and she clenched her teeth against the tears.

"Mind if I bring my book and sit with you?"

"Not at all—I just won't be much company."

Azalea nodded. "That's the best part about being friends for all these years. You don't need to."

Susana smiled. She knew this was Azalea's way of apologizing for harping on her all week. Part of her longed to call out her friend on the nagging, but Susana decided to simply accept the offer. "Thanks, 'mana."

Everyone got up and Esteban kissed Azalea before leaving the dining room. Enrique offered Susana a tight smile, then hurried after his friend.

"I'll meet you outside in a few minutes," said Azalea.

Susana stared at her laptop, unsure what to do. She knew Geneva expected her to call, but all she could think about was Enrique. They couldn't be farther apart. It was their thirtieth anniversary, and her husband was on a walk with his friend.

Pushing aside her sorrow, she considered her next move. Geneva's behavior was more and more aggressive, more like Peter Gelbarr's. Susana thought back about last night's determination to take her life back. *That didn't last long,* she sighed.

Was this what Desirée had to deal with? Susana opened LinkedIn and found Desirée's page. She didn't have her private email, but she decided to send her a message through the app. *It's midnight in California and she probably won't answer,* she reasoned, *but I'll try.*

Desirée, she typed, *I realize this is coming out of the blue, but I'd like the chance to speak with you about Liscia. I'm sure you know I've accepted the CMO job, but I'm finding that I have some concerns. Might you be available for a call or email?*

She was astonished to see a response within minutes.

I wondered how long it would take you to realize how evil she is. Call me.

Susana stared at the message, then called the California number.

"Hey, Susana," said Desirée, her voice gruff.

"Thanks for responding so quickly—"

"Look, let's forget the small talk. Here's the truth: Five years ago Geneva found out about the labor violations. She supposedly told the manufacturer that Liscia would pull all their business if it didn't stop. That's the last conversation we had about it, and I thought it was a done deal." She took a breath. "Stupid of me to believe her."

"So what do you think happened?"

"I think she lied her ass off," snapped Desirée. "I think she knew if she kept the company on the rails the CEO job would be hers in a few years and she played the long game. She's sneaky as hell and ruthless as they come. And she will use you until you have nothing left and discard you like garbage." She chuckled mirthlessly. "I know from experience and so do both of her ex-husbands."

Susana sat stunned, not knowing what to say. At last, she replied, "So how did you find out?"

"I've been in this business for decades, Susana. I can't reveal my exact source, but suffice it to say Geneva isn't exactly loved in this industry. Someone credible reached out to me just recently. I did some investigating and found out the source was right." She paused, then added, "I hate that people I care about are probably going to lose their jobs, but it just couldn't go on. I have kids that age myself. I couldn't look them in the eyes if I let this go."

The knot in Susana's stomach tightened further. "Thank you, Desirée. I'm sorry—"

"No apologies needed. I'm glad to be out of there. I suggest you do the same." And without another word, she disconnected the call.

Susana stared at the phone screen and looked up as Azalea approached.

"You okay?" asked her friend. "You look upset."

"Just trying to process all this drama," she answered. "I don't want to overreact."

"Do you want to talk about it? I promise to just listen and not lecture you. I know I've been a pain lately and I'm really trying to stop. You're a grown woman and you don't need me to tell you what to do."

Susana looked at her dearest friend. She really is trying, she thought. "I'm okay for now but I'll let you know when I'm ready to talk it through."

"You know I'm here when you need me."

"I do."

An hour later, Azalea stood and stretched. "This sun is putting me to sleep," she laughed. "Do you mind if I go upstairs and lie down for a bit before we go to lunch?"

Susana looked up from her laptop and shook her head. "Go ahead—you never nap. You must need it. I'll be done here soon and I think I'll do the same thing."

Azalea leaned over and kissed the top of her friend's head. "Love you, Suze."

"Love you, too."

Susana had no idea how long she'd walked.

She vaguely remembered opting for a walk over a nap, leaving the estate and wandering down the two lane road, heedless of direction. *I have no idea where I am*, she realized grimly as she surveyed the landscape.

It's been that way for a while.

She walked a few hundred yards more, then stepped off the road to lean against a rugged wall. Gazing out over a broad meadow she heard clanking bells and soon saw the waddling gait of dozens of sheep. She watched them meandering, seeming without direction, nibbling grass and baa-ing.

"What a mess," she whispered. Everything was unraveling. Only months ago, she was at the top of the world, her marriage, career, and friendships thriving. And now? Everywhere she looked was chaos, confusion, and hurt. It seemed like only yesterday she texted her parents the photo of her new business cards. They had been so proud of their daughter, accomplishing everything she'd aimed for, and proving that you didn't have to come from an Ivy League family to achieve greatness.

What would you think of me now, Mami? Would you be proud of me now, Papi?

Susana wondered if she'd simply aimed too high, if she'd let her ego push her too far.

No. She hadn't aimed too high.

I aimed at the wrong target.

She swallowed the bile in her throat and stood tall. Maybe Desirée was wrong. Maybe she really was just a disgruntled employee, lashing out. Susana resolved to give Geneva one more chance to prove herself and then she'd decide what to do about her job.

And then I'll concentrate on Kique.

She looked around, then headed back the way she came. The walk to the château was long.

32

At noon, the four friends walked across the château grounds to the neighborhood café. "It's really cool how the little hamlets all come together," said Azalea as they strolled. "Every week, there's a different meal and different entertainment—usually local music. Since it's hosted by the community, everyone takes turns volunteering to cook and serve. The food is all locally sourced and it's a wonderful opportunity to gather and enjoy the beauty of the village."

"Does anyone speak English?" asked Susana, her voice shrewish even to her own ears. "Or will Esteban have to translate for us?' She was still despondent, and the thought of struggling to communicate for the next few hours didn't hold quite the same allure as it apparently did for her best friend.

Azalea looked askance at her friend, but Esteban answered. "Many people speak at least a little bit of English. They love to practice and they'll be delighted to have new guests here, especially on your anniversary. Any excuse to celebrate!"

Susana glanced at Enrique, but his eyes remained fixed on the path ahead. Neither of them spoke, and she caught Azalea's wary look. She took a deep breath. *Just get it out*, she scolded herself.

"So look, I know it's not great, but I do have to make a call at one o'clock," she told them. She didn't even attempt to be apologetic. "I promise to make it quick, but I'll need to step away for a minute to be sure everything is squared away with my client."

Esteban exchanged a look with Enrique and Azalea sighed.

Susana hunched her shoulders and kept her thoughts to herself as she felt the familiar knot in her stomach joined by the beginning of a headache.

As they approached the café grounds, she could hear children laughing and the steady hum of adult conversation. They crested a hill and passed through a large grassy area where youngsters played soccer. The trees surrounding the field provided shade, and the breeze made her glad she'd worn a sweater over her sundress. They passed the soccer field, then walked down ancient stone steps onto another lawn, this one set up with tables and chairs. The stones were uneven, and Susana marveled that people walked or ran up and down without a care. Enrique reached for her arm, helping her down the stairs and she murmured her thanks. She wondered what he thought of the architecture, given that every building he designed had ADA requirements for ramps and handrails....

She needed some ramps and handrails for her life.

"This first group is all local women singing French folk songs," said Azalea. The four took their seats at a table as a dozen elderly women began to sing. Their harmonies belied their age—Susana was certain not a single one of them was younger than seventy, yet their voices were clear and ageless. She only half listened to the singers, instead looking around at the villagers. There was a mixture of young and old, everyone smiling and laughing and seeming at complete ease. Her reverie was interrupted when Azalea pointed to a middle-aged man walking from table to table. "That's the town mayor," she whispered.

"Town?" scoffed Susana. "It doesn't even seem big enough to warrant village status, much less a town."

Azalea's response was tinged with impatience. "Are you going to be like this all day?"

Susana bit back a retort as Esteban stood. "Shall we get some wine, Enrique? Ladies—what would you like? They have the local red and white available."

Azalea looked long at Susana, then answered. "White, please."

Susana sighed. She knew she was being unreasonable to her friend—to all of them—but she couldn't seem to shake her despair. Here she was, in a beautifully bucolic part of the world, with the people she loved most on earth, and she was being snappish and impatient. She forced a smile at Esteban. "Red, please." She glanced at Enrique. "And thank you."

The men moved off and Susana turned to Azalea. "Hey, I'm sorry. I know I'm not myself today. This stupid job—" She shook her head. "I just need to get through the next few days."

Her friend nodded, but didn't answer. The two turned back to listen to the elderly village women, an unfamiliar awkwardness between them.

A few minutes later, the band arrived and the party got underway. The children were shooed back to tables with their families, and everyone filled their plates with chicken and rice along with local salads, cheese, and bread. Susana began to relax, although her thoughts were never far from her dilemma. Enrique still hadn't said a word to her…and she had less than an hour before her call with Geneva.

She watched as children finished their lunches and ran nimbly up the ancient stone stairs to resume their games. Parents, grandparents, and singles remained to watch the band. With a drummer, guitarist, bass player, and a singer who also played a washboard, the group was actually quite good, she had to admit. Parochial, but fun. She didn't recognize any of the songs, but the melodies were catchy, and she found herself tapping her toes to the rhythm. She glanced occasionally at her husband, but Enrique steadfastly kept his gaze on the musicians.

One elderly couple—Susana estimated they were in their eighties—stood and began to dance. The villagers clapped as the two held each other and twirled about on the grassy area in front of the band. The couple, though, had eyes only for each other. He had one hand around her waist, the other clasped with hers. Susana felt a pang of longing. *What must it be like to be that much in love at eighty?*

She looked again at Enrique and this time he was looking directly at her, pain and love etched on his beautiful features.

Her pocket vibrated and startled her. She gave her husband an apologetic look as she reached for her phone. His jaw tightened and he turned away.

It was Geneva. She did the quick math—five o'clock in the morning in California. *She didn't even wait for me to call,* she thought crossly.

"I'm sorry," she said as she stood. "This is the call I mentioned."

Susana walked quickly to the stairs and swiped to answer the call just as the toe of her sandal caught on the rough stones. She tripped and slammed her knee, catching herself with her other hand and barely holding on to her phone. "Shit!" she growled.

"That's how you answer the phone with your boss?" asked Geneva. "Sorry to be a bother but we are having a rather significant crisis at your company." Her voice dripped with sarcasm.

My *company? I haven't even started yet.*

Susana righted herself and climbed the steps to the soccer field. "That wasn't directed at you," she said, her voice taut with pain. "I tripped just as I was answering the call." She felt an itching down her shin and realized her knee was bleeding. *Dammit.* "Hang on a second."

Susana looked around for a place to sit. The soccer game was rowdy with several spectators shouting their encouragement. She managed to find an empty bench under a tree and perched herself there. "Okay, sorry about that."

"Where are you and what is that godawful noise?"

She surveyed the field—there wasn't a quiet place in sight. The children shouted as they ran, kicking the ball from one end of the field to the other. "I'm at a neighborhood café and there are kids playing soccer." She glanced back toward the steps, knowing Enrique was mere yards away, yet there seemed to be miles between them. "It's part of my thirtieth anniversary celebration."

"Sounds like a lousy anniversary if you're celebrating around a bunch of screaming brats," mumbled Geneva.

Susana sat up straight and lifted her sundress up over her knee. Sure enough, she'd scraped it raw and blood ran in a line down her shin. *First my cheek, now my knee,* she thought morosely. *What a disaster this trip has been.*

"Anyway, I changed my mind. I need you here. There have been more articles today and I'm getting pressure from the board to make a statement. You need to get to California as soon as possible. As I told you last night, MPG isn't a problem anymore." She snickered. "I think they were eager to get rid of you."

Susana bit back an angry retort and tried to slow her breathing. "Geneva, we've been over this more than once. I'm on vacation in France. I get back to Barcelona on Monday and I have another week in Spain before I come back...*to Florida.*"

"That doesn't work for me, Susana." Geneva's words were clipped and brooked no argument.

Susana's jaw clinched and her hand tightened around her phone. She was pretty sure Geneva was right—Peter, at least, was keen to see her go. But for Geneva to go directly to MPG to get her released and then demand that Susana take on the responsibilities of her new role two weeks early? That took *cojones*—and a degree of disrespect that shook her. There had been no ethical way she could be employed by MPG and work for Liscia at the same time, but how was Geneva's interference any better?

She realized Geneva was still talking. "...crisis communications," finished the CEO. "So when can you be here?"

A cry grabbed her attention and Susana looked up to see one of the little girls lying on the ground. She'd collided with another child and taken the brunt of the impact. An older boy, maybe nine or ten, ran over to comfort her. Her little brown curls bobbed as she cried in his arms and Susana found herself entranced at the way he soothed her. *He must be her big brother,* she thought. Then it hit her: While these children were running and enjoying a gorgeous Sunday afternoon playing soccer, children thousands of miles away were stuck in sweatshops, eking out slave labor wages. She wondered who comforted those little ones when they cried. She swallowed hard, the headache now pounding her temples, her knee throbbing with pain.

What am I doing?

"Susana, can you hear me?" Geneva was testy. "Look, if it's money, I'll double your signing bonus and add another chunk of equity. We have to get on top of this and we need to do it now."

Susana's shoulders slumped and she whispered, "Geneva, is it true?"

"Is what true?" The CEO's patience was clearly running out.

She had to know. "Do Liscia's suppliers use child labor in Bangladesh? Did you hide it to keep your profits up?"

"You know damn well this is all Desirée's doing. She wanted my job and she didn't get it. This is nothing but petty revenge. I'm sick to death of answering this question. And I sure as hell shouldn't be getting it from you."

"But you didn't answer my question. I know Desirée is the whistleblower." She waited a moment before continuing. "I talked to her, Geneva. What I don't know is whether what she said is true."

The silence was deafening. At last, Geneva spoke, her words precise and harsh.

"We are not a couturier house, Susana. We are a luxury ready-to-wear company and our customers expect a level of price and quality that we have to maintain. Perhaps Chanel can sell blouses for three thousand dollars but Liscia is going to keep our price point below five hundred and never fail to deliver superior quality."

Susana gaped at the phone. She'd heard enough—Geneva's failure to answer her questions said it all. Her face went hot as fury engulfed her and she barged on, heedless of her words. "So what does your supplier pay these *children* for that superior quality? What's the cost to them to maintain your precious seventy percent margins?"

After another long pause, Geneva's voice was icy. "Those kids have no life, Susana. Their families are destitute. They make money that keeps them alive. And we have worked behind the scenes to build a school in the factory where they can take classes on Sundays. They don't just earn a living, they learn to read—"

"Are you fucking kidding me?" Susana exploded. "You work those *children* for six days and then pat yourself on the back for teaching them to read on Sundays? That's quite the comp package! Let me guess—you're matching their 401k contributions, too, right?" She stood and realized she was shouting and people were looking her way. Her hands shook and her breath was ragged.

"How dare you talk to me that way!" snapped the irate CEO. "Maybe take a step down from that ivory tower and realize what you've been offered here. You're what? Fifty? And never had a CMO job? Who the hell else is gonna give you this opportunity? I went to bat for you with the board, Susana. They didn't want a rookie executive but I convinced them you'd be a valuable and *loyal* member of the leadership team. I—"

Susana threw her phone and it landed mere feet from the goal. She stared at it as she fought back tears of rage. *I almost believed her. I almost went to work for that piece of shit. Desirée is right—she's evil.*

Then it hit her: *I am losing my marriage over this.*

She looked back at the soccer players, noting the little girl had brushed herself off and run back onto the field. The older boy was about to shoot the ball, but passed it to her instead.

She kicked it in for a goal.

I have been such a fool, thought Susana.

I need Kique.

33

Susana walked slowly back to the picnic area, wincing at the sting in her knee—and her heart. As she gingerly walked down the uneven steps, she looked out at the grassy area, now full of couples dancing. Young and old, the villagers twirled about, singing along with the band. Their carefree *joie de vivre* was in stark contrast to her anguish, and she felt painfully out of place.

When she was two tables away, she saw Esteban and Azalea rise to join the dancers, seamlessly flowing into the revelry. Esteban held her friend close, whispering something and Azalea threw back her head and laughed. The delight in Azalea's smile was like a knife in Susana's gut. Happiness for her friend warred with jealousy. *When was the last time I was that happy?* she wondered. *When was Kique that happy?*

She stood transfixed, unable to move forward as the charm of the afternoon unfolded and she finally—*finally!*—understood what Azalea meant. For Susana, this should have been a blissful vacation experience utterly different from her life in the States. For the dozens of people on the grass, it was just…Sunday. Could her life ever be this simple? She couldn't imagine it.

After a turn around the makeshift dance floor, Esteban stopped and whispered to Azalea, who nodded. He knelt before an elderly woman sitting on the outskirts of the lawn. Susana didn't need to hear him to know he was asking her to dance—Azalea's pride in her husband's gallantry radiated from her. The octagenarian regally inclined her head and accepted his hand, taking unsteady steps to join the dance. Azalea turned to Enrique, holding out her hand. He shook his head at first, but then shrugged his shoulders and rose, spinning her around and offering a wan smile. Susana watched them do an impromptu tango across the lawn and she could take no more.

I don't belong here.

She turned and fled for the château.

Susana ran to her room, heedlessly taking the stairs two at a time, her raw knee burning with every step, her head pounding. It was only when she reached the top that she remembered she didn't have a key to the room. She stared at the door, deflated and numb.

Why did I expect anything different? she thought morosely. *So close, but I just can't get in.*

There was no one in the château—everyone in the village was at the café enjoying the music and the camaraderie, so she slowly made her way back to the courtyard. She was sweating from running and took off her cardigan, turning toward the sun. She stood for some time, feeling the warmth on her face and the breeze on her arms.

She couldn't go back to the group. Her nerves were raw, her heart shredded. She was—what did Enrique say? *Unraveling.*

She was unraveling.

Susana walked across the courtyard to the indoor pool and opened the door. The dark was a welcome cocoon, the steam rising from the heated water. She slipped off her sandals and went to the bathroom where she dabbed her knee with a wet towel. After she cleaned the dried blood, she walked to the end of the pool, hiked up her sundress, sat down, and dangled her feet in the water.

Susana knew she was strong, certainly strong enough to overcome the disappointments and setbacks she'd suffered over the past months. But to have everything land at once—it was just too much.

She felt herself being crushed under the weight of every false promise and every bad decision. It wasn't just MPG and Liscia. She had to admit her fair share of the blame.

She thought back to her early days at MPG and her eagerness to distinguish herself as invaluable. Enrique had been in the early days of his career, too, and they both committed to long hours at work to establish themselves.

She kicked her feet idly in the water, remembering the twelve-hour days when they'd both come home exhausted. But they never failed to talk, usually while Enrique cooked and Susana tossed a salad. She would regale him with stories about a crazy idea her latest client had, while he'd tell her about some new architect in Europe who was creating breathtaking designs. They had high hopes and wild dreams about their eventual success, never failing to encourage each other—to believe in each other. They'd fall into bed, both determined to fall asleep quickly, yet many nights they found themselves wrapped in each other's arms, breathless and sated after making love.

Over the years, they'd continued to grind, as she called it, making the sacrifices to pursue their dreams and climb the ladders of their respective careers. For Enrique, that sometimes meant traveling to sites all over Florida to ensure buildings were completed according to his vision. For Susana, that increasingly meant working on the weekends to ensure MPG delivered flawless branding campaigns and product launches.

It also meant putting up with her mother-in-law's incessant complaints about her. She steadfastly accused Susana of being *una feminista,* her derogatory term that encapsulated everything she disliked about her daughter-in-law. *Yet Kique always had my back*, she remembered. "She's just an old-fashioned *vieja*," he'd say, patiently explaining his mother's position. "We've chosen our life and she has to accept it. I have no regrets. Let Antonio have a bunch of kids and she'll forget all about us."

But if things continued to fall apart with her husband, her mother-in-law was the least of her worries. She couldn't begin to imagine life without him. He'd supported her time and again as she took on new roles, new clients, and new responsibilities. He'd been her biggest cheerleader as she finally broke through into senior leadership. When MPG promoted her to SVP—the first woman and the first Latina to achieve the feat—he'd taken her away for the weekend, splurging on two nights in Key West where they'd lounged on the beach, drunk way too much champagne, and made love for hours.

But now when she needed him most, he wanted something different from her. She was angry with herself, but she was also angry with him. Why had he changed?

She thought back over Enrique's career path and the way she'd supported him. It hadn't been the same. While her husband had been sanguine about his slow but steady rise in the firm, Susana had bristled at what she saw as them holding him back, and she complained about every perceived slight. His affectionate nickname for her, *mi cardito*, started with her prickly and fiery complaints about the management at his firm.

Mi cardito. My little thistle.

And so here they were. Enrique was a partner in Cooper, Dallas, and Guerrero, his name on the wall and the letterhead—while she was out of a job.

Out of two jobs, she corrected herself, kicking her feet in the water. She replayed the conversation with Peter, his drunken and bigoted rant sending her into a fury. She thought about Steven's recurring reminders that he'd done her a favor by promoting her. She'd written the partners off as stupid, out of touch, old men— but then Geneva had done the exact same thing. In fact, the Liscia CEO's behavior was far worse. She'd lied and bullied Susana and made excuses for despicable behavior. Maybe Azalea had the right idea when she started Mora Communications. Maybe owning her own business was the only way to avoid the idiots and the criminals.

Who am I kidding? she thought. *I'm fifty-four years old and I'm not going to start a new company now.* She knew she had the skill, but her heart just wasn't in it. All her ambition and drive had come to naught and she was weary and heartsick and…

Afraid.

I'm afraid, she admitted. *I'm afraid of losing everything that matters.* She pictured Enrique's somber expression as they watched the elderly couple dancing on the lawn. *I should have ignored Geneva's call. I should have taken his hand and danced.*

Should have. Should have. Should have.

Susana leaned forward, her face in her hands. She winced at the pain in her cheek, the injury still tender after a week. She covered up the bruise with makeup, but it still hurt. *Same song, different verse,* she thought. *Cover up the bruises so no one sees how I'm hurting.*

As she sat up, a flicker of movement caught her eye near the door.

Enrique stood watching her, his expression unreadable. They looked at each other, neither moving. Her heart began to pound and she longed to reach out, to speak and erase the wounds between them. A sadness deeper than anything she had ever experienced overtook her and she had no answers or words.

The silence lengthened as Susana gazed at her husband, the man she'd loved for more than half her life. At last, she made up her mind. She was her *abuela's* granddaughter and she would fight for her family.

I will not let this slip through my fingers.

With tears glinting on her lashes, she patted the spot next to her. "Will you sit with me?"

Enrique stood for a moment longer, then moved to her side. "I saw you leave the party," he said as he sat down. "Are you all right?"

Susana closed her eyes for a moment and the tears spilled onto her cheeks. She glanced up and sighed. "No. No, I'm not all right. Not at all." She kicked idly, the warm water rippling around her bare feet. Her words were a whisper. "Everything has gone wrong, Kique. I've made so many mistakes." She looked at him, trying to gauge his reaction. "I'm sorry. I'm so sorry."

Enrique sat very still before answering. "I'm not trying to be a jerk, but I'd like to know what you're sorry for."

She felt a slight flare of anger but tamped it down. Pride didn't serve her well today. "That's fair," she murmured, looking down at the water. Then she straightened and looked directly at him. "I'm sorry that I let my career matter more than our marriage."

Enrique's eyes widened. "Wow. I didn't expect that."

She offered a rueful smile. "Again, that's fair. I haven't been terribly open to hearing criticism lately." She bit her lip, but the tears refused to stop. "I don't know what's happened to me, Kique," she whispered. "I used to be so strong and I've turned into this spineless person I don't even recognize. I used to have great boundaries but I've let Steven and Peter push me around for weeks. And lately, I just stood by while Geneva did the same damn thing." She turned a confused look to him. "What's happened to me?"

He looked sorrowful as he answered. "Do you want me to be honest?"

"Of course I do. I'm not stupid, Kique. It's obvious we're standing on the edge of a cliff with our marriage. There's no point in not being honest."

He nodded. "I think you took what we have for granted. We've always been there for each other—no questions asked. But when you decided you wanted the executive track at MPG, you never talked to me about it. You just powered through, taking on more and more and you never looked back to see if I was still there."

"But you—"

He held his hands up and nodded. "I know, I know. I celebrated your promotion and I was genuinely happy for you." He smiled sadly. "I was so proud of you. I *am* proud of you. I just wish we could have made the decision together. Because we're always stronger together." He shook his head. "I couldn't have stood up to my mom like I did without you. I wouldn't have pushed for promotions at work without your encouragement. We're strong alone, but we're unstoppable together, Susana."

She sat quietly weighing her next words. "You hurt me, Kique. You changed—it seemed like almost overnight. One day we were in lockstep and the next you were running down this path without me and you were angry that I didn't follow." She wiped away a tear. "What happened to you?"

Enrique looked away and when he gazed back at her, his eyes were brimming with tears. "I think I did the same thing. I think I took what we have for granted. I just assumed you'd see the value in us slowing down and spending more time together—traveling and taking advantage of the second half of our lives."

"Why didn't you just ask me?"

He frowned, then shook his head in bewilderment. "I don't know," he confessed. "I turned into quite the Neanderthal, didn't I?"

She looked at him without speaking. On one hand, she knew he was right. She'd barreled ahead without a thought, so consumed with her achievement that she never doubted his support. But she was right, too. He had made decisions without consulting her, without considering what his desires would cost her.

Enrique continued, "I'm sorry for my part in all this. I'm your biggest fan, Susana. You know that. I wish we could have talked things through, looked at the decisions from all the angles like we've always done. Maybe we would have come to the same decision—I don't know. We can't know now. What's done is done. But no matter what happens, I will always be in your corner."

Her heart dropped. "What do you mean, 'no matter what happens'?"

He frowned and blew out a breath. "You said it yourself. We're on the edge of a cliff."

Tears filled her eyes. *No, no, no.*

"Pull me back," she said, her voice a ragged whisper. "Don't let me fall." She reached up and cupped his cheek. "*Querido...por favor...te amo con toda mi corazon.*"

Enrique closed his eyes. "And I love you with all my heart, too. But I'm scared, Susana."

She put her other hand up to his face and leaned in, their foreheads touching. "So am I. But I have to believe we are strong enough. You're right. We're unstoppable. Please, *mi amor*...let's fight together."

He opened his eyes and they were filled with tears.

"Why now? What's changed?" he asked.

She sat back and took his hands—and she was grateful he didn't pull away.

"I was blind," she said simply. "Geneva is a liar. They've been using children in their production facilities and she's been covering it up. She's pushing me to leave MPG right now and come on board so I can be the—what did she call me?" She searched for the word. "Oh, yeah. Apparently I'm *pristine*. I have a spotless reputation that makes things easier for her."

Enrique made a disgusted noise. "She actually said that?"

"She did. Yesterday I tried to draw the line and tell her I couldn't be involved with her little press tour until I was officially severed from MPG. But then she had the nerve to call Peter and get me released early—without even asking me. And then she actually expected me to be grateful."

His eyes narrowed, but he didn't speak.

"So this morning, I decided I needed to know the truth and I talked to Desirée. She didn't pull any punches and she told me what she knew. She's disgusted by Geneva and what the company has allowed. When Geneva called, I guess I'd finally had enough. I confronted her and she danced around the questions until it was obvious she was lying. I kept pushing and she finally confessed—but tried to make it sound like she was doing those kids a favor!" She shook her head, still amazed at what had happened. "After a few strong words, I hung up on her. Actually," she sighed, "I threw my phone across the field." She was gratified to see Enrique grin. "And now your highly ambitious wife is unemployed."

She sat quietly under his scrutiny, willing herself to be silent as he processed her words.

"What made you stand up to her?" he asked.

She smiled sadly. "Partly because I am tired of putting my career in the hands of horrible people." She leaned her head against his shoulder. "But mostly, I wanted to be proud of myself—to be the woman I used to be." She looked up at him, her voice a whisper. "The woman who knows the difference between right and wrong. The woman who puts *us* first."

Enrique sat very still and then turned slightly to take her into his arms. "Are you sure?" he whispered, his lips brushing her cheek.

She nodded, unable to speak, willing her husband to believe her.

After a few moments, Susana felt his body relax.

He kissed her forehead, then her eyelids, his lips soft and tender. He gently kissed the bruise on her cheek, then brushed away the tears. "*Ay, mi querida*," he murmured. "*Eres la luz de mi vida.*"

Susana slid her arms around him as he pulled her into his lap. "Oh, love. I haven't been much of a light these past months. I'm so—"

He covered her mouth with his, softly and then harder. She responded immediately, digging her fingers into his hair, pulling him closer, desperate to reconnect, needing to find their way back to each other. Their tears ran together down their cheeks onto their lips.

I will not lose this.

34

Enrique's mouth slid to her throat, and she arched back, delighting in his touch, every nerve on fire. "I have missed you, my love," she whispered, her voice husky with longing.

"I love you, Susana. You are everything to me. I'm so sorry I hurt you. I never meant to—please forgive me."

"Yes, yes, yes…" she breathed against his lips.

She felt his need and it matched her own. She didn't know how long they would be alone…but suddenly she didn't care. She slid her hands to lift his t-shirt up and over his head and he raised his arms to help her. She leaned in, stroking his chest, her fingers brushing his nipples as he groaned.

"*Querido*," she whispered. "I need you."

He slid her off his lap and stood, holding out his hand, but she shook her head. "No. I mean now. *Here.*" She slid into the water and slipped her sundress over her head. She reached back and unhooked her bra, then stepped out of her panties as Enrique stood transfixed. When she began to unbraid her hair, he pulled off his shorts and followed her.

"Do you remember when we first bought the house?" she murmured as she reached for him. "We loved to make love in our pool."

"I remember."

"We were just kids," she said, pulling him close. "I love you more today than I did then." She touched his lips with her fingers, then slid her hand between their bodies to stroke him. Enrique's eyes closed and he touched his forehead to hers. He spun her around in the water, putting her back to the wall as he lifted her thighs, his mouth closing on hers. She wrapped her legs tightly around him and whispered into his lips, "*Te amo, mi vida. Por siempre.*"

"Forever," he answered, gazing into her eyes.

"*Apurete, querido. No esperes.*" Hurry, beloved. Don't wait.

"Ah, Susana," he groaned as he thrust deeply into her. "My Susana...."

She tightened her legs around his hips and they came together over and over, whispering their love, willing their hearts to heal as their bodies melded.

"Oh, Kique," she moaned, her body taut with desire. She arched back as he gripped her hair and their shuddering climax rent a cry from both of them.

You have unraveled me...but together we are unstoppable.

Enrique held her quietly, his breathing heavy. At last, he whispered, "Are you okay?"

She nodded, her head against his chest. "More than okay." She slowly unwrapped her legs and slid next to him. "And you?"

He cupped her chin and leaned down to kiss her. "I am," he said simply. "I have the love of my life in my arms and she loves me."

"Oh, yes, she does," she answered with a sigh, then looked around. "I don't want to leave, but we should probably get up to our room before everyone gets back." She lay her cheek on his chest and slid her arms around him. "Thank you, Kique. Thank you for loving me." She looked up at him, tears glinting in her eyes. "Thank you for fighting for us."

Enrique gazed at her, his lips trembling. She ran a finger along his jaw as he laid his head on her shoulder and cried.

After they changed clothes, Enrique and Susana headed downstairs to the courtyard. As they walked hand in hand to the dining room, Esteban and Azalea stepped out to greet them.

"We were just coming out to the terrace to watch the sunset," said Azalea. "What are you guys up to?" Her tone was light, but Susana knew her friend was concerned.

"We were thinking the same thing," she answered. "I'm finally all done with work—" she glanced at Enrique with a smile, "and we want to enjoy the rest of our anniversary with our friends." She was thankful to see Azalea's shoulders relax, knowing that her friend heard the implicit message in her words.

"There's bread and cheese and some wine in the kitchen," said Esteban. "I know I'm still full from that lunch. How does that sound?"

"That's perfect," agreed Susana. "Kique?"

Her husband squeezed her hand. "Fine with me."

Azalea beckoned to Susana. "Will you help me in the kitchen?"

"Sure." She leaned up to kiss Enrique. "Be right back. You want white or red?"

"Red, please," he answered, a smile playing on his lips.

The women went into the kitchen where they assembled a tray of the bread and cheese Céline had left for them. They grabbed two bottles of wine and glasses, and Susana started back towards the doorway when Azalea stopped her.

"Suze? What happened? Why did you leave the café?"

Susana looked at her dearest friend and her heart swelled. She'd been a lousy friend for weeks—but Azalea hadn't stopped trying to reach her, even if she'd been clumsy and harsh at times. She set the tray down on the counter and held out her arms.

"It's a long story, *amiga*," she said as they hugged. "But it has a happy ending." She grimaced. "I know I haven't listened very well and you've just been trying to help. I'm sorry."

Azalea's eyes widened. "You're not just my best friend, Susana. You're like a sister to me. You know I love you." She frowned. "And I haven't been the best at showing you that."

"I love you, too, *hermana*," answered Susana. She picked up the tray and nodded to the doorway. "C'mon…let's get out there with those hot Latin husbands of ours and I'll tell you everything."

"So that's the last of it, I suppose," finished Susana. She was exhausted from telling the story but felt a sense of peace getting it all out. Now they all knew everything.

The friends sat quietly on the terrace, two empty bottles of wine on the table between them. Esteban looked serious, while Azalea wore a pained expression. "I'm just horrified," she said at last. "How could anyone treat children that way? And then try to drag you into the whole mess? It's despicable." She shook her head. "What is wrong with people?"

Susana shivered and pulled her cardigan closer. "Could we go inside? It's getting chilly out here."

Enrique stood and took her hand. "Coffee, everyone? It's not as good as Esteban's, but we could warm up indoors."

"I saw some wood by the fireplace," noted Esteban. "What if we made a fire and sat in the salon? Doesn't seem like anyone is ready to go to bed yet."

The four friends went in and the men set about starting a fire. Azalea and Susana made coffee, then carried the mugs into the salon where a small blaze was beginning to grow and warm the room.

Susana sat on the love seat closest to the fireplace, wishing she'd dried her hair before coming downstairs. She sipped her coffee and then leaned back, her head on Enrique's shoulder. "Mmm," she murmured, closing her eyes. "That's better."

"So what now?" asked Azalea, her question breaking the silence. "What will you do now?"

Susana sat up and shook her head. "I'm not sure." She looked at her husband. "But Kique and I will talk it through and figure it out. We both have some big decisions to make.

"But this evening, we're going to enjoy our anniversary."

Esteban stood. "Would you excuse me for a moment?" he asked.

They nodded and he stepped out of the salon.

"Anyway," continued Susana, "I know I made some stupid decisions and I'm determined not to repeat them. I have teams at MPG I don't want to leave high and dry, but I'm not sure what the agency will let me do. I definitely want to talk to Lauren at the very least. I never formally started with Liscia, so I don't really have any responsibility there. "

"What about with law enforcement?" pressed Azalea. "Geneva admitted what she did. Surely they'll want to talk to you."

Susana mulled her friend's question. "I don't think there are any legal issues here. It's in another country and with another company," she answered. "But the ethics committee on Liscia's board will surely grill her and I think there are compliance issues in California. They'll probably have to reissue reports. At any rate, it doesn't involve me."

Azalea's eyes filled with tears. "Suze…those kids. I can't stop thinking about those kids."

Susana's throat tightened. She thought back to the boy in the Anduze plaza, the little girl on the soccer field. What Liscia had done—what Geneva had allowed—affected real lives, real children. It wasn't theoretical for Azalea, Susana realized. She was a mother and now a grandmother. The entire disaster hit far closer to home for her friend.

Susana rose and knelt next to Azalea's chair. "*Hermana*," she whispered, taking her friend's hands. "Yes. I will talk to the state regulators. I'll do whatever I can to help."

Azalea nodded, her lips tight as the tears pooled in her eyes. "Thank you," she whispered.

Esteban returned and stood next to his wife. "Everything all right?" he asked.

Azalea nodded and stood. "We should go up and let these two enjoy their evening," she said. She squeezed Susana's hand and then hugged Enrique. "We love you," she said.

As the Obregons left the salon, Susana and Enrique sat back down on the sofa. When the small fire began to die down, Enrique used the poker to put out the last of the flames. The room was warm and cozy and the couple sat quietly watching the embers.

"Happy anniversary, Kique," she said softly.

"Happy anniversary. Are you ready for bed, my love?"

Susana nodded. Even after thirty years, she was very ready.

Enrique reached under the mat outside their door to retrieve their room key.

"Why did you leave it there?" Susana asked, puzzled.

"I didn't," he answered. "Esteban did." He didn't answer her questioning look and instead opened the door to their suite.

Inside, the bed was turned down and rose petals were strewn across the sheets. The nightstands both held candles, their flames dancing in the darkened room, and a tray glinted with champagne flutes and a bottle of Dom Pérignon. A small glass plate held two gold dusted truffles, and a scroll tied in gold ribbon rested on Susana's pillow.

She gasped at the display. "Kique—I—"

He took her in his arms and held her close. "Happy anniversary, *mi reina*."

My queen.

"This is beautiful…I don't know what to say." She turned to look again at the bed. "You and Esteban take the prize for the whole Latin lover thing," she chuckled. "This is incredible." Then she frowned. "But what if…?" Her voice trailed off as she considered how badly the day could have gone.

"I was prepared to drink the whole thing by myself until I was completely wrecked. Or smash the bottle against a stone wall." He hugged her again, then whispered into her hair. "I much prefer sharing it with you."

Susana reached up to kiss him. "Just one minute," she said. "I have something for you, too."

She went into the closet to retrieve the journal. "I didn't have time to wrap it," she apologized, then smiled ruefully. "Oh, hell… let's be honest. I didn't make time. I was a bit too caught up in my own garbage." She handed him the slim leather volume. "But I do hope you like it."

Enrique took the journal from her and ran his finger over the embossed cover. "I love it," he said, looking up at her. "It's perfect."

"I know I wasn't at my best that day," she began, struggling for words. "But the way you looked at that bridge—the awe and passion when you described it to us…. It made me love you even more." She looked down, then back at the face of the man she adored. "You are brilliant and I love seeing you excited about teaching. It was…

magical watching you." She shook her head. "I don't know how to explain what I mean—"

"I know what you mean, *querida*," he answered, his voice soft. "I feel the same way when I see you in the middle of a big project, that amazing, creative brain of yours just firing on all cylinders. It's part of why and how we love each other." He looked down at the journal again. "I will treasure this forever." He gestured at the scroll. "Now open yours."

They sat on the bed and Enrique moved the tray. Susana untied the ribbon and rolled out the parchment.

It was an architectural drawing of a small building. She looked closely, noting her husband's fine handwriting. The structure wasn't large, but it held a kitchenette, windows on all sides, and a small loft at the back.

"What is this, Kique?" she asked.

"*La oficina de la reina*," he answered. "We have plenty of room in the backyard and my queen deserves an office space better than the kitchen table or the spare bedroom. If you want it, I'll pull the permits and we can start construction when we get home."

Susana looked down at the plans, her eyes filling with tears. "But I don't have a job, Kique. I don't need this anymore."

"Oh, my love. I have a feeling you need this more than ever."

Susana stifled a yawn after sipping the last of the champagne. "What a day. Between the wine on the terrace and this champagne, I can barely keep my eyes open," she told Enrique.

He reached up to wipe a trace of chocolate from her lip. "Nice try," he teased. "You're not getting out of making love with your husband on your anniversary."

She glanced at the clock. "Well, there are only twenty minutes left in the day," she noted. "What are you waiting for?"

"Challenge accepted," he grinned. He picked up the tray and the gifts and placed them on the writing desk, then looked back at her. "You're still dressed?"

"Challenge accepted," she responded with a laugh as she stood.

Enrique's face grew serious. "No, let me." He slipped off her sweater, running his hands down her arms, then slowly pulled her tank top over her head. She stood very still as he slid his fingers into the waistband of her leggings, peeling them off her. "*Mi hermosa esposa*," he whispered against her thighs.

A shiver ran over her skin, and Susana reached to undress him.

"No, *querida.*" Enrique stood and reached to undo her bra and slip off her panties. He took a step back and gazed at her, love plain in his eyes.

Susana looked back at her husband. She was naked in every sense. She had nearly lost this man—over what? A drive to achieve, to succeed beyond her grandmother and her parents, to prove herself to leaders who neither cared for nor valued her? She could—*she would*—stand naked in the face of a love this powerful.

She undressed him slowly, kissing his warm skin as she slipped off his clothes. When he, too, stood naked, they gazed long at each other, the candlelight flickering off their skin.

Despite the odds, they had fought for each other, fought for their marriage. And they had finally come back to themselves, to what they truly valued.

At last, Enrique swept her into his arms. "Forget the clock. We have all the time in the world, *mi cardito. Eres la amor de mi vida.*"

She was the love of his life. And he of hers.

35

One year later….

Susana sat back and stared at the large monitor on her desk. The logo wasn't quite right, but she couldn't put her finger on what bugged her. She took a long drink of her coffee and turned in her chair.

"Come look at this. What's wrong with it?" she asked.

Lauren turned away from her desk and rolled her chair over the cool tile floor to Susana. She looked at the screen and laughed. "Easy. Wrong typeface," she said simply. "We're not girly but we're not macho, either. It has to be clean, elegant, and powerful. What if we did *Las Tres Latinas* in a handwriting script and marketing in all caps?"

"I like that idea," nodded Susana. "Should we call Azalea? She's the font guru."

Lauren looked at her watch. "It's five o'clock in Barcelona—isn't that siesta time? Is she gonna be up for a call?"

Susana was already pulling up FaceTime. "If she wants to be a founding partner of this agency, she'd better be."

Lauren smirked. "Okay, *Geneva.*"

Susana shot her a withering glance and then turned back as Azalea's face came onscreen.

"*Hola, amigas,*" she said brightly. "*Que tal?*"

Susana snorted a laugh. "Oh, look who's finally bilingual."

"Hey, Azalea," said Lauren, leaning into the camera's range. "How's it going?"

"Very well. How are *mis mujeres favoritas?*"

Susana couldn't stop laughing. "Now you're just showing off. Hang on—we want to show you something." She shared the graphic image on her screen and asked, "What do you think of this? It's not quite there yet, right?"

Azalea frowned as she looked at the logo. "I'd like something more feminine," she said. "But not girly, if that makes sense. We're three strong, professional Latinas—"

"That's what I said," broke in Lauren. "I think we stack it. *Las Tres Latinas* on top in a handwriting font and marketing on the bottom in all caps—*mas fuerte.*"

Azalea nodded. "Strong. I love that."

"What if we dropped the *Las* and just did *Tres Latinas?*" asked Susana.

Lauren looked thoughtfully at the screen. "Yeah, that might give us a nicer composition—"

"But did you notice that *Las* has all our initials in it?" asked Azalea. "I know we aren't using it as an acronym, but it does stand for Lauren Azalea Susana."

Susana grinned. "I never would have even noticed that—"

There was a knock and Enrique leaned in the doorway. "Sara's here with Toby. Just grabbing her stuff out of the car."

Susana nodded as she began changing the fonts on the proposed logo, then glanced out the window to see Sara, baby on her hip, walking to their office.

Sara walked in and handed the infant to Lauren. She leaned over Susana's shoulder and smiled at the screen. "Hi, Azalea! How's Toby's favorite Spanish auntie?"

"Things are great. Where's our boy?"

Lauren held up the dozing baby and Azalea grinned. "He's getting so big!"

"He fell asleep in the car," Sara said. "I was hoping he'd stay awake until we got here but he was out in two minutes."

"Esteban and I will be there in another month and I want to cuddle that precious little man," Azalea answered. "I just found out Tomás and Emily are pregnant again. Can you believe Amelia is almost two?"

Sara laughed. "You're in full on grandma mode, aren't you? What about Landon? Still single?"

Azalea rolled her eyes. "That boy dates like it's his job, but there hasn't been anyone special."

"Well, you never know when the right one sneaks up on you, right? Anyway, can't wait to see you." Sara looked at Susana. "Okay if I nurse him in the spare bedroom? He's ready to eat and I hope he'll take a nice long nap so I can get these papers graded."

Susana nodded and Sara blew a kiss at the screen. "Anyway, sorry to interrupt your big important business meeting."

Lauren laughed as she handed the sleeping infant to his mother. "Yeah, so important. That's us."

Susana smiled and looked back at Azalea onscreen. "Okay, I'll mess around with more typefaces and send you some mockups with and without the *Las*. They'll be in your inbox when you wake up."

"Sounds good. *Abrazos, guapas!*"

Susana rolled her eyes as they ended the call. "I guess all we had to do was start a business to get her to speak Spanish. She could barely put two sentences together when we were in Spain last year." She stood up and stretched. She looked around at *La Oficina de Reina* and smiled. "I love working from home. This office is just the right size for all of us."

"Must be nice to have an architect as a husband," said Lauren as she settled back into her chair. "This place is fantastic."

"I still want to do some decorating," mused Susana. "Get some artwork on the walls, maybe some more plants. I saw some nice Diego Rivera prints that would be perfect. I want to have a nice backdrop for our video calls."

"Sounds like we need to sign an interior designer as a client."

"You know any?"

Lauren grimaced. "Nah. Guess we're stuck doing it ourselves."

Susana nodded and smiled at the younger woman. "So, it's been a month now. Any regrets about leaving MPG?"

"Are you kidding? After the way they treated you, there was no way I was staying. Not gonna lie—it was nice to get a few months with the promotion and the raise, but I'm much happier now. Oh!" She clapped her hands together. "I almost forgot to tell you—you'll love this. Douglas left and is starting his own agency. I heard he's trying to poach a few of the junior account folks, but no one seems interested."

"No surprise there," answered Susana. "With that ego, he's not terribly attractive—for employees or clients."

Lauren lifted one eyebrow and continued with a grin. "And speaking of clients, I don't know how you got around the MPG non-compete clause but I'm not even a little bit mad that Thompson Toys is our first client."

"I just had to wait the year," answered Susana. "It worked out in our favor, giving me time to get this place set up. So how are things with you and Jayson?"

Lauren paused. "Honestly, I'm not sure. He asked me to move in with him, but I love my freedom. Since Sara got married, I have the house to myself and it's pretty damned awesome. You know he's older and never married. He's ready to settle down and I'm not sure he's gonna wait for me." She grimaced. "I'm not even sure if I'll ever be ready, so you need to find a way to keep his business if we break up."

"If he's that fickle of a businessman that he'd dump us if you break up, I don't want him. The work we do doesn't have anything to do with his personal life, *amiga*."

Lauren looked skeptical, but nodded. "You're right."

Enrique poked his head into the office and smiled at his wife. "I'm heading out, babe."

Susana looked at Lauren. "Be right back." She stood and swatted her husband on the backside. "I'll walk you to the door, love."

Lauren shook her head. "I don't know what happened in Europe, but you guys are borderline disgusting. You're like newlyweds."

Husband and wife laughed and walked out of the office, hand in hand.

"He's out like a light," Sara told the couple as she emerged from the spare bedroom. "I'll just let him sleep and check on him again in a bit." She grabbed her backpack from the counter and headed toward the backyard. "I love working over here with you guys," she said. "Enrique, you're a genius. That office is perfect."

"It's great to see you all enjoying it."

"I'll be out in a minute," added Susana. She squeezed Enrique's hand. The office *was* perfect—big enough for all four women when Azalea was in town, cozy enough for Susana on her days alone. Enrique had designed the space exactly as Susana outlined, with built in desks and bookshelves, and ample light and storage. It was glorious this time of year with the windows open yet snug during Florida's rainy season when the skies unleashed. Her architect husband had followed her requests perfectly, even designing a Murphy bed-type conference table that could be used when the women needed to spread out sketches or work side by side. Susana marveled at his creativity every time she walked in.

More than creativity, she thought. *It was built with love.*

"So did you see the news this morning?" Enrique asked as they walked to the front door.

"I did. After I talked to the California regulators, they uncovered even more of her lies. They're coordinating with the Department of Labor and it sounds like they're shutting down the factory." She made a face. "But there will be another one up and running in no time, I'm sure. There's no shortage of greed in this world. I just wish she'd end up in jail."

"Well, the board did fire her," he replied. "Good luck ever getting a job anywhere else with that history. Did you talk to Desirée again?"

"Yeah, she's fully engaged with the investigation. She's even talking about writing a book." Susana shrugged. "We're never gonna be friends, but I am thankful we're on the same side." She slid her arms around him. "And I heard something else this morning."

"Oh?" he answered.

"Peter is retiring. I suspect the other partners forced him out. Even after a year, they're probably still scared I'll report him."

"And do we care about Peter?" he asked, nuzzling her neck. "Or Geneva?"

Susana tipped up his chin and met his mouth with her own. "Nope," she whispered, then slid her tongue along his lips.

"*Ten cuidado, chica*," he murmured. "I haven't left yet."

"I'm never being careful again," she said, taking his face into her hands. "Not when it comes to loving you."

"Hold that thought. I'll be home by six," he promised. "Make sure Lauren and Sara are gone by then."

"I'll meet you in the pool," she said, lightly sliding her hand down his chest to his thighs.

Enrique growled softly. "Ah, woman. What am I going to do with you?"

"Oh, I can think of all sorts of things," she whispered.

He reached down and clasped her hands. "*Te adoro, mi cardito.*" He kissed her soundly, then opened the door.

"*I adore you, too*," she whispered as he left. She smiled as he blew her a kiss from the car, then turned back to her office. It felt good to reclaim herself. No more compromises, no more self-doubt. She was finished with trying to prove herself to anyone.

With Azalea and Lauren, she'd build a new creative agency.

And with Kique, I'll build a life.

ACKNOWLEDGEMENTS

This book challenged me in so many ways.

First, my life is nothing like Susana's. I have gone through two divorces—married fifteen years the first time and nearly twelve years the second. While I don't personally have the experience Susana and Enrique had, I got to see my parents. They would have celebrated their fifty-first anniversary two weeks after my mom died from cancer in 2011. Their marriage was far from perfect, yet I was fortunate to watch them work through their hard times and love each other deeply, especially the last ten years when my mother was so sick.

Second, I needed to do a lot more research for this story. I knew next to nothing about the garment industry or its dirty secrets around forced and child labor. Thankfully, my friend Diane Osgood, PhD is a pioneer in sustainability and climate impact strategy. She is the author of *Your Shopping Superpower* (2025, Health Communications Inc, distributed by Simon and Schuster) and generously gave of her time and expertise to get me up to speed. I'm deeply grateful for her help. Any errors in the scenes between Susana and Liscia are mine alone.

Lastly, Susana is clearly everyone's favorite character. My wonderful beta readers were not happy during parts of this story! No one wanted to see her get bullied by the Miles Porter Gelbarr partners—nor did they enjoy watching her lose her way. There were ferocious bits of feedback after her phone call with the drunken Peter. Everyone loves Susana's strength and grit, so it was tough to see their favorite allowing the executives at MPG and Liscia treat her so badly, or to see Enrique take her for granted.

But this is a romance novel, so we all know there's a happily ever after.

Thank you to my wonderful editor, Michelle Meade. Perhaps Susana's most fervent fan, she made sure that everyone (especially Azalea and Enrique) treated the hero appropriately and got their comeuppance when they didn't. Thank you also to the one and only Samantha Sanderson-Marshall for her incredible design. Readers adore these covers, and I think there were as many fans awaiting this latest artwork as they were the story!

I am very grateful to my long-time readers who have fallen in love with these women. A special thank you to Janis Farmer, who has faithfully read every single draft. Your encouragement means the world!

Thank you to Alison Cooper, who is pretty much Susana IRL. Your gutsy, sassy approach to life has been a great model for her character and a blessing to me.

Let me take a moment to single out the wonderful people of the Cevennes. It's no exaggeration to say that my visits to the Feliz Café changed my life. There is something so pastoral, so idyllic about a small community gathering around food and music that suffuses one's soul. The time I was able to donate to the café meal by baking bread pudding with my writing friends (thank you again, Diane!) remains a highlight of my visits.

As always, my thanks to Ted, my loving husband who never fails to encourage me to keep putting pen to paper—or fingers to keyboard. It is pure joy to experience my own late in life love story. We may not get thirty years, but we make the most of every single day and I am grateful.

And to all the fans of the *Blooming* series: Thank you for following these wonderful women. I hope that you have Azaleas, Saras, Susanas, and Laurens in your life, those who prove that the most profound lessons bloom in the hearts of women who open themselves to friendship and to love.

"You said you didn't want kids."

Lauren's face was hard, her voice sharp. "We had this conversation a long time ago and we *agreed*."

Jayson shrugged, his expression only mildly apologetic. "I thought I was sure. But I was wrong."

He reached a hand out to her but she didn't take it, instead leaning back in her chair and taking a deep drink of her wine. Her hand shook slightly with anger. *Dealbreaker*, she thought. *This is a dealbreaker.*

"Can we talk about—"

"No!" Lauren set her glass down hard, the Pinot Noir splashing onto the white linen tablecloth. She closed her eyes for a moment, calming herself. "No, Jayson. We can't." She looked up at him, her brow furrowed. "We talked about it already and we don't need to talk about it again. It's clear that we don't have the same goals for ourselves or this relationship."

"People change, Lauren—"

"Not about this," she hissed. "Not about something this important. You've known from the start that I had no interest in having kids. I like my life. I have a great job and I thought I had a great relationship." She felt a familiar tingle in her hands, the anxiety finding its way to her extremities. *Not this*, she thought. *Not this.*

"We do have a great relationship. Two years, babe. That should count for something. You know I love you. How many times do I have to ask you to marry me?"

"Well, you certainly don't ever have to ask again," she muttered.

"Lauren. Please. I love you. I want us to be together."

"Not *us*. You want us *plus a baby*. Which means you don't want me—you want the me you think I could be." She shook her head. "The me that doesn't and won't exist. I'm not a mother, Jayson." She tossed her napkin on the table and stood, gathering her purse and coat. "Don't get up. I'll get a cab."

Jayson Rivera stood and looked at her, his expression sorrowful. He raised his hands, then dropped them to his sides. "I'm sorry."

"Yeah. Me, too."

She forced herself to walk to the door, overcoming the inclination to bolt. The evening was chilly as she left the restaurant, and Lauren pulled her coat close as she shivered. A couple stepped out of a cab as she approached the curb, and she raised her hand to catch the driver's attention. She got in and gave him her address, then settled back, still seething.

She was startled to feel tears on her cheeks and angrily wiped them away. What was there to cry about?

She considered texting her best friend. But Sara was a happily married schoolteacher with a toddler and Lauren wasn't sure she'd get the encouragement she needed tonight. *Besides*, she thought, *it's eleven o'clock and Sara's sound asleep already*. Little Toby was teething and not sleeping well these days. Lauren wouldn't disturb her.

She contemplated talking to Susana instead. They'd been friends before Susana was her boss at Miles Porter Gelbarr, the marketing agency where they'd both worked—and where she'd met Jayson. Once Lauren and Jayson realized they were interested in each other romantically, Susana had pulled her off the Thompson Toys account where he was vice president of marketing. When the women left MPG to start their own firm, Thompson Toys was their first client.

Oh, damn. Lauren's stomach dropped. *What if he fires Tres Latinas Marketing?* She shuddered at the thought of losing their biggest client. Thompson Toys currently accounted for, what? Forty percent of their revenue? *Maybe more*, she admitted. She had no professional connection to the account—Susana managed the relationship to avoid any impropriety—but they were a small agency and losing that retainer would be a significant blow. She took her phone

out of her purse and considered texting her friend and business partner, then decided to wait. *I'll tell her in person tomorrow*, she thought.
She leaned her head against the window, suddenly spent.

*What does it say about our relationship if I'm more worried about
the professional backlash than I am about losing my partner?* If she were
honest, she'd had doubts for months, starting when Jayson asked her
to move in with him. When he escalated his request to a marriage
proposal, she rationalized her reluctance, assuring herself that while
she did love him, she'd just bought her new condo and she was content with the status quo. Now she realized the truth. She'd sensed it
wasn't a forever thing.

And tonight it almost felt like a relief.

The next morning, Enrique nearly plowed into Lauren as
he walked out the front door, her hand raised to knock. "Oh!" he
exclaimed. "Sorry—I didn't expect you this early." He glanced at his
watch and looked quizzically at her. "Do you guys have something
going on today? You're never here at eight." He chuckled. "Half the
time Susana is barely out of bed by now."

Lauren shook her head. "Nah, just thought I'd get an early start
on things." She walked into the foyer as he held the door for her. "Is
she out back?" The women worked together in the spacious backyard
office Enrique had built for his wife.

"I think she's in the kitchen," he answered as he passed her.
"*Que tengas un buen dia.*"

"*Gracias.* You, too." Lauren wasn't sure how good of a day it
would be when Susana learned they might lose their top account, but
she smiled and waved as Enrique walked to his car.

"Hey, *chica*," said Susana as Lauren entered the kitchen. "You're
early. What's up?'

Lauren looked at her friend and business partner. Susana was
dressed in leggings and a pullover sweater, her hair gathered into a
ponytail. She wore no makeup and still wore her Uggs slippers. *Guess
no meetings today*, thought Lauren.

"Well, I need to tell you something," she began, her voice hesitant. "Might not be anything, but we should be prepared."

Susana set her coffee cup down on the counter and leaned
back, crossing her arms. "Okay. That sounds ominous."

Lauren bit her lip, then continued. "I broke up with Jayson last night. I don't know if it will affect our business with Thompson Toys, but it might."

Her friend frowned. "Are you all right? I'm a lot more concerned about you than Tres Latinas. I thought you guys were serious."

"I'm okay. I think it's just run its course. I realized last night that we weren't going to be…permanent?" She winced at the question in her voice.

"Did something happen?"

Lauren took a moment to respond. What did happen? She didn't really want to discuss it with Susana, no matter how close they were. The whole baby thing was too painful, too confusing, too… well, whatever it was, she didn't want to think about it, much less talk it out. *Cram it and jam it*, she told herself. *Same old story.*

"Not any one thing. I think I just realized we weren't meant to be together forever. He's asked me to marry him three times now and I figured that if I haven't been able to say yes, it must not be right." She forced a laugh. "I mean, I'm forty years old. Maybe I'm just not the marrying kind. He deserves to find someone who wants that." She trailed off, then rallied. "Anyway, just wanted to tell you."

Susana looked long at her friend, then sighed. "Okay. I get that you don't want to talk about it and I'm not gonna push you." Her eyes softened. "But please don't keep this to yourself. You know I'm here—and not just for work. We're friends, Lauren. *Amigas del corazón, no?*"

Lauren nodded, too unsure of her voice to respond.

Susana continued. "*Bueno.* Then let's have that business development conversation this morning. Whether or not we lose Thompson, we need some new clients. Grab some coffee and let's talk about the Chamber of Commerce breakfast next week."

The two women took their mugs to the office and Lauren set her bag down at her desk, grateful to her friend for changing the subject. She pulled out a notebook and turned to Susana. "Okay, tell me more."

"There's a monthly breakfast meeting at the Chamber," answered Susana. "A different company sponsors it each time and they make a presentation to the group. It's not long—you'll be there for maybe an hour and a half, but I think it would be good to start meeting some of our local businesses. We don't need a bunch of big clients but we could sure use a handful of midsize ones."

"Wait—you want *me* to go to the meeting?"

"Why not?"

"I've just never done anything like this before," confessed Lauren. "I'm not sure what to do."

"Well, the truth is, the only one of us who's done any face to face busdev is Azalea, and she won't be here for another couple of weeks. So we need to learn for ourselves how to pick up clients." Susana sipped her coffee. "You'll be fine. Just be friendly, hand out business cards, and talk about Tres Latinas Marketing. How hard can it be?"

Need to know what happens next?

Sign up at cindyvillanueva.com or follow on
social media to receive preorder info for

the final book of BLOOMING: The Series

Coming in 2026!